CW00351445

Cambridge Libraries, Archives and Information Service

This book is due for return on or before the latest date shown above, but may be renewed up to three times unless it has been requested by another customer.

Books can be renewed -
in person at your local library

Cambridgeshire
County Council

Online www.cambridgeshire.gov.uk/library

Please note that charges are made on overdue books.

Previous works by Fran Smith

Best Wishes, Sister B

Fran Smith

The Power of Cake

Further letters from Sister B

THREE HARES PUBLISHING

First published in Great Britain in 2017
www.threeharespublishing.com

A CIP catalogue record for this book is available from the British Library

Three Hares Publishing Ltd Reg. No 8531198
Registered office: 17 Plumbers Row, Unit D, London E1 1EQ

Print ISBN 978-1-78745-037-0
Ebook ISBN 978-1-78745-038-7

Typeset and printed via Type & Tell.

I blame Chris for this one, too.

Previously...

The remote East Anglian convent of St Winifreda-in-the-Fen is home to an international group of religious sisters from different orders and even different faiths. Visiting sisters from around the world are always welcome. About half the permanent residents are officially retired and live in the Father Edward Wilson Centre, cared for by the others.

The buildings of the convent are not in good repair. Last year the roof leaked, the drains broke and there was an infestation of rats; worst of all, part of the ornate bell tower fell down. The church authorities, who had not taken much notice of St Win's for the past 200 years, decided it was no longer practical to support the convent. Financial advisers proposed closing it down and disbanding the retired sisters to care homes. Intermediax, the company in the business units up the lane, offered to buy some of their land for a car park.

However, the sisters, led by their dynamic new Reverend Mother, decided they had a mission to stay, so, in a bid for self-sufficiency, they opened a shop, converted some neglected outbuildings into bed and breakfast rooms and began selling crafts online. Their best-selling items are nunpegs; wooden clothes pegs dressed as nuns.

Sister Boniface runs the shop, known officially as Ye Olde Convent Shoppe (nobody can remember whose decision that was). She is helped by Nesbitt, an odd teenager who just arrived one day and started work. Nesbitt worked unpaid for a while, and then when they realised they were exploiting her, the sisters managed to organise an apprenticeship and she is now training as a chef under the guidance of French Sister Clementine.

Last year it was Sister B's turn to be convent correspondent for handwritten letters, and the Sisters Worldwide Correspondence Circle allocated her Emelda, an independent sister working in the remote Peruvian Andes. Emelda comes originally from Suffolk, but now travels forests and highlands teaching and nursing in remote communities. An energetic mountaineer and explorer, her life is full of drama and adventure, but she is homesick for the Fens and longs for gentle news of the daily round of convent life.

The usual arrangement is for the Correspondence Circle to allocate travelling sisters a different correspondent each year.

1

St Winifreda-in-the-Fen
September 2nd

Dear Emelda,

Fabulous news about the tiny boxes your workers make from fruit peel: we have sold 120 to someone in Finsbury Park who wants to use them for an art installation. It was the artist himself who rang, so I asked him what sort of installation it was.

"It's at the fluid stage right now," he said, "so I can't commit, but think Ai Wei Wei."

To be quite honest it was the image of a panda that popped into my head, and then I remembered who Ai Wei Wei was, and we've been speculating about it round the convent ever since. Perhaps it will be a drift of little boxes, like the ceramic seeds at Tate Modern, or perhaps he will fill each one with a separate tiny artwork – who knows? Whatever he does, you are £120 to the good, but we will need the other 40 as soon as you can post them. I explained about their long journey and he said there was no hurry. Hardly anyone says that these days.

The retired sisters are hard at it filling orders for nunpegs this week because someone put a photograph of one in a Sunday colour supplement. A journalist called Cee Delaney said they were 'terribly cute' and that was all it took. I hadn't seen a Sunday colour supplement for years, but Mrs Odge bought one in and we studied Cee Delaney's favourite things together. All the supplements have this sort of article, apparently, where someone takes a few bits and pieces and they are prettily photographed and the details of how much they cost are written next to them so that people can buy them. I said, "Is this what newspapers do now? Isn't that more like a catalogue, really?"

Delphine Odge just said, "You have to move with the times, Sister. I used to make my own puff pastry."

We keep expecting to catch a glimpse of you in the new television documentary about the Amazon. Whenever the presenter is lying in a Yanomami hammock or following a hunting group with blowpipes, we are peering into the background wondering whether you will be there running the netball tournament or taking the seniors through their irregular verbs, but no luck so far. I know the Amazon is on the large side, but we keep looking.

Although you only ever see the presenter himself, there's probably a crew of a dozen encamped in giant caravans somewhere not far away. Once on Autumnwatch they showed the infrastructure that was needed to film deer rutting and woodmice nibbling in their burrows and it turned out to be a small village of electronics set up in half a dozen steel containers bristling with aerials and strung around with cabling. There were about twenty staff whose job was to sit and watch hidden cameras all day and night in case a woodlouse or a squirrel did something interesting. Rather disillusioning, actually.

Eustacia thinks I am naïve. "Well, how did you think they did it?" she asked me. "You probably think The Archers is just microphones hidden all over Ambridge."

Most of Cee Delaney's other favourites were so expensive that it was easy to believe a decimal point had been put in the wrong place. There were riding boots at £1250 and a cashmere shawl at £675, so perhaps that's why the nunpegs (£5.60 for 6) have been so popular. Now the cathedral wants several dozen for its shop as well, and according to their regional buyer on the phone, "Once you get into the cathedrals, you're well away. It'll be National Trust next, and you know what that means."

Actually, I didn't know what that meant, so I asked, and he said, "National Trust! That's countrywide outlets and a better class of customer altogether. £10 is small change for National Trust members! There's people'd kill for a space on their shelves, but let's not run before we can walk, or count our chickens."

Undaunted by the metaphorical overload, Sister Martha is branching out and designing nunpeg variants. Besides the ordinary nunpeg (Nunpeg#1, as she lists it) there are now Summer Nunpegs, wearing the white habit and Jolly Nunpegs, who are more padded. I had a few reservations, but online shoppers are very keen on clothes pegs dressed as nuns, especially the jolly ones.

Ted, the supervisor, has Animal and Baz doing community service on the hedges this week. They are especially good at anything that involves chopping or cutting back. The delicate work, like pricking out seedlings, was always done by Alphonsus Dunn, our nice young hacker, but he's finished his sentence now.

"You know what, I miss that Alphonsus," Animal remarked, over a custard tart in the Shoppe. "He was all right for a posh boy. Bought us biscuits sometimes and everything."

"Yeah," Baz agreed, "I never liked that la-de-da music of his, though. Give me a nice bit of Meatloaf."

"Sorry," I said, "we haven't got any meatloaf."

"No, you're all right, Sister, it's a band. She thought you meant meatloaf!"

They roared with laughter, elbowing each other in the ribs and nearly choking on their food.

"We miss him too," I said, when they settled down. "He

was a good worker."

"Done you a nice little website, didn't he?" Baz said. "Brainy. Probably got some cushy desk job now. Employable, he is. Not like us."

"You're good workers, too," I said. "Look at all the clearing you did around the Pigpens. Those brambles had practically covered the houses, but you soon put paid to them."

"Yeah, we know what to do with a billhook," Baz said.

"Yeah! Chopping! We can do chopping!" Animal agreed, demonstrating vigorously.

Ted had come into the Shoppe to find them. He's a stickler for timekeeping: army training.

"There's hedges wanting to be cut out here, when you two have finished basking in the glory," he said.

A beautiful sunrise here this morning. All the fields are ploughed now and the flocks of commuting crows and jackdaws wheel around before deciding where to head for breakfast. There are loose little groups of fieldfares and redwings coming over too. They love the windfalls in the orchard. We left two trees at the far end for them this year. These visitors are very shy. One always sits on guard on a high branch and warns the others at any hint of danger. At the first alarm call they fly off, small silhouettes across the soft pink sky.

It's much cheaper to describe autumn than to film it.

I needed no catering van and no containers full of high-tech equipment for that little word-picture. Of course, I can't offer the thrill of live action, but frankly, Emelda, once you've seen one rutting stag you've seen them all. They wee on their own feet – I wish I hadn't watched that part now.

Best wishes,

Sister B.

2

St Win's
September 4th

Dear Emelda,

A proper Fen blow is in progress as I write this. It *whapps* against the convent walls and moans through the chimneys. The poplars in the garden walk are swaying and tossing their silver-lined leaves up and down like dancers shaking their skirts. Today it's oddly warm so it doesn't cut through you like a winter wind, it just tries to tear off your veil. Or if you are one of our lady customers, it does wild things to your hair between the car and the door. Older lady customers avoid this with a practical headscarf, like the Queen – someone who knows a thing or two about the Norfolk wind – but most of the others just have the authentic East Anglian windswept look.

Last winter, when it was really cold, we started making hot chocolate in the back kitchen here, and selling it to the frozen fieldworkers who bustled in during the breaks in their long shifts. They loved it. So I'm wondering whether we have room to sell hot drinks more often this winter.

All this speculation is because we might be getting

a makeover. Over there in the jungle you might have missed the whole makeover idea. I know I had, until it was explained to me. Our local magazine journalist, Tilly Matthews, of Wonderful Homes and Beautiful Country Gardens Magazine, a rather flighty young woman, but kind-hearted and helpful as well as being a regular and rather extravagant visitor to the Shoppe, helped us decorate our B&B rooms very cheaply. She loves the convent's 'look'. She photographs the paint peeling off the doors and worn flagstones from time to time and sighs over them in delight. Where you or I might see a bumpy floor or something in need of a nice coat of paint, Tilly sees something shabby-chic and timelessly distressed.

She was looking round the Shoppe the other day, while waiting for her Sachertorte, when she said, "You know what, Sister B? The whole Shoppe needs pulling together. You need a look. I have an intern who's itching for a little project. Can I let her loose?"

I know what Tilly is like when she gets going, so I was a little wary. I said, "What would it involve, exactly?"

"Oh not much, she'd probably just come over and take some pics and then make one or two plans. Then when you've agreed, she'd bring a few chaps in and carry it out. You'd end up with a lovely-looking shop and Zelda would have her first four-page makeover feature

– win-win!"

"We're very basic here," I said, "very plain."

But Tilly was in full swing. "You know what? It's a pity you haven't got space for a little café or whatever. We could get you a few tables. I see bunting. Bunting's very Downton, very First World War, everybody loves bunting right now."

It's quite hard to understand Tilly when she goes off like this. I have no idea who Downton is, but between you and me, I like bunting too. I think it's from being in the Brownies.

I said, "We couldn't afford any expense, Tilly."

"Are those *venison* sausages?" Tilly said. "I can't say no to some of those! No cost to you, Sister B. We'd provide the props and materials. Anyway, you think it over and I'll pop in next week with Zelda. Ooh! *Scotch eggs*. Yummy! I'll have a couple of them too – no, make it three."

She's a slip of a thing but she's quite hard to stop. I mentioned my anxieties to Rev Mother on the way to supper and she said, "What can we lose? Let's go for it! It's probably a sign that we should open a café. We must be open to opportunities, Boniface. Make your own plans too. If she comes up with anything peculiar you can tactfully re-direct her."

Rev Mother is just back from a workshop –

'Leadership in a Crisis' – it's made her very decisive.

So this morning I am here with a piece of squared paper pacing out the floor, planning, but the more I try, the less I realise I know about decorating. So far my ideas are white walls, white woodwork and perhaps – very daringly – a pale blue door. I like blue. I was never allowed to wear it as a child. It drained all the colour out of my face.

And speaking of drains... last week one of the baths wouldn't empty and no amount of plunging helped. We had to call in the plumber and the further he investigated, the more work he found needing to be done. At least £800 worth. We knew the pipework in general was in bad repair, but £800 is a lot more than we have available. It's what Rev Mother calls a little challenge to our prayer-focus. So this evening and tomorrow we have special meditations in the hope that one of us will be inspired. We have several baths and two showers still functioning, so, as long as you avoid rush hours, it's perfectly possible to be well-washed at St Win's, thank goodness. Sister Prudence called it a First World problem last night, and she was right.

The lawyers are still locking horns over how much our little piece of land in King's Hedges is worth. We try not to be distracted by it. So when I caught Bob Fairbrother studying our giant cardboard fundraising thermometer, I was cheerful.

"What news, Sister, of the future of St Win's? You had me worried last time I asked. I need five walnut gateaux and a Sachertorte for next Tuesday: international delegation. Oh, and I'll take a couple of those little custardy things for elevenses."

"I think it's just a matter of time, now," I told him, "before it's settled. We have great plans."

"Well, as long as the Shoppe keeps flourishing, I'll be happy," he said. "Sister Clementine's cakes get a mention in every feedback form I get. The Finnish delegation posted photos on Facebook and six more of their colleagues booked the course."

"Do they really come from Finland for your courses?"

"Finland, Thailand, Korea..." he shrugged nonchalantly, "I used to charge lots less and aim at customers from the East Anglia region, but since I quadrupled the price and started posting videos on YouTube they come from all over. The material is just the same – and it's good, though I do say so myself. If I couldn't market a marketing course, I wasn't showing a very good example, so I set to and did it."

"As a marketing professional, Bob," I said, "do you think there would be enough customers for a little café here at St Win's?"

Bob raised an eyebrow. "With proper coffee?" he asked.

"Is that essential?"

"Definitely. You need a barista machine."

"Are they expensive?"

"Probably, but if you had one, I'd come and so would my clients."

I am enclosing a photo of some of our chrysanthemums. Aren't they lovely? Carmella has had a great success with her cut flowers this year. She and Pavel bring armfuls into the Shoppe every morning. The rich gold and dark velvety reds sell very well. I'm not sure whether you have chrysanthemums in Peru – you certainly have dazzling orchids, according to the internet. We pray for your work and we don't expect many letters, but let us know you're well if you can.

Best wishes,

Sister B.

3

St Win's
September 7th

Dear Wanderer in the Dangerous Jungles,

We're very impressed with your plan for an up-country trek, but are you sure going alone is a good idea? Perhaps someone else could investigate the rumours about the terrible working conditions of the poor loggers? Or the settlement could spare a few warriors to go with you? In photographs they are well-armed and hardy-looking, they look like the right sort of companion for a trip to what I see on the internet is called the 'lawless zone'. Obviously, if you have a call to go, you must, so we are sending some very rugged Wellington boots and some Rescue Remedy.

The boots were donated by Mrs Odge, who went mad and bought herself a brand new pair recently. Bright red with white polka dots. We were quite taken aback. Replacing a pair of perfectly serviceable wellies is usually sign of a lottery win around here.

"It was in King's Lynn," she told me, as if that explained it all. "They're fleece-lined and it was a special offer – it's not all mad indulgence."

Now, Emelda, strictly speaking, Sister Bernard

should be your correspondent this year, but there's been a hitch. Rev Mother is very keen on keeping our professional training up to date. As part of her 'St Winifreda's Renewed' campaign, we've had a training audit, and Sister Bernard asked to brush up her organ skills and went on a course at the cathedral. They were so impressed that they took her on their composition course and now she's composing something for a competition. We're very proud of her, but she's working night and day and has no time left for letters, so you're stuck with me until she finishes. Sister Clara has taken over as our day-to-day organist temporarily, which is fine as long as we don't try anything with a key change or too many twiddly bits.

"You can carry on with the letters, can't you Boniface?" Rev Mother said at convocation, "You'd be lost without your scribbling."

I said yes, gladly, but I thought the idea was that the recipient might want a different correspondent for a change.

"Oh no, Emelda likes your letters, I've had something about it from Sisters Worldwide." Rev Mother hunted through a pile of papers in front of her. "I left it on my desk, dear, I'll show you later."

Your next set of tiny boxes arrived safely and are stowed in the stock shed over by the kitchens, some ready for our artist and the rest for email orders. We loved your photo of Raulito, the canoe postman. Our whole correspondence depends on that canoe, that paddle, his determination, his strong arms and his continued sobriety. Bless his heart!

First frost last night, and now the sky is clear and the sun is streaming into the Shoppe. The grass shimmers with the sunlit dew. A blackbird is jumping into Carmella's neat pile of raked leaves, scattering them violently left and right, looking for breakfast.

A serious storm is forecast for tomorrow. *Storm of the Century Alert* according to the Daily Express, although they did say that last week too. The wind has already blown all the walnuts off the tree, which is handy as long as you remember to wear gloves when you pick them up. I did not, so now I have dark brown palms and fingernails, which will take a fortnight to wear off, according to the most pessimistic estimates. I'd heard that walnut skins contain a very effective dye; until now I thought it was an old wives' tale.

Carmella and I have lashed down anything that might blow away in the garden, including the lids to the feed bins, which were found three fields away after the last storm. Even so, I don't imagine our bad weather is much compared to what you encounter in the Peruvian rain forest. I looked online and it seems warm, where you're going, but also malarial. Long sleeves and nets at night, Emelda, don't forget! But you know all that, of course.

This morning there was a queue of shoppers outside when I came to open the Shoppe – not something I'm used to at all. They all bought baking things like bicarbonate of soda, self-raising flour and icing sugar. Storm warnings bring out the baker in everyone in Hog Fen, it seems. But it turns out to be a competition – the Three Fens Bake-off. The theme, apparently, is 'mellow fruitfulness'. A lot of the ladies bought toothpicks, and I thought perhaps this was because their cakes were so mellow and fruity that they might stick to the teeth, but Nesbitt explained this was because you use them to hold the more elaborate cake sculptures together.

"I'm going for a cascade, a sort of cornucopia," I heard one lady explain to another. "Handpainted marzipan fruit and foliage tumbling from a horn of plenty in lemon sponge layered with white ganache."

"Nice." said her friend. "Mine's a pair of asymmetrical ellipses representing the equinox. The filling is mango and papaya crème fraiche with pomegranate jus."

Sister Clementine, our French cook, overheard this and made no remark, simply placing three perfect walnut cakes on their stands and leaving them to speak for themselves. The English attitude to food will always exasperate her, I fear.

We have lapwings in the fields around us this year. They are mysterious birds, flocking onto the new green wheat and then suddenly wheeling up into the sky in patterns. They perform starling-like evening displays, rising and falling in aerobatic shoals and whirls. Their cries are mournful and always seem distant.

An unidentified donor has given Sister Carmella a very handy waterproof cape. It appeared in her toolshed on Tuesday. I helped her cut off its label, which showed someone in the Arctic, smiling. The cape is huge, a very simple design – just a roomy rectangle with a hooded hole for the head. Perfect for covering Carmella – who works in all weathers – from top to toe. She is delighted with this new garment and has worn it most days since.

I was moving the outdoor displays under cover this morning when I heard the lapwings' haunting cry against the wind and thought how strange and atmospheric it was. Then I heard it again and again, and realised perhaps it wasn't lapwings. Looking in the direction it came from, I saw what appeared to be a tarpaulin caught in the wind being hurtled along the path at a terrific rate. On closer inspection little feet were cantering along underneath; it was Carmella. The wind had caught her poncho and was turning her into a kite. A couple more big gusts and she'd be airborne!

Luckily Pavel and Animal – far and away the two largest people ever to be found on convent grounds – were passing the Shoppe at that moment and saw what I did. They sprinted down the path among tornadoes of leaves, caught Carmella by one arm each and wrestled the madly flapping cape over her head, so she was restored to normal gravity. Even on its own, the cape took the two men several minutes to restrain, but eventually they crushed it into a small bundle and now it is bagged and confined to the potting shed on windy days. It may make people smile in the Arctic, but it is clearly not designed for the kind of winds we get at St Winifreda's.

"You was lucky not to lose that small gardening one," Animal remarked afterwards. I gave the rescuers a cup of tea for their trouble. He nodded towards Carmella, who was already back at work pushing her wheelbarrow past the Shoppe. This time her trusty Cambridge United scarf was securing her veil.

"Sister Carmella is almost blow up to heaven!" Pavel said.

"Well, up to Newmarket, anyway," Animal agreed. "I'll take one of those custard things too, if you're offering."

Rather a lovely pastime for me this afternoon: nutcracking. The community service workers collected the rest of the fallen walnuts earlier. Ted made them wear not only gloves, to protect from brown hand-dying, but also hard hats, to avoid being knocked out by any falling walnuts – a genuine risk: Hermione was hit by one dropped by a crow on her way to the green bins yesterday. Now we have three or four buckets of nuts, all needing to be shelled. I have been appointed chief sheller, as I can do the work out at the back of the Shoppe. And very satisfying it is. I have a hammer and a piece of wood with a shell-shaped dip in it, an extremely useful item which just appeared by the till this morning. All I have to do is bash the shell of each one in just the right way to pull out the walnuts. I have developed a crackshot hammer aim and achieve extraction of a perfect whole nut about 80% of the time. I am probably far too proud of this new skill, but if walnut shelling ever becomes an Olympic event, I'm fairly confident of a medal. It is enjoyably noisy work, but the shells fly everywhere, so we are a bit gritty underfoot. Nesbitt pointedly put the dustpan and brush in my sightline. Piercings or no piercings, she runs a tight ship, or rather a tight Shoppe.

Yours,

Sister B (Official Convent Correspondent for Hand-written Letters for another year – as long as you don't mind – and East Anglian Walnut Sheller of the Week)

4

St Win's
September 9th

Dear Emelda,

It is a beautiful bright clear wintry day. The hedges are transparent now, and the small birds are flocking to the feeder. Do you remember the lovely chicks we raised so proudly in the spring? Five tiny peeping babies, they were, who entertained us by rushing about after their mother all summer long. We had hopes of a few more home-bred layers, but then they started crowing and fighting with each other. Four of the five are cockerels! The odds were against it, but there we are. They are handsome birds, developing glossy tail feathers and proud red combs, but they eat a great deal and we already have a good cockerel, so they will have to go. We are not certified to sell them in the Shoppe – regulations are strict – but we can eat them ourselves, which just leaves the little issue of dispatching them, as they put it in the chicken-rearing book I found in the library. Killing is not the word the professionals use. Several ways were described. All sound quite quick and painless, but none of us can face it. Carmella, who grew up on a Polish farm, killed (sorry, dispatched) any number of birds in her youth, but when I mentioned it to her she just gave me a stern look and went back to the leaf raking.

I keep thinking I could do it – and indeed, that I *should* do it – as the birds know me and would not be alarmed until the very last moment... but then I can't bring myself actually to picture the very last moment, how, where, or what with. I am praying for guidance on this one. Luckily Jean-Paul our old cockerel has stopped crowing while he moults. When he starts again, all four of the young ones will try to out-crow him. Five cockerels at once will not be good for the B&B business, so something has to be done soon.

At convocation on Monday Rev Mother presented our accounts for the year. She has put the whole lot on a spreadsheet for the first time. We all know it has taken her several weeks of work because she had to learn how to use the computer, how to make a spreadsheet and how to make a set of accounts all at once. She used little videos from the computer and kept coming back from the library van every Thursday with arms full of *Accountancy for Dummies* and *Spreadsheets in 2 Minutes a Day* type of books. It hasn't, to be honest, put her in the sunniest of moods. But it's done now and we all studied the serried ranks of neat figures last night. The presentation was lovely, but the contents were not.

The accounts ought really to be very straightforward. Hermione keeps our books and we do regular bank statement reconciliations – see how the technical terms slip off my pen – but in actual fact they never are. Money is a bit like egg white – strangely static in some areas and very runny and difficult to contain in others. Whenever a boundary is drawn, there will be leakage just inside or outside it to fool the unwary. But we're winning, and when the accountant arrives from the diocese to audit, we confidently expect to have worked out where that odd 43p has gone and why cheque number 231 (but mercifully no money) is missing.

It's dreadful when everything is reduced to figures. We looked at our year's efforts in the Shoppe, for example, and saw a terribly small profit. The Pigpen B&B's and the handmade goods, on the other hand, were nice little earners. Even so, there is no hope of any repairs to the convent buildings unless the money comes through from the little piece of land near Cambridge which we believe is ours. Meanwhile a puzzling slope is appearing in the floor of the chapel at one corner and in the wet weather a small puddle appeared.

I have to remind myself sometimes that you've never been to St Win's. Our dear chapel is plain in its decoration, but rather grand in scale. It's lofty and could seat about a hundred sisters in comfort – well, relative comfort: the benches are hard, obviously. There are altogether only forty-two of us now, but that number includes the twenty-four who are residents of the retirement centre and not mobile enough for the big chapel except on special occasions. They have their own little chapel with wheelchair access and a carpet. So usually we are fewer than twenty in the big chapel. We tend to use the front pews only. There isn't any heating that works and sitting together might conserve our body heat, like those penguins on the documentary. It was fascinating: all the male penguins put their eggs on their little feet and tuck them into their belly, then they all stand in a big huddle and wait patiently for several weeks blasted by icy blizzards ruffling their feathers until the females come back from fishing.

Oh dear, you can see how easily distracted I am from accounts and structural problems. Give me penguins over crumbly architecture and spreadsheets any day.

Anyway, the upshot of all this labour is that (a) we are now completely self-sufficient in book-keeping terms and after convocation we all have a much better idea of how the finances around here work and (b) it's perfectly clear that we definitely have not got enough money.

This may not sound like a breakthrough, but it means that for the first time in three hundred years we need not rely on anyone from the diocese to keep accounts for us. They can, and will, come and audit them, but essentially we are in charge ourselves. Even if it was a long and difficult struggle to confirm something we knew all along, we now know it in detail and on a spreadsheet. This is progress.

"Why is it taking so long for our money from the Poore Pasture to come through?" several of us asked at convocation.

"Huh!" Sister Eustacia said, "They don't part with the stuff without a struggle. Even if it is rightfully ours."

"But even so," I said, "it's been months."

"I checked with Mrs Dunn," Rev Mother said, "there's been a hold-up. She wasn't sure about the details."

"We will need to do something about the chapel floor soon," Sister Bernard said. She visits it even more than the rest of us because of her organ practice. "The puddle is getting bigger and it's making the whole of one corner damp. If it's not sorted out, I'm afraid the floor tiles will be undermined and it will all become much worse."

"I'll ring tomorrow," Rev Mother said. "Now I need to talk to you about the Bishop. He's very keen on training, as you know, and he wants to send us a visitor, a Sister Joy Vernon. She's on a management course and is looking for a small religious house to use as a case study."

"What sort of case study?" Eustacia asked.

"The Bishop didn't say. He just asked us to make her welcome and share as much information with her as possible."

"Hope she's not a spy."

"Now, Eustacia," said Rev Mother, "that doesn't sound very welcoming."

"The Diocese seems pretty keen to close us down," Eustacia said. "At least this time they're not trying headhunt you for some boarding school in Zurich."

"They were perfectly gracious when I turned that offer down," Rev Mother said. "I think we should make Sister Joy welcome and give her all the information she needs for her study."

Nesbitt has been in the Shoppe very early this week. She was expecting Mrs Dunbar, the apprenticeship manager from the college. Nesbitt is always anxious, despite the fact that she is obviously doing very well. Mrs Dunbar is, I must admit, a rather intimidating figure. Stern-faced and carrying a clipboard, she ticked things off a long list as she interviewed Nesbitt. After five separate sheets had been signed, Nesbitt was sent back to work in the kitchen and Mrs Dunbar came over and reported that all was well and that our apprentice was making good progress, considering.

I thought the 'considering' must be considering her reading and writing. Nesbitt has worked very hard, but she has never found it easy or quick to do these things. She can read perfectly well, but it takes her a long time. She can write too, but never chooses to unless it's unavoidable. I looked it up and it might be dyslexia, which is a very complicated condition. It might also just be a natural bent towards practical, tangible skills and away from static things like words on paper. Perfectly understandable either way.

"We're quite impressed with her work ethic," Mrs Dunbar said. "She has overcome a lot, but she sets herself a very high standard. Only the occasional lateness, but, given the circumstances, we make allowances. There are limits, obviously, but we try to be as flexible as we can."

"Does she have difficulty getting to college?" I asked. "She's never late at the Shoppe."

"No, we run buses," said Mrs Dunbar, "as far as I know there's no difficulty with that. No, she manages her responsibilities well for someone so young. We're quite satisfied."

I thought no more about it except that Nesbitt should be congratulated.

"They seem very pleased with you at the college," I said, the next time we were alone in the Shoppe.

"Yeah. Good," said Nesbitt. She looked tired.

"Is it going well?"

"Yeah," she said, "it's alright. Quite easy so far. We've done a lot of food hygiene and safety stuff. I already knew most of it because of that course we did."

"And do you enjoy it?"

"Yeah. It's alright. Not bad. I like the cooking here best."

"With Sister Clementine?"

"Yeah, she's alright. She never gets cross, but she makes me get things right. We done viennoise last week. Wicked."

Wicked – this is Nesbitt's highest term of appreciation.

"So it's going well?"

"Yeah. We need more fruit cake wrapped, shall I do it?"

"Oh no, I'll do that. I was just wondering how you find, you know, the practicalities of getting there to college and managing your work and your studies," I said, "it must be quite a lot to deal with."

"Yeah. It's OK though." Then after putting some sandwiches into a neater display, she said, "Why? Did Mrs Dunbar say something to you?"

"No," I said. "She was full of praise. I just thought you might be feeling the pressure. You're obviously working hard and making a good impression. I wouldn't want you to overdo things, that's all. We're very proud of you,

Nesbitt."

She gave me a sideways look. "Right," she said, re-aligning the cheese and onion. And then quietly, looking down at the ham and mustard she repeated the word. "Proud. Right." She shifted her shoulders. "I need to get over to the kitchen now. We're doing crême pâtissière."

"Of course," I said. "I didn't mean to hold you up."

She took her white chef's apron from behind the door and put it over her head. She only wears it in the kitchen, she keeps another one for the Shoppe. As she reached behind her back to tie it, she turned.

"You give me a job, Sister B. Nobody else would, but you did. It's a big thing."

And she left, pausing on her way out to turn the Shoppe sign from closed to open. As she tied the apron I thought she looked even thinner than usual. We might be over-working our apprentice.

I mentioned this over the supper washing up to Sister Prudence. She is a head teacher in Kenya, and used to young people.

"She looks tired," I said, "she's young, and I worry that the course and the apprenticeship might be stressful. She doesn't read well."

Sister Prudence thought about this and then said, "What is her family situation? It may be something at home that's worrying her."

"She lives with her mother and younger brothers, I think." I said.

"You don't know for sure?" Prudence seemed surprised. She lifted pile of plates into the cupboard.

"No, she's very shy. She has never talked much about home. She's never talked much at all, really."

"Well," said Prudence, "she has every right to her privacy, but it might be worth asking gently whether everything is all right at home. You could just give her the chance to talk."

After supper was cleared I went with Sister Mary Martyr and helped her to clear up the chapel puddle. It was muddy and cold and it took a long time, but we enjoyed the work because Sister Bernard was doing her organ practice. She never really has a chance to shine in our little services, they're all fairly routine hymns with modest accompaniments, only the occasional twiddly introit allows her to hint at her musical skills. But practising for the competition, she literally pulled out all the stops and the organ boomed until the pews trembled, whilst at other moments sounding as gentle as a tiny air harp. It was wonderfully impressive. It even drowned out the cockerels for an hour or so.

Best wishes,

Sister B.

5

St Win's
September 12th

Dear Emelda,

Outpatients visit today. I used to just load the retired sisters into the minibus but since I wrote it off on the A10, it's back to public transport, and I honestly think the invasion of the Falklands was easier to organise than getting four elderly sisters to different clinics at different times of day and back by bus.

I leave you to imagine the number of phone calls it took to negotiate all the appointments onto one day, but finally Mother Hilda's chest clinic was at 9.13 am; Sister Rosemary was at the podiatrist at 12 noon; Dymphna's ears were at 2.46 pm and Mother Gertrude's orthopaedics at 4.28 pm. It was always going to be a long day.

We took sandwiches and flasks to avoid paying the terrible prices they charge – I suppose they have to fund the NHS somehow, but £3.25 for a cheese and pickle sandwich – they ought to be ashamed! And anyway I don't think the money goes to the hospital; it might be Costa Coffee or Little Burger Picnic who ought to be ashamed. And the hospital staff have to buy their food there too, so they are paid the barest minimum and then sold hugely expensive lunches. It's all wrong! You can tell my nerves have taken a beating.

So I put our supplies into the rucksack and we set off to walk to the bus stop at 6.45 am. There is only one bus a day and it's at 7.15 from the turn off the main road, and that's 20 minutes walking briskly and half an hour for hospital patients – even ones as game as ours. It was lucky we were well-wrapped because the winds were straight off the tundra. The electronic display board the Parish Council invested in was telling us the next bus was the '213 to R@£4!&' and was 19 minutes late – it's always broken, but never quite broken enough to be certain that you can ignore it. We relied on the old-fashioned method of squinting up the road instead. There used to be a shelter, but a lorry misjudged the corner, so now you just stand there on the roadside, lashed by icy winds and splashed by black arcs of freezing water thrown out by passing HGVs. We said a few rosaries to pass the time and the bus was only 16 minutes late. After that it was plain sailing all the way to the Park and Ride outside Cambridge. I don't know whether you remember this, dear, but East Anglian country bus rides are always a little bit longer than elsewhere because every single passenger pauses to thank the driver on their way off. It's a touching tradition, but (Lord forgive my impatience) I do occasionally wish they'd do it a bit quicker.

You may not be familiar with the concept of Park and Ride – it means big fields on the outskirts of town are turned into car parks, and buses drive the passengers into town instead of people taking their cars. They're strange places. Nobody seems to know yet whether to model them on a bus station or a visitor attraction ticket office. The architectural style suggests they commissioned someone young and optimistic after a competition. The one we use looks like a Bauhaus Martian spacecraft. It's cheaper to buy your ticket from the machine than to pay the bus driver. With five of us, the saving adds up, so we had carefully brought exactly the right amount of change, but when Dymphna attempted to use it, one of the pound coins was rejected. No reason we could see, but the machine simply spat it out. The bus arrived, everyone else climbed aboard and the driver was beginning to tap his fingers on the steering wheel. We didn't have another pound coin to use. All we could do was keep vainly pushing the same one back in. It was a stressful moment until an enormously tall boy in studded boots and a black leather cloak cut like a bat's wings stepped forward and offered one of his.

"Give this one a go," he said.

"There's nothing wrong with it, it's just the machine." I said, trying to give him the reject coin.

"You're alright," said vampire boy, "this one's on me. All Goths together, like."

Mercifully it worked, the machine chugged out its ticket and we hurried on. Even so we were slightly late for the first appointment and if anyone had needed to have their blood pressure taken, it wouldn't have been good.

The receptionist at the chest clinic said, "You're late. Shall I tick 'transport difficulties'? Only I need to give a reason."

"I waited three hours last time I came," Mother Hilda pointed out, "and now I'm 12 minutes late and you want me to explain why? That seems harsh."

"Would you be wanting a complaint form?" asked the receptionist.

"We've been travelling since 6.45," I tried to explain.

"I'll tick 'transport' then. The clinic is running about 20 minutes late."

"So it doesn't matter, then, that we're 12 minutes late ourselves?"

"No, as it happens."

"So why did you have to...?"

Without looking up from her screen, the receptionist sighed. She beat a short tattoo on the desk with elaborately painted fingernails. "Yeah. It's two different systems. On the computer? Appointment lateness is one and running times is another. I just follow the instructions on the screen, yeah?"

I kept Mother Hilda company in the waiting area. She had a little doze after all the excitement of the journey and I had a look at a two-year-old copy of Vogue, which was the only reading material not about model aeroplanes or embroidery. The models were grim-faced, glaring and skeletal with huge puffs of knotted hair. They lurked in grimy alleyways, dark circles painted around their eyes for the authentic slum-dwelling madwoman look, in dresses worth the equivalent of a small bungalow in Hog Fen. I thoroughly enjoyed it.

By 10, nobody had gone from the waiting room, despite a lot of nurses passing up and down. The receptionist looked at her watch and left. There were three other patients waiting now. We continued to wait. Then the phones started to ring. They rang, stopped, rang again. When one phone stopped, another started. This happened several times. Finally I decided it might be something urgent, so they needed to be answered, and the next time one rang I picked it up.

"Hello?" said a brisk voice, "Is that the chest clinic?"

"Yes, it is," I said, "but there's nobody at reception."

"So who are you?"

"A visitor," I said.

"What? Who told you to..?"

"The phone keeps ringing and there's nobody else to answer it. Perhaps I can take a message?"

"What? No! I'll phone back later."

Next ring. This time I said "Hello? I'm not the receptionist, I'm a patient, actually I'm the friend of a patient, but there's nobody here at reception. I can take a message..."

"A patient? A patient, did you say?"

"The friend of a patient. I can't help very much, but I could take a message."

"But where are the receptionists?"

"I don't know, I'm afraid. There was only one and she just left."

"Good God!"

"So you could leave a message if you like."

"Great Scott, I never heard anything like it! What's this place coming to?"

Every caller was either horrified or burst out laughing, so I probably wasn't as helpful as I intended to be. Luckily the doctor called for Mother Hilda before much longer and I was able to make my escape and go and see Rev Tim in the chapel.

Rev Tim is always rushed off his feet, but he still finds time for a chat, and always talks as if you were the only person who mattered in the world, and remembers tiny details you have told him; my definition of a saint.

"So how are things at St Winifreda's?" he asked, over a cup of tea from his flask (he can't afford hospital prices either). I brought out our convent-made Armadillo biscuits, his favourites. We always bring him a few.

I said, "We're fine, Tim, only a bit worried about building repairs and struggling without the minibus." He had been a frequent visitor to the ward when I was recovering after the crash.

"Wouldn't the insurance money help?" he asked.

"It would help, but only by a fraction. It's difficult without. We had to leave before 7 am today."

"That's too much," he said. "Won't they provide transport?"

"Perhaps they would, but we don't need it. We're not ill, these are just check-ups. We don't like to ask for transport unless we really need it, Tim, the NHS hasn't got money to burn."

"Well, no, but I think they could spare a car for a quick run to Hog Fen. I know the organiser. I could give him a ring."

"Oh no," I said, "thanks anyway, but we have return tickets. And how are you and the other chaplains?"

"Well it's non-stop." he said. "We support everyone;

patients, families and staff and all of them stressed for different reasons, it's a lot to keep up with. I don't know when I was last home for supper. You can't say to someone desperate to talk – oh I can't listen to your heartbreaking story just now, it's my turn to cook the spag bol tonight – can you?"

While we were talking there was an odd scrabbling sound coming from the corner of his office. Now there was a little squeak too.

I said, "Tim, you don't think you have mice, do you? Only I've heard rodent sounds a few times at the convent and that sounded like one to me."

"Gerbils," he said. He leaned over and pulled a cover off a cage. "Long story. Little boy in Mercia Ward. They're the only thing that cheers him up. His mum and dad were bringing them here every day on the bus, but the bus company wasn't too sure it was allowed and besides they had to pay an extra fare, so I offered to keep them here." The little animals were springing playfully about in their cage. "It's breaking all sorts of regulations, but everyone's pretending they haven't noticed. Are you making any visits, while you're here?"

I said yes, I'd offered to see one of Father Humbert's parishioners as Humbert had turned his ankle on the dry ski slope.

"Oh Lord, don't let Humbert take up skiing!" Tim

THE POWER OF CAKE

said, walking me to the door, "Somebody stop him, quick. Talk about accident prone. That man could break a bone sitting on a sofa!"

"He was there with the NEETs," I said. "It was in a good cause."

"NEETs?"

"It stands for Not in Education, Employment or Training."

"Bit hard to see where skiing might fit their lifestyle, but I suppose it's a long-term thing," Tim said. "Humbert has a heart of gold, but he's a danger to himself. Send him my best."

Then it was off to Ward 9, Southgate Ward, to see Mr Wilkins. I knew nothing about him, except that he was 91, terminally ill, and had no family. I was expecting something quite sad. His bed was empty when I arrived, so I went to ask at the nurses' desk, fearing the worst, but as I passed a door in the corridor I heard a quiet knocking and a polite little "Help!"

"Hello," I said at the door.

"I can't get out," said the voice, "I'm locked in. I tried pulling the emergency cord, but nothing happened. I've been here half an hour."

"Are you alright?" I asked. "Shall I call a nurse? I'm just a visitor."

"I'm fine. I'm not hurt," he said, "I'm just locked in."

I could see the lock was a very straightforward one, so I thought I might give it a try. I opened it quite easily using the rejected pound coin I still had in my pocket. The door flew open immediately and Mr Wilkins – it turned out to be him – burst out, laughing. He was astonished to see me. "What? Oh look, I've been rescued by a nun! A nun who can pick locks! What a turn up!"

He was a tiny man, but spry, in a vast dressing gown. He laughed so hard he had to lean against the wall. "Where d'you learn a trick like that, Sister? I thought I'd be needing the fire brigade!"

So the visit to Mr Wilkins started very merrily and so it went on. We giggled about horseracing (his old world), locksmithing (my father's career), and hospitals, especially the entertainment to be had in Southgate Ward – there was plenty of it, if you knew where to look. There was a Somali nurse who sang to them at night to help them sleep, there was a beloved ward assistant from Romania, who was so beautiful that she lit up the ward and was also willing to make a cup of tea at any time of day. Best of all there was a doctor who prescribed Guinness every night as a tonic.

"Are you sure?" I said, "That sounds a bit unconventional to me."

"As I live and breathe! Only a small bottle, mind you, but it doesn't half cheer the place up. Proper doctoring that is."

Mr Wilkins is very ill, but not in the least downhearted. "I was at first," he told me, "but then all of a sudden it just fell away and wasn't worried any more. I can't say why. Nothing religious, Sister, saving your presence. I just suddenly saw the funny side. I'm 91, I've had a few regrets, but on the whole I can't complain. My life's been good. I've ridden a few winners; had my share of fun; met some great people; made a bit of money. I'm lucky."

The gift of Mr Wilkins' good cheer took me right through the arduous business of rounding up the elderly sisters, queuing for the first bus, waiting 45 minutes for the second and enduring the icy blasts of the Hog Fen winds for the walk back to St Win's. We were half way along the lane, and it was beginning to sleet, when a large car slowed alongside and an expensive window slid down, revealing our neighbour, Roger Collis, of Intermediax, the company up the road.

"Looks as if you ladies need a ride," he said.

I was about to say, rather ungraciously, "No thanks, we're nearly there," but the other sisters were already climbing aboard enthusiastically, so we all had a few minutes' heated luxury before we were home.

"What's the delay?" Collis asked, when I'd helped

the sisters out and was closing the door. "You really do need a new vehicle of some sort, don't you? Surely the insurance...?"

"Not enough," I said.

Collis looked out of his heated windscreen into the driving rain. He narrowed his eyes. "I'll give it some thought. Quick, get them inside before they're washed away."

From start to finish the hospital visit took 10 hours and 45 minutes, but there was hot soup waiting and twelve new internet orders for nunpegs (one from Lichtenstein!), so we soon recovered.

Good luck in the mountains. We loved the photograph of the waterfall. Is abseiling down it really such a good idea, though?

Take care!

Best wishes,

Sister B.

6

St Win's
September 15th

Dear Emelda,

Rev Mother has decided we should all be bolder and embrace change more willingly. It's one of the recommendations she brought back from *The 21st Century Sister – Religious Women Going Forward*, her latest conference. She also brought back Sister Doris Riley from the Little Sisters of the Common Faith in Los Angeles. Sister Doris (incidentally not a *little* sister herself, at all) is a psychotherapist researching religious groups. She offers free counselling in return.

Not everyone was keen. "Why would we need that? We have managed several hundred years without the services of a head shrinker," Eustacia said at convocation, "surely prayer offers us all we need."

"I just thought it would be interesting to have Sister Doris's services available to us," Rev Mother said.

When we met Sister Doris we could quite see why she was a big name in psychotherapy (which she is, apparently). She is very gently spoken, but somehow very penetrating. She seems to know all about you after only five minutes' conversation. It's a little unsettling.

"You must find it very inconvenient, managing

without a vehicle," she said to me, when she came into the Shoppe.

"We all do," I said.

"But for you, especially, as the driver. It was a role you enjoyed..."

"Well, yes, I did."

"You like driving?"

"Yes, I do. I always have."

"It represents...freedom, perhaps, to you..."

"I suppose it does," I said.

"And now it is gone."

"Yes. Only temporarily, we hope."

"And you have been feeling a little below par since..."

"Who said that?"

"I was just imagining how it would be to lose something that represented so much. Your life is quite enclosed, you stay here most of the time, and then your one means of seeing the world is removed..." said Sister Doris in her soft Californian accent.

"I don't think it's that serious," I said, "I am happy here, and busy."

"Oh no question about that," Sister Doris said, she was examining nunpegs on the handmade crafts display, "very busy, no doubt about that at all."

"And it's not as if I took the van on jaunts when it was here. I usually drove the retired sisters to their appointments at the hospital or delivered vegetables."

"Of course…"

"Or went to a supermarket occasionally or over to collect chicken feed from the farm, or to borrow the rotovator or collect someone from the station…"

"All very useful…"

"I never went far, really," I said, "just local trips, routine things."

"Yes. Those are the things we miss most, though, aren't they, if they are taken away from us?" She picked up a nunpeg, straightened its headdress and placed it carefully back.

"I suppose they are," I said.

"And your accident, that must have been…"

"Well, I was lucky really."

"Of course you were."

"Wonderful treatment and so on."

"But no van to climb back into."

"No."

"Well, sister, I won't keep you. I see customers on the way."

And she left. It was an odd feeling, Emelda. It was as if she had gently nudged a door open in my heart and I needed to go in and look around. I rather wished she hadn't.

There was a meeting today with the Bishop and

his team. I was in charge of biscuits. I went for the Conservative Older Person's Serious Occasion Selection, which is Garibaldis, Nice and Custard Creams, plus a few of Nesbitt's homemade Convent Crumbles, but no Gingernuts – too frivolously crunchy.

I readied the plates of biscuits and was just about to carry them over, when the door of the Shoppe opened very quietly and a sister I didn't recognise slipped in. She was a small figure in a short grey habit. "Boniface?" she asked, striding over.

I said yes, that was me.

"I'm Sister Joy Vernon. I'm part of the Bishop's team; his management consultant. I specialise in PR and media relations. Are you the one dealing with the media for the convent?"

"The media?" I said. "No, I don't think..."

"Only I heard you'd set up a magazine feature... Beautiful Homes and Lovely Country Gardens Magazine?" She pulled a phone from her pocket and stroked its surface. "Ah yes, here it is. Tilly Matthews contacted me."

"Oh that," I said, "yes, Tilly has suggested a make-over..."

"Yes. Not going to happen," said Sister Vernon. She held her hand out as if to stop traffic. "Sorry; no can do. Not pre-cleared, you see. I don't want to be difficult, Sister, but to be honest, the rules could hardly be plainer."

I was confused. "Rules?" I asked her. "What rules? I don't understand."

"You can't just go publishing media stories left and right without consulting. Who knows what they might write?"

I said, "She offered to carry out some work. It wouldn't cost anything and I thought…"

Sister Vernon smiled, "You can't be expected to understand the media implications of a feature. To you it's a simple matter of a bit of help with smartening the place up – and goodness knows it needs it," she said, looking about her, " but I have the corporate perspective to take into account. If you go running features saying the place is shabby and in need of a make-over, what does it say about the diocese as a whole? Why should St Winifreda's benefit from such an opportunity when there are other diocesan buildings far more in need of it? Do you get my meaning, Sister? Am I making this clear?"

"But surely…" I was struggling to follow her.

"It's the implications, Sister. I know it's hard for you to see the bigger picture, but from where I stand a feature like that does far more harm than good. Far more. It sends out all the wrong messages. It's not what we want to signal to the world at all. We have a very comprehensive PR plan. You can check it any time, it's online. We're all about modernisation and community integration this year. Seriously, Sister, the wrong message at the wrong time can undo months of strategic planning."

I was stunned. "But, isn't a little café a good example of modernisation and integration with the community?" I asked. "It will be members of the community who come and eat here, after all."

Sister Joy looked into the distance and pursed her lips before slipping her phone back into the folds of her habit. "A café is neither here nor there," she said, sweeping a look around her, "obviously you'd need professional help and wherever do you imagine the customers are going to come from? No, it's the uncontrolled media exposure I'm concerned to avoid. Bishop Tom understands. I'm going to leave it there."

And she swept out, the door banging behind her. The open/closed sign flew off, crashed down and spun across the floor.

Nesbitt came in with a tray of sausage rolls.

"You alright, Sister B? You look a bit..."

"I'm fine," I said. "What do you think, Nesbitt, about using that bit of space for a few tables and opening a café? It's just a thought."

"A café? Our own café? What, we could serve lunches and proper meals, you mean?"

"Do you think people would come?"

She was arranging the sausage rolls and didn't even look up, but I could tell from the back of her head that she was smiling.

"'Course they would," she said. "There isn't a café for miles. People'd love it."

The smell of fresh baking immediately began to have its irresistible effect on the workers in the offices up the lane. They can't possibly be able to sniff a sausage roll from half a mile; sometimes I suspect them of having hidden cameras. Whatever method they use, they are here within a minute of something special arriving, and today was no exception, so we were busy for the next hour, selling. I didn't really get a chance to think any more about Sister Joy's warning until later.

At convocation Rev Mother declared that the Bishop wanted Sister Joy to start attending our convocations.

"Oh, watch out," said Eustacia.

"Now Eustacia, we've talked about maintaining a positive attitude, I think," Rev Mother said.

"I'm not feeling very positive either," I said, "She was very annoyed about Tilly's make-over feature. Said it wasn't part of the PR plan and it wasn't going to happen."

"In so many words?"

"Yes. 'No can do,' she said."

"Did she say why?"

"There's a PR plan and this wasn't part of it, and they didn't want people's attention drawn to the shabbiness..."

"Oh now we're getting to it..." Eustacia said. "They think it might make them look bad."

"She may be right," Rev Mother said. "It would look as if they weren't supporting their convents."

"Well, they're not!" several sisters said at once. "They're not supporting us at all!"

"No, so I suggest we ignore Sister Joy and go ahead as planned," Rev Mother said, "besides, we shouldn't mistake the strictures of Sister Joy with the Bishop's real view. In my experience very good and noble people are often surrounded by fearsome staff. The Dalai Lama's people are probably absolute rottweilers."

We all thought about that for moment. Her theory certainly applies to doctors' receptionists, I thought.

"Did you show him the drains?" asked Eustacia.

"Yes, drains and the chapel were both discussed," said Rev Mother, "all they can do is to add our repairs to the long list of work needed in the diocese. Naturally, we come way below the Grade 1 listed buildings and the cathedral, so there is not much chance of any money.

There was an offer of a loan. I'm not keen, but we may have to think about it."

"Is being in debt necessarily a terribly bad thing?" Hermione said. "It's a way of life these days. Students have loans to pay back; people have mortgages, if they're lucky enough to be able to buy somewhere to live. Having a loan to repay would put us in the same boat as most other people, and we shouldn't be afraid of that. We should share life with the people around us as far as possible, shouldn't we?"

"And we'll be able to pay it back, anyway, as soon as the money from the Poore Pasture comes through. And surely that can't be too long now. Any news from the lawyers?" asked Sister Bernard.

Rev Mother sighed, "Mrs Dunne's confident, but there's no telling how long it will take. Oh, and the accountant – Mr Wooler – says he needs to go through some more of the financial records. In fact, he's back on Wednesday, which reminds me, Hermione, he says our security arrangements need updating. He wants a secure room for records and a fireproof safe inside the room. Data Protection insists on it, or fire regulations, or both – he wasn't quite clear. Can we find him a room? He'll supply the safe."

Hermione looked puzzled. "I can't imagine which regulations make all that necessary," she said.

"He could use the Retreat Cell off the library landing, I suppose," said Rev Mother, "that locks, doesn't it, Boniface?"

"Yes, it has a special lock."

So, it looks as if we might be taking out a loan for building repairs for the first time in the history of St Win's.

But then, as Mrs Odge would say, you've got to move with the times. Shame about the make-over, though. I was looking forward to a bit of bunting.

When the plate came back from the meeting they'd left all the biscuits untouched, except the Convent Crumbles. At least they know a good biscuit when they see one.

Best wishes,

Sister B.

7

St Winifreda-in-the-Fen
September 17th

Dear Trekker with Mules in Mountains and Rainforests,

Pavel has a new toy, a shredder for garden waste. He must have bought it himself, it certainly didn't come from our funds. Its motor is in the background all day long. He and Carmella have shredded all the cuttings from the hedge, the tree prunings and the veg garden waste into tiny pieces for the compost heap. It's brilliant stuff, our compost. It looks like chocolate cake after a few months and Carmella can make anything grow in it. We don't use chemicals, but we're not strictly organic, which means our veg have all the lumps and bumps of real organic veg without attracting the premium prices. From the shopkeeper's point of view this is a great pity. I often have to explain the less-than-perfect appearance of, say, a carrot or potato, or the presence of an earwig in an apple (or six earwigs in one memorable case – I had to give that customer a free cauliflower).

Hari Menon, my Retail for Beginners tutor from the college, shook his head at the veg display when he came last week.

"They are good food, Sister, I know, but frankly they

are not tempting to the eye. The sales of these gnarled little vegetables, especially some which are – forgive me for saying this – also a little wrinkled and past-it in their appearance. The sales of these things, despite their undoubted nutritional merit, dear Sister, will not be profitable, I am afraid."

Hari is always tremendously diplomatic.

"But Hari, our whole principle is that we sell our own homegrown produce here in the Shoppe," I said.

"Indeed," Hari said, "and an honourable principle it is too, Sister, and one I wholeheartedly support, but there is more than one way, I believe the saying has it, there is more than one way to swing a cat."

For a moment I thought he was suggesting selling pets. I must have looked surprised.

"You could cook with these vegetables that cannot be sold. Your cooks do wonderful things with cakes and pastries already. They could perhaps create a few savoury dishes also. A simple vegetable curry, or dhal would be my choice, but you will know the dishes that would attract your customers better than I. Value adding, remember, Sister. Always value adding!"

He's right about the wonderful cakes and pastries. Nesbitt is working on Danish pastries this week. They look delicious.

"These are going to be popular," I told her.

"They take a long time because of the yeast," she said, sliding the tray into the cake cabinet. "I started these at 6 am."

She had scarcely finished lining them up before the door flew open and in came the masons. The tower workers are a brilliant crowd. In the fiercest weather they are out there with Pavel in their high viz jackets and helmets. They were measuring and taking photographs before, but now they have begun the actual repairs. It begins with quite a lot of destructive work, as they had to take down all the loose and unstable masonry to begin from a firm foundation. There never was much of a firm foundation to the bell tower, so a lot of it has gone now.

Their work is cut out for them, but they seem to enjoy it enormously. That's what you get with specialists, I think – for these are folly tower repair specialists and until we met them we had no idea such a thing existed or how utterly undaunted they are by a gothic monstrosity that has been raining down monumental stonework for a century and a half.

All around their work area at the foot of the tower there is now a display of gargoyles. They are an impressively horrible sight. Close up their grimacing faces are remarkably varied. There are scowls and snarls and some that seem to be shrieking. There are beaks and bared teeth and rolling eyes and lunging talons and scales and lolling tongues all in a row. Any evil spirit coming up our lane would be stopped in its tracks, if we believed in any such thing, which in this rational age we, of course, do not. We have to admire the detail and craftsmanship that went in to making them as appalling and fearsome as this, though.

Pavel oversees the project, but the Archer and Snow team are led by Ollie, who is himself a fitness and healthy diet man, buying only fruit and green tea from the shop; he brings his own salads in a plastic box. The other stonemasons, Ellie, Derek and Marshall, on the other hand, are first in any queue for fresh cakes. They have walkie-talkie radios and I've definitely heard them send cake alerts from the scaffolding.

"Derek to Marshall. Over."

"Marshall here."

"Cakes being delivered to shop. Over."

"What kind? Over."

"Looks like apple turnovers. Over."

"Roger that. On way. How many turnovers? Over."

"Just two for me thanks. Over."

"Roger and out."

Mr Wooler, the diocesan accountant, is here again, auditing. This means two things are needed: Garibaldi biscuits and moral support for Hermione, whose job it is to act as his assistant. Mr Wooler is very inclined to find fault with our book-keeping arrangements, no matter how meticulous Hermione tries to make them. Yesterday I saw her run into the garden on three occasions and beat the clump of stinging nettles by the compost heap with a bean stick. It's clearing the nettles rather effectively, but I'm not sure it really works as therapy for Hermione – she looks shattered.

"Whatever is he doing?" Sister Gertrude asked at convocation. "Surely it would only take ten minutes to look over our books? We're hardly a multinational corporation, it's all in one little ledger isn't it?"

Hermione sighed. "Don't get me started. He's insisting on a handwritten ledger and an electronic spreadsheet – which is fine, it doesn't take long, but then he disappears into the Retreat Cell with them and spends all day with the door locked. I have to knock when I carry him his tea."

"The cheek!" Eustacia muttered. "I'd give him what for if he asked *me* to bring his tea."

"He says it's because of data protection."

"It that true? How much security can be needed? We have no money and a set of accounts that show it. Why does that need protection?"

"It's all in the regulations, he says." Hermione shrugged in resignation. "He really just wants to be left alone. He works away in there on his little computer and I just take him tea or coffee and listen to his complaints every now and then."

"Makes you wonder what he's up to in there," Eustacia said.

"Well, whatever it is I hope it leads to some more funds," Rev Mother told us. "We've got another round of dental appointments coming up, and we really must think about a vehicle."

"Oh, and he wants to come and look at the Shoppe records tomorrow," Hermione added.

Sure enough, Mr Wooler appeared in the Shoppe at precisely 11, walked straight behind the counter and helped himself to our ledger. He flicked through it, tutting.

"There are anomalies, I'm afraid. And I need specimen signatures from everyone."

"What sort of anomalies?" I said, "Perhaps we can put them right together. It's really a very simple system."

"You don't need to tell me that, I can see how simple it is." Mr Wooler said. "As an auditor, it is not my job to 'put things right', my job is to..."

At this point he suddenly jerked upright as if electrocuted and stared wild-eyed around the Shoppe.

"Is that a wasp?"

I listened. I couldn't hear anything.

"I hate the things."

"Oh dear," I said, "are you allergic? It's not wasp season."

"Not allergic. I just can't abide the filthy creatures... there it is again!"

He began swiping the air with the documents he was carrying. "I can hear it, it's here! No, there it is! I'll get it."

He sprang to one side, swung a great arc and delivered a blow like a tennis serve above his head, then leapt round and did the same on the other side, uttering war cries of "Yrrrah!" and "Gotcha!" For several minutes he windmilled about the Shoppe in a frenzy, beating the air, knocking over a sack of potatoes and sweeping a whole row of nunpegs off a windowsill.

"Mr Wooler," I said, from behind the counter, where I had taken cover, "Mr Wooler, I don't think there is a wasp here."

"People always say that!" he yelled, careening past, "I'm often the only one who hears them. People are just deaf to the disgusting things."

He aimed a sharp blow at a light fitting, which flew apart, followed by a vigorous backhand to the door, sending the open/closed sign flying to the ground, then froze in the middle of the Shoppe and peered breathlessly about, narrow-eyed, brandishing his paper weapon. "I'm always right. There's always one somewhere. I'll find it!"

He tiptoed around, examining corners, then hurled himself at the front window beating above his head to left and right until, satisfied, he stood back, dusted himself off, and began to examine his papers and then the floor, presumably for the remains of a squashed wasp.

Despite looking very carefully, he found nothing.

"It's fallen between the floorboards," he told me, "they often do that." And without another word he walked straight out of the Shoppe.

Nesbitt had witnessed all this from the back kitchen.

"Did *you* hear a wasp?" I asked her.

"There wasn't one," she said. "I reckon he's a nutter."

I couldn't get the incident out of my mind. I was still trying to mend the light fitting when Rev Mother came into the Shoppe for the cellar key. She teases me about my habit of carrying the convent keys – many of them large and ornate – around on an ancient ring and chain. "You're like a medieval jailer, Boniface!" she said.

"We all have our quirks," I said. "At least I don't cause havoc thrashing about after imaginary wasps." I told her about Mr Wooler's little episode.

"Perhaps he's under a lot of stress," she said, holding the steps as I tried to put the lampshade back together,

"I find spreadsheets very stressful. I can hardly imagine what it's like to work with them all the time."

"We must pray for Mr Wooler's patience, as well as our own, Rev Mother."

She gave me a funny look and left with the cellar key. She's on rat duty this week, which means checking the baited traps. This is the time of year they find a nice dry convent very appealing and start taking up residence unless we're very vigilant.

We happened to be reading from Ecclesiastes this evening: "He that diggeth a pit shall fall into it; and whoso breaketh an hedge, a serpent shall bite him."

Wasps weren't mentioned, nor were light fittings, but I couldn't help thinking of Mr Wooler.

Best wishes,

Sister B.

8

St Win's
September 19th

Dear Emelda,

I was on my way to the chapel for prayers last night when, passing the long passageway, I heard a distant sound. I couldn't identify it and, not wanting to be late, kept going. Rev Mother wasn't at prayers, when I looked around. Her pew was empty. This was unusual, but not in itself cause for alarm. Her office has the telephone, so occasionally a phone call or some other intrusion keeps her away.

It was chilly in the chapel, as usual, and its own smell of polish and prayer books with a hint of candle wax and chrysanthemum – the finest smell in the world – was calming our thoughts, even if there was a note of mould in there too, when between hymns I thought I heard the same indistinct thumping. It was rhythmic and slow, but persistent. I dismissed it from my mind as determinedly as I could, but it was definitely still there in the background of both readings. My pew is nearest Hermione's. I caught her eye. She had heard it too.

As we filed out, Hermione and I left the line of sisters filing towards the refectory and headed towards the sound. We didn't speak, but I think we shared the same worry, because by the time we were at the long passageway we were beginning to run. The knocking came again, clearly this time. It was coming from the open cellar door. Hermione got there first and immediately blocked the entrance with her arm. She had seen the wooden cellar steps in pieces below. The rotten timbers had fallen apart half way down and there, lying at the bottom in the dim light of a single bulb we could see Rev Mother.

"Be careful! Be careful of the stairs!" she called. "I fell. Don't come too near!"

We leaned over and peered in.

"I think I've broken my ankle. I heard it crunch," she said, matter-of-factly. "The stairs gave way beneath me. We'll need an ambulance. I've been banging on the wall for an hour. I was afraid someone would come running and fall in after me."

It was a complicated rescue because the ambulance crew couldn't get down the cellar steps and sent for the fire brigade, who arrived in two huge fire engines and had to use ladders and the kind of stretcher you'd need to airlift someone off a mountain.

We made cups of tea because, while the main part of the team was in the cellar, there were a lot of fire officers who could only wait upstairs. There is something very touching about someone in bulky safety clothing taking off a big helmet before drinking their tea. They were mad about Nesbitt's lemon drizzle, I must remember to tell her.

Eustacia went in the ambulance and rang us from A and E. Rev Mother has broken her left ankle and her right wrist. The right ankle and left wrist are both badly strained. Whilst the injuries themselves are not terribly serious, thank the Lord, they are completely disabling. She can do nothing for herself.

Tomorrow we'll organise the hospital visiting rota and get to grips with this latest "little challenge to our prayer schedule", as poor Rev Mother Elizabeth would no doubt call it. She has suggested Sister Prudence as her deputy. Prudence is the obvious choice as she is a Rev Mother in Nigeria, leading a large sisterhood, and running a school in Nairobi. Managing a little place like St Win's for a while should be a piece of cake to her (so to speak).

Best wishes,

Sister B.

9

St Win's
September 21st

Dear Emelda,

Thanks for your last letter. We loved hearing the details of the trek so far. Mud, mountains, dripping forest, searing heat – it reminded Sister Bernard of her Duke of Edinburgh award. Little Raulito, whose canoe is also the postvan, ambulance and bus service, is our new hero. We picture him paddling undaunted up vast swollen tea-coloured rivers to tiny outposts marked by only the glimpse of a palm-roofed house, and leaving letters under the stone you mentioned – the one he marks with a plastic bottle on a stick.

Sometimes I rather envy your internet-free (indeed electricity-free) existence out there in the jungle. No irritating virus warnings popping up to give you mysteriously threatening messages every two minutes, which has started to happen on our big computer. *"Do you wish to reboot in safe mode?"* (Do I? Who knows? It sounds quite attractive.) You suffer none of the bleeps and chimes and ringings that punctuate the lives of people with electronic devices. On the other hand, we're not likely to be bitten by a poisonous spider or kidnapped, so I shouldn't complain.

I was at a Teaching Pronunciation workshop

today with Very Clever Jenny over at the college. The other students all kept looking at their little phones, they burbled and twitched and buzzed all the time. Eventually I asked why. They showed me the phonetic alphabet displayed on them: their phones were giving them all the answers. No wonder they all seemed to know so much more than I did.

At break time Samira, my neighbour, showed me a game called Angry Birds. You flick cartoon birds from a catapult and use them to kill little piggy cartoon creatures. I got through three levels before I realised something very addictive was taking up residence in my brain and quickly passed it back. I said, "Samira, when you only half kill the piggy things, they have black eyes and bruises. It's a little bit violent, isn't it?"

She said, "Right. If anyone ever asks you to look at Grand Theft Auto, you'd better say no. You might be all right with Where's My Water, though."

Anyway, I definitely need to raise my game when it comes to the International Phonetic Alphabet, so forgive me if I practise a little.

We really look forward to your letters /letəz/, Emelda. Life at St Winifreda's is far flatter without your news. We don't go looking for excitement, obviously, but we enjoy a little of it when it comes our way. And winter is ahead, with all its cold winds and chilblains /

tshilblenz/. A glimpse of Peru now and then is a great treat – mountains! – wonderful even to think of them. But we know your trek takes you far away from the nearest post office – it's bad enough finding one round here, they are as rare as Great Auks these days, so we don't expect you to write very often.

We're even more aware than usual of the contrast between your roving life in the wild rainforests and ours here at St Win's at the moment because we are marooned without transport. On Monday Sister Eustacia and I went along to a garage to look for a new minibus. We saw Trevor, the Sales Manager (his name was on his badge) sitting in the middle of the vast showroom at a desk surrounded by unnaturally clean vehicles. He looked up as we approached. Trevor's professional skills include instant assessment of approaching customers, I imagine, because his face fell fairly obviously as he saw the two of us. We were a lot less likely to spend £75,000 on a vehicle than the very smartly-dressed man who followed us in.

Trevor nodded to us without moving but as soon as he saw this other customer he bustled over and welcomed him fulsomely. The gentleman looked puzzled and then said, in a delightful Italian accent, "But why you don't talk to these religious ladies? They was here first."

"Well, I thought they might like to..." Trevor gesticulated vaguely at the gleaming vehicles around us in the showroom.

"You should hask them!" the man told him. "Hask them first. Good morning, Sisters," he said very graciously to us, "this gentleman will talk to you first."

Outsmarted, Trevor had to make the best of it. "What can I interest you in, ladies?"

"Which is your cheapest minibus?" asked Eustacia, confirming his worst suspicions.

"You mean people carrier?"

"Is that what you call them now? We need to fit in six to eight."

Trevor led us outside and round the back to the furthest recesses of their stock of cars, where the least expensive second-hand vehicles were stored. He trod carefully in his shiny shoes; there was mud. The prices on the windscreens were still shocking.

"These are far too much," Eustacia said, with her usual Yorkshire clarity. "We are replacing a very old minibus that was written off in an accident. The insurance isn't nearly enough for one of these."

The Italian man had followed, and listened to the conversation.

"Oh!" he said, "You have an *haccident*?"

"Boniface here in a wheelchair for three

months." Eustacia told him, "multiple fractures."

"*O Dio!*" said the man, "but this is terrible!"

"Had to be cut out by firemen, didn't you, Boniface?"

"*Madonna!*" he cried, crossing himself. "And now? Are you well?"

"Oh, I'm fine now," I told him.

"If I could just…" Trevor was trying to get to business.

"Your old vehicle. What was hit like?" asked the Italian man.

"Oh very old." I said. "It was time it went, really, but it was our only means of transport and we have to get the elderly sisters to the doctor's and so forth. Only the insurance money wasn't much. Not nearly enough for one of these."

"We'd better be going," Eustacia said. "There isn't anything here for us."

"Where is your place…your house-a?"

"The convent? Hog Fen, Saint Winifreda's."

"I like to come and see you," said the man. "Soon I will come, yes?"

We said he'd be welcome and headed back to the bus stop. There are only three buses a day. It is surprisingly difficult to go car shopping by bus – you'd think someone would spot that hole in the market.

Later I was loading pumpkins into a customer's car when a very sleek low-slung vehicle pulled up outside the shop. It was the Italian.

"Ah Sister, you have a lovely place! Look at these beautiful buildings! And your tower – she is magnificent!"

"Well," I said, "she will be when she's repaired."

"But you are a long way from the town. You need a car. You must have a car."

"Well," I said, "we will have one as soon as we can find one that is cheap enough."

He followed me back into the shop and looked around. He seemed delighted with what he saw.

"You have fresh eggs! You have good bread. Real bread! You have cakes! Your cakes are wonderful! Is like Italy!"

"We have very good cooks," I told him.

"It makes me feel homesick!" He inhaled shop smells of bread and cake. "My aunt is a sister, a Benedictine, in Rome."

"Oh that's wonderful," I said.

"I am so proud of her," he said, striking his heart in a very Italian way. "I have a traditional family. Is an honour to have a family person in the Church back home. Unfortunately I myself am not religious. My name is Ferrara, Antonio Ferrara. You heard of me?"

"No," I said, "should I have?"

"Good. That is good. In Italy people know me, but

here only football people, I think. I look on your website," he said. "It say you can give English lessons. Is true?"

"Yes. I'm one of the teachers."

"Ah, you are a teacher, Sister! How is my English? Tell me, what do you think? Be honest!"

"Well..."

"Is terrible. Yes?"

"No," I said, "it's not terrible. It's good, very good."

"But my accent is terrible. No? And my grammar also, eh?"

"No, no," I said. "Not perfect, perhaps, but very good."

"People don't understand me. Is my accent, yes? Is bad?"

"It's a lovely accent," I said, "but, yes, it is quite strong, I suppose."

"So! You give me lessons. Improve my accent. I want to sound like a Royal Shakespeare! Like the husband of the Queen! You give me lessons. But don't tell nobody, eh? I want them to have a big surprise. They will say, 'Eh Antonio! Your English is perfect! We understand everything what you are telling us!' Is a deal, yes! Now goodbye, Sister, I must go to Birmingham. My assistant will ring about lessons, yes?" And pausing only to buy a walnut cake, he left.

So that's a new student to add to our register. And a good chance for me to practise my newly-learnt pronunciation teaching methods. We'll start with the silent h: /ɒnest/, not /hɒnest/, Antonio.

/ɪnglɪʃ/ pronunciation can be very hard.

And now I must rather anxiously prepare for an exercise class. Sister Prudence heard me mention that the physiotherapist prescribed regular vigorous exercise for my recovering legs and signed me up. She didn't actually ask me first.

"Boniface, I have put your name down for – oh, I have forgotten what it's called – some kind of exercise to music. It is on Wednesdays in the village hall. I saw a poster. They gave us a lovely discount. You can walk there, it will only take half an hour."

"It might be Pilates," Hermione said, when I told her, "that's very good for your core."

"Or Zumba," Sister Bernard added, "that's all the rage, I read it in *Hello* magazine. Don't look at me like that, one of the B&B guests left it behind. Lots of WAGs do Zumba. We'll have you on Strictly yet!"

Strictly? WAGs? Core? Zumba? A whole language has been invented when I wasn't looking. I didn't understand a word. I need to put on the convent's shared tracksuit and search for shoes suitable for vigorous dancing. I'm guessing wellies don't qualify.

Best wishes,

/sɪstə bɪ¨/

10

St Win's
September 25th

Dear Emelda,

A letter came yesterday from the Sisters Worldwide Writing Circle. It said,

"Dear Sister Boniface,

Congratulations! You have been nominated for the Sisters Worldwide Correspondent of the Year Award. Your correspondent, Sister Emelda Griggs, nominated you, and we are pleased to inform you that you have been awarded the Copia Prize, which means you are through to the next round. Here is your prize committee commendation:

"In writing more than sixty letters in a single year, Sister Boniface has far outstripped the basic requirements of the Writing Circle and given her correspondent enormous support and entertainment. The average number of letters written by members of SWWC is 6, so with 60 letters, Boniface's performance vastly outperformed anyone else's.

We have no hesitation in recommending her for the Copia Prize for the highest number of letters written."

Sister Prudence started to chuckle when she read it.

"Were you anticipating such an award?" she asked.

"No," I said, "I've never heard of it before."

"It is quite an honour, anyway," Prudence said, by now giggling aloud. "Even if you are being awarded for quantity rather than quality! It is most impressive that you find the time, Boniface, you certainly have enough work to keep you occupied. When is it that you do all this writing? Sixty letters, that is more than one a week!"

I felt rather guilty when she put it like this.

"Have I misused my time, do you think?"

"Misused it? Why do you ask that?"

"Well, perhaps I should have been using it for prayer or meditation or self-improvement in some way?"

She composed herself with an effort. "You were using your time to support a Sister who is on a difficult mission in a lonely and dangerous place. You are a major source of support to her and together you have set up a trading charity that raises funds for some of the poorest people on the planet. I believe it is high time you considered your letter-writing a form of work as well as a form of devotion in its own right, Boniface. Anyway, is there a prize?"

I looked back at the letter. "Yes, look, a voucher for a computer shop."

"Well," she said, chuckling, "we can let Sister Bernard loose with that in PC World, she will be very happy."

"Can I buy a few stamps too?"

"Only if they sell them in PC World. No! I am joking! Of course! You must have stamps, envelopes and a whole new A4 pad. Congratulations!" She was really laughing now. "Sorry, Boniface, but you must see the funny side. There's something a bit amusing about getting an award for writing *a lot!*"

Prudence mentioned the prize at convocation, and my dear sisters gave me little round of applause. They are all thrilled for me, although ever since they have been trying to make me feel better about the award being for quantity, saying things like "Well done, Boniface, I'm sure the letters are very *well* written as well as very *often* written!" and "Congratulations, dear, it's getting a *lot* of letters that is the important thing isn't it?"

I'm hoping they will stop now. The combination of being damned with faint praise, and congratulated for something I did with ease and enjoyment, is a little uncomfortable. I haven't won an award since the Fourth Year Girls' Skipping Race Silver Certificate. Deirdre Ronson carried off the gold. She is a violinist with the Hallé Orchestra now – and probably runs Médecins Sans Frontières on the side. Deirdre won some sort of commendation or award every week in her youth. She'd know how to handle this.

I wonder if Hilary Mantel feels the same? Do people say, "Well done, Hilary, for writing such *lovely long* books"? *Wolf Hall* is doing the rounds at St Win's. We have little time for leisure reading so it's moving very slowly, and should reach me by the May-after-next at the current rate. Hilary will probably be on to the next queen by then.

Another problem is that – like any such recognition – the Copia Prize brings with it a list of duties. One is to run a Creative Letter Writing Workshop at the SWW annual conference in London. They will pay travel costs so of course I am happy to do it, but completely stumped as to what to tell them. The sum total of my letter writing technique is this: *Write Down What Happens.*

Saying that certainly won't fill 50 minutes.

Anyway, thanks for the nomination, but enough with the prizes!

Yours, wrong-footed, but a bit thrilled too,

Sister B.

11

St Win's
September 28th

Dear Emelda,

This morning Nesbitt was wrapping sandwiches when she remarked that we have seen very little of Hermione in the Shoppe lately. Our novice is so engaged in her research for the History of St Winifreda's that she rarely emerges from the library. She threw herself into her work after Alphonsus completed his sentence and stopped coming. It's more than three months since he left now. I dropped into the library later, to see how she was, and found her sitting on the floor among a tidal wave of papers.

"Can I help?" I said. "I have an hour, Nesbitt's doing a stock-take and Mrs Yu cancelled her lesson today."

"You might have a look at these," she said, and thrust a handful of documents towards me. "These are the letters from the box labelled Bad Things."

"What sort of letters are they?"

Hermione shrugged. "Most are warnings of one sort or another. Sometimes the sisters are reminded about a bill they should pay, but it isn't usually money. Often they're warnings about a regulation. They contravened a lot of orders and regulations, apparently. For example," she pulled a letter from her pile. "This one tells the Rev Mother of the day that she is not supposed to give money to causes other than those approved by the Diocese." She read aloud: *"I would remind the sisterhood that grants to the poor must always, under all circumstances, be approved in advance and in writing by the Benevolence Committee. Such decisions must not be made* ad hoc *for fear of the misapplication or duplication of grants and donations."*

"So they gave money away?" I asked.

"Well, I can cross-reference a lot of these letters with the account books, which are always very neatly kept. This one, for instance, seems to refer to a donation of three shillings and fourpence to 'Miss T. Morton'. She picked up a huge dusty ledger and pointed out an entry in elegant copperplate handwriting. It said, *'to Miss Theodora Morton, destitute vagrant woman, three shillings and fourpence for clothing and food.'"*

"And they didn't like that?"

"No. Every time the books are inspected – and they seem to be inspected very often, at least twice a year – there follows a series of letters of complaint. The sisters just seem to give up reading them at some point and start throwing them into the box and locking it."

We stood in the peace of the library, surrounded by the heavenly smell of books and beeswax polish.

Sunlight filtered down from the high windows around us. I thought of all the generations of sisters who had studied and meditated there over the years. "How long did this go on for?" I finally asked.

Hermione waved a hand over the piles, "About a century!"

"And all these letters are complaints of one sort or another?"

"They seem to be. The sisters harboured the destitute, they fed the poor, they gave away their produce, they allowed vagrants to stay in a lean-to outside the west wall, they allowed men to work in the gardens – which was not permitted at the time – and they seem not to have sent anyone to represent the convent at any of the meetings the Bishops called. The Bishops always seemed very fond of meetings."

"And nobody from the convent ever went?"

"Well, I guess not, as they never even opened the letters."

"What a wilful lot they were, our predecessors."

"Well, they were very popular with the people in the villages, who seem to have given them money, even though they were generally very poor themselves. The account books are full of small donations. People just arrived and handed over a few coins. Lots of them did it quite regularly, a sixpence here, a shilling there.

Even so, the sisters were terribly poor. Quite a few of them kept journals, I've been reading them." Hermione sighed. She pointed to a bookshelf where she had lined up the journals of assorted shapes and sizes. "Sister B, I don't know whether this life is for me."

She took one of the little volumes off the shelf, opened it at random and read an entry:

'November 10th 1903

On this day Sister Catherine fell and was gathered unto The Lord whilst in chapel. We think it may have been the cold. She was so light that we hardly even needed two of us to carry her to the infirmary. When Doctor McWhinney came, he signed the certificate and put 'malnutrition and pneumonia' as the cause of death. We have run out of tea, and had to have barley grounds again this evening. They look like boiled floor sweepings and probably are just that, as they were donated by Farmer Winton after he cleared his old barn. God forgive me my greed and my ingratitude and please welcome the soul of dear departed Catherine.'

I said, "Hermione, I think it would be better if you took a little break from this work for a day or two, dear. It is not good for your spirits to be always indoors. Why don't you go for a walk or come and help me check the mail order stockroom? We have so many nunpegs now that we need a better system for organising them."

Hermione showed no sign of responding to this. "It's Alphonsus, Sister B. I miss Alphonsus. I think it must be that."

"Yes," I said, "we guessed."

"Did you? I was hoping it wasn't obvious."

"It wasn't obvious. It was Nesbitt who noticed. We could see that you got on well with him. We guessed you would probably miss him once he left."

Hermione looked down at the letter she was holding in her lap. "Do you know, Sister, it actually hurts. Real physical pain, I don't mean metaphorical stuff, I mean it actually is a pain, roughly in the heart region. It's always there. It's funny that such a clichéd idea should turn out to be accurate. Humiliating. I'm embarrassed. I don't seem able to control it. I should be able to set it aside and go on, but I wake every morning and a horrible grey sadness just floods me from head to toe."

Tears began to run down Hermione's cheeks. I sat on the floor beside her.

"Is there anything we can do to help?" I said.

"No." She blotted her eyes rather matter-of-factly. "Nobody can help, except by being patient. I am just waiting, trying to find out what it means for me, and what I need to do. I love it here. I love life here at St Win's. I have always wanted to be part of a community like this one. But now it seems so much more involved. I suppose until recently I hadn't really been aware of what it meant giving up. A partner, children – it's a huge choice to make, to consciously choose a life without them."

"Yes," I said, "it isn't for most people. There are plenty of ways of living a good life without being in a convent, Hermione. It's a big world, it needs good people out in it."

She sat, among the pile of sad letters and heart-rending diaries, dust motes drifting around her.

"Have you ever regretted...?"

"No," I said, "I can't say I have, but I've seen others who did, and who suffered. I've known many who left and found other lives, happy lives, elsewhere. It isn't easy. It isn't meant to be easy."

"I don't know what to do," Hermione shrugged and pushed the little diary back onto the shelf, "and I can't make any sort of decision. It's awful. I can't decide whether to have porridge or corn flakes, never mind how to set the course of the rest of my life. I just don't know anything anymore."

"You know a lot about putting things in order," I said. "I'm sorry I can't help, but perhaps you can help me. Mr Hedgby has lent me his labelling machine – that funny thing that prints little plastic labels. I know how fond you are of labels. Come and help me sort nunpegs and pipecleaner priests. You can be in charge of labelling. A change of scene. I can offer that, at least."

Hermione blew her nose. She took a deep breath and straightened her back. "Can I stick them on the boxes and put them alphabetically?"

"Whatever system you like," I said, "as long as we can find them fast enough to get the mail-order parcels out. My own filing system is a bit..."

"Creative?" she suggested, "Random? Improvised? Ad hoc?"

"Yes, well. All of the above, I'm afraid," I said. "Come on, these dusty old papers have waited centuries, another afternoon won't hurt."

"Can I actually *print* the little plastic labels on the machine?" she asked, wavering.

"You can do the printing, and the sticking, and decide what every label should say. I have a set of brand new plastic boxes. There's also a laminator, for the larger signs."

I think it was the laminator that swung it. No orderly person can resist a laminator.

"You're on," she said.

We had a happy time sorting nunpegs and pipecleaner priests into the right boxes, stacking the boxes and labelling them. The logic of Hermione's labelling system is impeccable. A newcomer can now find exactly the right nunpeg with two minutes' training and almost no effort at all. It's a filing triumph. We packed the latest order – 25 pipe cleaner priests and 27 nunpegs (why the disparity, I wonder?) in record time and parcelled them up for Newcastle.

I still wonder at the way this online ordering works, but apparently it does. And at least poor Hermione was able to forget her situation for a while.

We're praying for the right decision, so there's nothing to worry about, really, but it's sad to see such a good-hearted and genial young woman struck down. It isn't the natural order. I'd recommend a chat with Fr Humbert, but he's having his tonsils out this week, poor man. We're sending ice cream. Pistachio is his favourite. Each to their own.

Best wishes,

Sister B.

12

St Win's
September 30th

Dear Emelda,

Farmer Odge has ploughed and harrowed the fields around us to such neat, dark brown evenness that it looks even flatter than usual round here. He likes things tidy. We had to sprint out and emergency pick blackberries last week when we saw his man approaching with the mighty hedge flaying machine. He'd have smashed every one of them to atoms in a second if we hadn't got them first. Sister Bernard is planning blackberry vodka – we can't sell it in the Shoppe, but we can certainly give it away as presents.

Sister Joy joined us for the first time in convocation last night. She arrived in her silver car carrying a briefcase. As we settled in the common room, Sister Prudence welcomed her and she flipped open her laptop, glanced round and said, "So who usually takes the minutes? I didn't receive mine."

"We do not minute our convocations," Prudence said.

"I see," said Sister Joy, "that is... unusual. But then I know you pride yourselves on your *unconventional* ways here at St Win's. You won't mind if I take a few notes?

Oh, and I have a little announcement." Sister Joy arced a smile like a lighthouse beam from right to left around the group. "The Bishop has suggested that I manage the convent whilst Rev Mother Elizabeth is indisposed. Just to lend a hand in your time of need."

We were completely taken aback by this and sat in stunned silence until Sister Prudence smiled back at Joy Vernon and said, "That will not be necessary, Sister Joy. Rev Mother Elizabeth proposed that I should lead St Winifreda's while she recovers, and the sisterhood agreed."

"Oh, but the Bishop was quite clear," Sister Joy told her, "he thought it would be most efficient and most helpful if I were to..."

"That is not how we arrange things at St Winifreda's," said Sister Prudence. She spoke slowly, with her usual crisply perfect enunciation.

Sister Joy took her eyes away from Prudence and smiled round at us all again.

"But Sister Prudence – excuse me from saying this, and I hope you won't take it the wrong way – but Sister Prudence is only a visitor. Surely the convent needs someone with a longer-term view at the helm."

Sister Prudence was perfectly still in response to this. She sat straight-backed with her hands folded calmly in her lap before saying, "It is perfectly true that

I am a visitor. I am a visitor from Kenya. Perhaps it is this that worries you? I am told that you are deeply concerned about the public face of the convent. Perhaps my face is not the kind of public face the Bishop had in mind."

Sister Joy blinked. She shifted her knees under her laptop. "Of course, the convent is free to make its own leadership choices," she said eventually, "it was just an offer, in case you wanted *professional* advice. Either way, the Bishop has appointed me to write a report about St Win's for the next major diocesan council."

"What sort of report would that be?" asked Eustacia.

Sister Joy was back on firm ground."We call it a 'Potential and Possibilities Report."

"And what's that when it's at home?"

"It's basically fact-gathering and interviews. I try to build up a really sound, in-depth, 360 degree picture. It enables a fully informed decision to be made about the longer term. Nothing to be concerned about. This would be your chance to feed your views into the decision-making process. You could call it a consultation."

A puzzled silence followed this, before Prudence said, "Thank you, Sister Joy. I would like us to move on now. You wanted to ask something, Hermione, I think."

"I wanted to ask whether anyone had heard from Mr Wooler," Hermione said. "He left saying that he would be back very soon, and giving me a long list of documents he needed to see, but he hasn't come back. I've rung his office several times, but they just say he's not in. He hasn't finished signing off the audit completely. I need to get hold of him."

No-one else had heard from Mr Wooler, so we went on to discuss the dental repair fund. Mother Martha and Sister Annunziata are both due a visit to the dentist, but funds won't stretch to it at the moment. The elderly sisters are all due for check-ups too. They are so determined not to cause any expense that they have stopped mentioning their teeth altogether, but we can tell they need work because mealtimes are so slow and none of them dares tackle the crunchier biscuits any more.

After Sister Joy had snapped her little laptop closed and left – she always leaves early – Sister Bernard said, "There is one piece of good news. Someone sent us a cheque for £5,000. I found it in the post this morning."

"That is most generous!" said Sister Prudence, returning to her usual smiling self, "do we know who it was from?"

"The cheque is signed by A.J. Wilkins, but there's no note."

I remembered the hospital visit. It must be Mr Wilkins the ex-jockey I let out of the bathroom. What a lovely man.

Now we have to decide whether to spend it on teeth, plumbing or chapel repairs. But that decision is for another convocation. We ended on that happy note.

On the way out I heard Eustacia say, "Well that told Sister Joyless! That put her in her place."

Sister Prudence smiled up at Eustacia, who is about a foot taller, "Eustacia," she said, "it would be better not to stoop so low as to call anyone names, but I agree we will need to keep a watchful eye on her. She will not be happy about a set-back like that. "

And now I must go and check the rat traps – they need a watchful eye too.

Best wishes,

Sister B.

13

St Win's
October 4th

Dear Emelda,

I looked up the weather in your region this morning. Apparently it rains there from December to March, all day, except when El Niño comes and brings the *really* bad weather. Our chapel puddles and drain problems seem very small compared to your daily challenges. We all pray for you every day, and so do the prayer circles online and across East Anglia and indeed the whole of this country and the home countries of all the sisters here at St Win's. It's quite an engine of prayer when you think about it – these are prayer professionals, Emelda, remember you have a very strong team on your side.

I looked out of the Shoppe window this morning and saw a very large black vehicle – somewhere between a car and a tractor, pull into the yard. Its windows were blacked out. The driver, when she unfolded herself gracefully, also wore sunglasses. Here in the Hog Fen the sunlight is rarely strong enough to need such precautions. The lady was as fine, tall and delicate as a giraffe and picked her way over on very high heels. Inside the shop she lowered her sunglasses onto her nose and looked from left to right, smiling.

"Are those sundried tomatoes?" she asked.

"Yes," Nesbitt told her, "Sicilian."

"And the Dolcelatte?"

"From Cremona."

"Well!" she declared. "I wasn't expecting this. Not here. And the cakes! Are those *natas*?"

Nesbitt was beginning to enjoy herself. She continued arranging ciabatta on the display counter and answered very casually.

"Yeah. Homemade. Brazilian recipe."

"He said you were a find!" declared the glamorous customer.

Nesbitt went on stacking lunches for the office workers, who would be arriving any minute. I could tell from her shoulders that this pleased her, but she said nothing.

"How delicious! I'll take half a dozen natas to go," said the elegant visitor.

I popped the little cakes into a box and handed them over.

"I'm Antonio Ferrara's PA, by the way, Carla Dacosta. I'm here to book Mr Ferrara's English lessons. He tells me you are the teacher. Is there somewhere we can sit down with our diaries?" She smiled and looked left and right.

The Shoppe has one seat, in the storeroom, where there is a single stool. It was impossible to imagine this delicate creature in a storeroom. I was about to take her off to the guest parlour when Nesbitt rushed round the counter and produced two folding chairs and a little round folding table – from thin air, as far as I could see. She unfolded them and dusted them off, saying, "I'll bring the coffee"

My diary, you may not be surprised to learn, was a lot emptier than Mr Ferrara's. Whatever his work is, it involves a lot of travelling, but we soon booked a few lessons. Nesbitt conjured up coffee in stylish little cups I'd never seen before.

"Antonio is looking forward to the lessons," Carla said. She flipped open the cake box and peered inside. "I have to eat one of these! Will you join me?" I declined, but Carla ate her nata with great gusto. For a slim, glamorous woman she was a very enthusiastic eater. "Wow! This is wonderful! Did someone here make this?"

I pointed to Nesbitt and introduced her. "This is Nesbitt, she's training here as a chef."

"*Nesbitt!*" said Carla, giving the startled Nesbitt a hug, "You are a real cook! It is a gift and you have it. Oh sorry, I am Italian. Great food makes me hug people! Now, Sister, about working with Antonio."

She sat down again at the little table, crossing her

legs. One of her gorgeous shoes slipped off at the heel and hung from her toes. "He's a lovely man, I've worked with him for 23 years. In Italy first and now here. Really, he is a great person, but his English accent is awful. We all adore him, but we don't really expect you to make it any better. There is no hope. You know how it is, some people can lose their accent in a very short time, but others...." she shrugged.

"Should I take him as a pupil, then?" I said. "Perhaps it is wrong to do so."

"No, not at all. You can help in all sorts of ways, you know, a little grammar and so on, but you shouldn't feel bad if he makes only a little progress – or none. He is so busy. Besides, you know, the accent is like a trademark. He always says he wants to speak like the Queen, but nobody would like it if he did."

She looked around at the Shoppe. "It's so nice here, Sister, so peaceful. Have you thought of having a little café – over there, say?" She waved an elegant hand. "Ah, forgive me! My family is in the restaurant business, I imagine a restaurant or a café wherever I go. But really, with a few little touches, it could be lovely. And how much do you charge?"

"Charge?" I was distracted by the café idea and lost the thread.

"For your lessons?"

I told her the usual rate.

"But Antonio will want to pay more than this," she said.

"But that's the rate," I explained, "it's the same for everyone, except the people who can't afford anything at all."

"Right," she said, "OK. I'm going to write you a cheque and you just put it in the bank." She wrote out a cheque and folded it before handing it over. "Don't forget, Antonio is keen for this to be discreet. He doesn't want the press printing stories about how bad his English is, even though a lot of people have probably worked it out for themselves by now. And when you do decide to have a café, talk to Carla first. I will help you. Just call, Sister! Ciao! And ciao, clever Nesbitt!"

Sister Bernard and Eustacia bustled in at that moment carrying nunpeg orders.

"Who's the film star?" Eustacia asked, "You were called stick insect if you looked like that at my school."

"Yes, and how glad we are that times have changed!" said Sister Bernard. "Now, we need to consult you about Alphonsus Dunn. We need some changes on the website and we need him to make them. We've been talking and we must not allow him to work for us voluntarily, but we don't know how to pay him. Any ideas?"

"Gah!" A cry of surprise came from Nesbitt, who

had carried off the cheque to put in the till. "How many lessons is this man having?" she said, waving the little piece of paper.

We all looked, and the cheque was for approximately twenty times what we were expecting.

At convocation we wondered what to do about the huge overpayment, but clearly Ms Daconti wanted us to have the money, so we decided to thank the Lord and use some of it to pay Alphonsus for more website work.

This explains why I am reading through a pile of pronunciation textbooks /tekstbukz/. We'll start with h. They recommend inventing tongue twisters: *Harry is hungry and angry as he hurries home to help hammer the honeysuckle and hoe the angular hornbeam.*

You might try that one on your loggers, though come to think of it, I've always found *Sue wishes she could see Spain again, but shifty Sean will soon shoot her if she does* is the one to go for if you want to test a Spanish speaker's mettle! Use with caution and only if the loggers are in a good mood! I've known it to make estrong eSpaniards moan and beat their heads on the desk.

Hasta luego,
Sister B.

14

St Win's
October 7th

Dear Emelda,

Please excuse the wobbly writing. This is the trembling hand of one who has recently survived a Paquita McMurray Salsa Workout. I'm used to her now, but the first few times I thought I had stumbled into a crazy lights-on South American nightclub run by a Colombian madwoman who had forgotten most of her clothing. The music blares and twenty or so ladies of all shapes and sizes transform into strutting Latin divas. They arrive in sensible warm coats, then throw them aside to reveal astonishing outfits, all acid-coloured and skin-tight. If anyone ever wanted to see well-set-up Fenland females going all out, Wednesdays at the village hall would be the place to come! Paquita can do things with her hips that no Englishwoman can aspire to, but we're not letting that stop us.

The first time I went she said, *"Don't worry about nothing. Chuss let your body feeel the music. Chuss feeel it. Your feeet know what to do. Your heeps know what to do, chuss let them do it! Stick out your chest and have fon!"*

Every detail of this little speech contradicted the

ground rules I generally live by, but they did so with such utter thoroughness that it seemed silly to carp. I was either going to stay and let my body feeel the music, or I was going to keep my coat on and walk home keeping my dignity, but losing my muscle tone. I stayed because (a) the physiotherapist recommended regular exercise – my legs still haven't completely recovered from the car crash, (b) the convent had paid in advance, and (c) it turns out I am a complete push-over for Salsa music. I've no idea where that came from, I've never been closer to South America than Hastings, but I absolutely love it. The minute Paquita started the first dance blaring out for the warm-up, I was hooked. I stopped caring about the too-big tracksuit; I stopped worrying about whether or not I could follow the steps; I stopped wondering whether the lyrics were quite as rude as they seemed to be, and I danced like a... well, probably like a turnip bouncing downstairs, if I'm honest, but like a Colombian queen of salsa *in my head*. I have never been so exhausted or grinned for so long at a time in my life. I *merengued* all the way home. It's been four weeks now and I can get almost half way through the class without having to lean on the wall and gasp. I usually set off on the wrong foot, and I can only do half the moves, but I feel fitter already.

My classmates are lovely. They worked out where I

was from without being told.

"You can't dance in that thick tracksuit, Sister, it's too hot. You need some leggings. Are you allowed leggings?"

"Well, I'm not sure..." I said.

"I can bring you some of mine. I've got loads."

"I've got a couple of tops you can have," said her friend. "Nothing fancy. We can't all carry off Dayglo strapless numbers like you, Evelyn, can we? Even if they are in Extra Extra Large!"

I showed the outfit they gave me to the other sisters at convocation. The top is lime green and acid pink with swirls of sulphurous yellow; the leggings are black with luminous stars.

A few sisters looked a bit doubtful, but Eustacia said, "If it was free and it's what you need to get fit, then I can't see any problem."

"Are there any men at the Salsa?" asked Sister Mathilda. "I was thinking about... well, about modesty, I suppose. Call me old-fashioned."

"No men," I said, which is true, though the caretaker seems to pass through more often than is strictly necessary.

"Modesty is a personal matter," Sister Doris said. "It should be entirely up to you what you wear and what you do while you're wearing it. No big deal."

As to the lyrics, Sister Bernard speaks Spanish. She listened last week, and said, "Well, plenty of frank sexual invitation, but nothing unholy, Boniface, in fact a lot of it is rather sweet. I should just get on with it."

Honi soit qui mal y pense, was the general feeling.

What with the public transport marathons required these days to get elderly sisters to the dentist or GP, and taking on a few extra language students to boost the cashflow, I haven't been in the Shoppe as often as usual lately. A lot of the work has fallen to Nesbitt. Last time I was there Bob Fairbrother came in to order cakes for his next international seminar, but not as many as usual.

"Only three, Bob?" I said.

"Yes, this is the Masters Advanced Pro Marketing course," he said, "I sell it on its exclusivity, so I can't have more than about five students at a time."

"Oh. That's actually quite a *lot* of cake for five people."

"Yes, well, it's hard work, and they seem to appreciate it. Especially the Danes, they love a bit of cake. But I won't be ordering any more for a while, I'm writing a book. No more seminars after this one."

I manoeuvred his Walnut Special into its box. "What sort of book, may I ask?"

"About marketing," he said. "It's the next step in my career, I've decided. A best-seller. I need to turn myself into a global brand. The go-to guy. A well-respected book is vital for my credibility."

"Well," I said, "I can see that, but won't it take up a lot of your time? You'd have to do a tremendous amount of research, I imagine."

"No. Three weeks, I calculate," he said. "Four at the outside. I've been reading up on book-writing. I've done the research. It's simple enough if you make a plan and stick to it. I did consider outsourcing, but that's less authentic. I couldn't rely on anyone fully capturing my unique persona."

"No," I said, "it certainly would be difficult to capture that accurately."

"I've already got the outline made. I start the actual writing on Friday. My main challenge right now is the title. I need something with very high SEO and it needs to be original, searchable and absolutely spot on. Problem is I'm not really a word person. I'm more action-oriented."

"Ah, yes, that would make it difficult," I said.

I often find my thoughts drifting off when Bob's explaining.

"I thought of *Niche Marketing for Beginners*," he said. "What do you think?"

"Well," I told him, "it has the strength of being plain, at least."

"You're saying it's a bit bland, aren't you?

A bit...*vanilla?*"

"No. I mean, I know nothing about this sort of book at all," I said, "but it isn't a title that would jump out at you. Perhaps that's what you want, something unassertive and reassuring."

"No, that is not what I want at all"!" said Bob. "I want something that turns heads, pulls you up short and makes your hand reach out and grab it off the shelf! And the online equivalent. That's what I want. I want it to be irresistible!"

I handed him his three cake boxes. "What would I know, Bob?" I said.

"Mind if I keep running titles by you?" he asked. "I think you've got a bit of a feel for this, Sister."

"I'm sure I haven't," I said, "but of course, I'm happy to help."

That was three weeks ago. Since then Bob has dropped in most days. Without seminars to run, he has taken to coming over for his lunch and he's very talkative. He chats to people in the Shoppe far more than he did before. Once he was always in a hurry, but now he positively hangs around. He sits at the table that nobody got round to putting away. Eats his lunch there. And seeing him do so, other people do too. He was always glossily well-groomed when it came to teaching roomfuls of international delegates his Five Steps to

Better Marketing, but now he is unshaven and seems to be wearing the same black tracksuit for days at a time.

"How's the book going, Bob?" I asked yesterday.

"Not so bad," he said. "What do you think of *Finding the Marketing Needle in the Haystack* as a title?"

"Doesn't really do much for me," I said. "Sorry."

"No, you're right," he said, looking crestfallen. "It's hard work, this writing. I'll take two ham and cheese baguettes, a sausage roll, and four of those Portuguese things."

"Oh, you've got visitors?" I said.

"No, they're for me. Writing makes me eat. How about *Chasing your Millionth Marketing Star?*"

"No," I said, "that's a bit..."

"...over the top? Schmaltzy? Tinsel town?"

"Vague. I was going to say it was a bit vague."

"Yes," he agreed. "I knew that one was a long shot."

Takings are quite good lately. Nesbitt has perfected several varieties of Danish pastry and started turning out chocolate brownies as well. The saying about selling like hot cakes turns out to be true. We get through five dozen of each some days. Lovely smells wafting irresistibly about make people settle on the chairs and stay. Oddly enough, the number of tables keeps increasing. At first there was one small one with two little chairs, then last week I counted and there were three tables and eight chairs. This morning there are five tables and 12 chairs. And they match. I have no idea where they're all coming from, but people have started eating at them.

Tuesday is my turn on the chapel floor cleaning rota. The mud keeps on building up and we keep mopping it away – it's like a parable. It was on my way back with an empty bucket that I saw Nesbitt sitting on the storeroom stool. I should explain that Nesbitt almost never sits down in the Shoppe. She is never still, usually, so seeing her sitting, and from a distance holding her head in her hands, was very unexpected. She leapt up at my approach and was back at work washing the floor when I opened the door. I said, "I expect you'll be glad of a little holiday now, Nesbitt, you'll have a few days over half term, won't you?"

"Yeah, college has finished now," she said, still mopping.

"So you can rest a bit." I said.

"There's a lot of essays," she said, sounding grim.

"Not over the holiday?"

"Yeah, they reckon that's when you'll have the time."

"But you need a break."

"And my brothers are all off school. Bit mad at home."

"If I could ever help, in any way. With an essay or anything...I could type them for you, if that's allowed," I said. I couldn't think of anything else.

She paused from her mopping for a moment. "My Mum's not been well."

I said I was very sorry to hear that.

"It might be something serious, they don't know. She's having tests."

"If you need to have some time off, just let me know. They'll understand at the college. I can explain if there's a problem. I could talk to Mrs Dunbar."

She hated that idea.

"No, don't do that. She might... I don't want her to... I just want to keep going as I am."

"Fine," I said, "that's fine, but let me know if there's anything you need and why not go home early now? I can easily finish the floor."

"I will go," she said, "they've all got a bug at home, they need me to make their tea."

And she left, running up the lane in a flurry.

Pronunciation class with Antonio this evening. Carla is quite right, he makes very little progress. His aitches are all over the place, but he is still an enthusiastic student in his way. He is keen on imperatives at the moment.

"How can I say this, 'Focus yourself! Give me more attacking! More fast'?"

"Speed," I said, "not fast; speed is the noun."

"Ah! Give me more *speed*! Act what I say to you! Listen me! Work harder! How can I say this, Sister?"

I said, "Antonio, I'm sure people would understand what you just said. It was perfectly clear and forceful."

"They don't understand me. I think this is because there are Scottish men there and also some from Liverpool. They don't understand my accent."

"Scottish people could understand that well enough, Antonio. Liverpudlians could too."

"No! I tell them what I want, many times I do this, but they don't understand nothing."

"I expect they do, really."

A look of astonishment crept over Antonio's face.

"You mean they are....? What is this word...?" He circled his hands rapidly in the air.

"...pretending?" I guessed.

"They are pretending? Is not true they don't understand me?"

"It's just an idea." I said, "I can't be sure, obviously."

"*Porca miseria!*" he said, under his breath.

It seemed a good idea to change the subject.

"Let's try a listening passage now," I said, and chose a rather peaceful one about wildflowers in Cornwall.

I hope I haven't got anyone in his office into trouble.

Best wishes,

Sister B.

15

St Win's
October 9th

Dear Independent Traveller to Far-Off Andean Logging Camps,

A beautiful frost this morning. Under a bright sky it glistens on the grass and turns seedheads and cobwebs into icy sculptures. Birds are flocking to the feeders. They're well fed at St Win's. Magpies, woodpeckers, pheasants and partridges all enjoy a bit of left-over cake, as well as all the usual garden birds. I like the cock pheasants, who stroll fastidiously over the grass, trailing their tails and looking haughty, but easily fly into squawking panic, all dignity lost, if anyone walks by.

The dear ducks, on the other hand, plain white and stoical in the face of almost any weather, are unhappy in a freeze. They stand along the bank looking mournfully down at the ice, wondering where their beloved pond has gone. Pavel, who dotes on them, gets up early to break it on his way to work. Pond ice-breaking on a frosty morning; it's a very characteristic sound, echoey and high-pitched.

This morning the masons were removing the

bell from the tower. When the top part of the tower collapsed, the bell fell directly downwards, rather neatly, through two wooden floors and a rickety staircase (which we still climbed quite regularly – a fact that makes the masons shudder whenever they think of it) and came to rest just inside the doorway. It hit flagstones at the bottom and was damaged. It isn't large, just a little angelus bell, but it still weighs a fair amount and they brought in an impressive crane to move it. I couldn't resist watching, you know I like a vehicle.

There was something very sad about it being taken away. It had been up there for hundreds of years, ringing out prayers and services and tolling deaths. Just getting on with its work. Nobody paid much attention to it, except that its sound punctuated our days and was as familiar as the wind or the cries of the birds. I thought of all the sisters whose deaths had been marked by its ringing, like our dear twins last year, and all their predecessors. I thought of all the sisters who had trudged out in all weathers and hauled on the rope, as I had on many occasions. *Ora pro nobis*, the simple inscription says. It's gone now, off to the foundry to be tuned and re-cast and generally put back in order. I can only imagine the expense, but the Folly Towers Association do not flinch at it.

No bell, half a tower and a chapel with a puddle,

that is our situation at the moment, but are we downhearted? No! Well, we weren't until this evening, anyway, but more about that later.

"A lot of people, when they re-cast a bell, add an inscription," Ollie, the site manager told me, as we watched the crane. "You might want to think about it."

So I have passed a very pleasant half hour (alright, a very pleasant *hour*, if I'm strictly honest) looking up inscriptions on bells. With no difficulty at all, Hermione found half a dozen books on the subject on a rather seldom-visited shelf in the library. Most of these were written by vicars in the 19th century, and a wonderfully disputatious lot they were. They often disagree with each other in print and clearly if Rev James Somersham FSA had met Rev A H M Filby MA FSA in a bell tower there would have been strong words exchanged over the interpretation of some of the medieval inscriptions, which are delightfully odd in their spelling and often dedicated to saints nobody can find on record. My favourites were HAL MARI FUL OF GRAS and LOVE HORTETH NOT, with IHESUS BE OUR SPID 1598 coming a close second. Some are very sweet: I KATHERYNE GODDES DERLYNG TO THE MARI SHAL I SYNGE, and some are very (if you'll excuse a pun) appealing: I MEAN TO MAKE IT UNDERSTOOD THAT THOUGH I'M LITTLE YET I'M GOOD 1782. If we keep to tradition we should probably go for FOLLY TOWERS ASSOCIATION ME FECIT, but that's a big inscription for a small bell.

I have a soft spot, I must admit, for saints nobody has ever heard of. I like to think they were just quiet saints whose holiness took the form of keeping a low profile whilst performing miracles of a modest local kind.

"Like curing warts?" Hermione suggested, when we talked about this.

"No dear," I said, "that's witchcraft, isn't it?" We were sorting Nunpegs.

"I like lower division saints too," Hermione admitted. "My favourite at the moment is Saint Guthlac of Crowland who lived as a hermit in the Fens and was attacked by Welsh-speaking demons. Luckily, he knew Welsh and was able to fend them off. He had a sister called Pega. For some reason having a sister called Pega makes him irresistible."

"Did he cure people?"

"Yes, he cured agues. He ticks all the boxes, good old Guthlac. Wilgefortis is another good one. She grew a beard and mustache so that she wouldn't have to marry."

"It's good to see you laugh, Hermione. Are you feeling a little more cheerful now?"

She looked down at the jolly nunpeg she was holding. "I think I'm just closing part of myself down," she said, finally. "It works. In a way."

I went to find Sister Doris on the way back. I might suggest she have a word with Hermione. I'm no expert, but shutting part of yourself down didn't sound right to me. Doris agreed.

The retired sisters have been producing nunpeg variants again. We now have white wimple nunpegs and nunpegs with pipe cleaner arms, so they can wave. Nunpegs are a strangely unstoppable idea. Sister Mary of Light's latest design is Matryoska Russian Doll Nuns; five little nun figures that fit inside one another. She has a team of three painting them, and we have already had to ask Alphonsus to take them off the website because we can't keep up with demand. Someone in Helsinki ordered 20 and cleaned out our entire stock in one order.

Last night at convocation Sister Joy listened to our discussion of dental worries and bell inscriptions, then said, "Through the Chair, and with your permission, obviously, I'd like to run through a few technical issues. Regulatory things."

She handed around an official-looking document with a long list of items on it. The first was *"Use of male workers. Proposed: male workers should be discouraged from working on convent grounds, except in emergency situations. Religious community/closed house regulation 125/6301, Norwich, 1954."*

We all read our papers and looked back at her, confused.

"I'm just going to go ahead and say this," Sister Joy told us, "to be honest, there are a huge number of regulations being infringed here at St Win's. We've got to start somewhere..."

"Start what somewhere?" asked Sister Bernard.

"Start bringing this convent back into line with official guidelines. I mean, I truly believe people have just been making things up as they go along around her for decades."

"But the Community Service workers," I said, "we can't manage without them."

"There is no issue with Community Service workers, they are supervised and temporary, and their work is by way of rehabilitation. The Bishop actively encourages such arrangements. No, it is Mr Chez...Shesh...Zesh... Pavel, as you call him, who is the cause of concern here."

"To whom is he a cause for concern?" asked Sister Prudence.

Sister Joy ignored the question.

"Pavel is our builder. He is supervising the tower repairs," said Sister Bernard, "his work is essential."

"Yes, but I see him in the vegetable garden, I see him in the chicken run, I see him coming and going all the day long. Anyone would think he lived here," Sister Joy said.

"He does live here. He lives in the third pigpen house. He renovated it himself. He was homeless, you see..." Hermione began to explain.

Sister Vernon held up a hand. "Please," she said, "however this arrangement came about, you surely can't expect it to continue. It is wholly unacceptable for an order of religious women to have a man resident among you."

"He's not among us, he's in the pigpens," Hermione started to say, but Joy Vernon turned suddenly towards her.

"I believe you are a novice in this community."

"Well, yes," said Hermione, "I am."

"Novices do not speak at convocation."

Hermione blinked. Several of us began to speak, but Sister Joy waved our words aside.

"If you look at item 6, it clearly states that only a sister who has completed her vows can speak at convocation," Sister Vernon replied, helpfully holding up her document and pointing to the paragraph.

There was general confusion and muttering. Sister Joy looked from one of us to the other intently.

"I'm sorry, sisters, but I am minded to write in my report that what I have found here at St Winifreda-in-the-Fen implies the kind of poor discipline and compromised standards that lead to convents failing. Surely we are agreed that these regulations reflect the very highest and most holy ideas of how a religious house should be run?"

"Are you suggesting that we make Pavel, who mended our roof, who is overseeing the repairs to the tower, who is endlessly helpful and generous with his time, who helps us with the many repairs the buildings need, who digs the garden, who chops our firewood – are you seriously suggesting that Church regulations insists that we make him homeless?" Sister Bernard asked.

"Of course not," replied Sister Joy, stretching a little smile, "that would be inhumane. I am simply saying that he has no business living on convent grounds. He can find accommodation elsewhere, like any other worker. Now, since I can see you need time before responding, I'll take my leave. It's getting late. I think we all need time for reflection. I suggest you read these regulations carefully before we table them for further discussion. My prayers are with you."

Sister Joy strode to the door and went to make her usual crisp exit, but for some reason the door handle resisted her. She muttered, switched her laptop to the other hand and tried again. Still the door refused to budge.

Hermione, who was nearest, jumped up to help. "Allow me," she said, "perhaps a lowly novice can be of some little use, after all."

Sister Joy left without looking back. We all listened as her footsteps clattered down the stairs and the side door banged behind her.

Ollie the engineer also told me, as we watched it being driven away, that removing a bell was considered terribly bad luck in the old days. He said this as we were standing surrounded by a horde of terrifying gargoyles. I laughed at the time, but now the thought makes me shiver.

Good luck with the loggers. We haven't had a letter for some time. Let's hope Raulito hasn't fallen off the wagon (or out of the canoe). Write when you can, we need cheering.

Best wishes,

Sister B.

16

Dear Wanderer,

This morning Mrs Odge rushed into the Shoppe looking flustered.

"We've got a bit of a crisis at the village hall," she said. "There's a lunch club for pensioners – we're expecting 14 of them, but the roadworks in the village seem to have disrupted the electricity supply and none of the cookers are working." She clutched her chest and puffed aloud. "We were wondering – the food's all prepared – we were wondering if there's any chance of using your kitchen for a couple of hours. Only they look forward to it and several of them don't get a hot meal otherwise. It's quite an important event for them. They'd be upset if we had to cancel at the last minute."

Our cooks, Clementine and Gertrude, were only too happy to help. Initially the plan was to cook all the dishes in the convent kitchen and transport them to the village hall, but that meant a relay of cars and probably not very hot food when it arrived. When Sister Bernard saw the problem, she said, "Why not just bring the lunch club here? At least the food will be hot. We have acres of space."

So carloads of pensioners were delivered and shown into the refectory instead. I carried their cups of tea and it was very jolly to see the tables bustling. The villagers had a lovely lunch – Sister Clementine 'adapted' the ready-made meals in some inimitably French way, they smelt delicious – and everyone had a little outing as well. Success all round. And our retired sisters couldn't resist joining in, some of them hadn't eaten in mixed company for decades, so it was a red-letter day for them. Mother Gwendolin, who's nearer a hundred than ninety, said she hadn't laughed so much in years. It made us realise how rarely the elderly sisters have a chance to socialise.

Our refectory and kitchens are on a vast scale – easily enough space to cater for a hundred people at time. We only ever use a corner of them these days. Why not put them to good use? So Sister Bernard and Mrs Odge have agreed that until the village hall kitchen is mended, the pensioners' lunch club can come here.

After they had eaten, many of them enjoyed a stroll in the gardens. I must say it was a change to look out of the window and see a group of old ladies and gentlemen strolling up the avenue. They loved the gardens and pleased Carmella enormously by admiring the vegetables with expert eyes. It was another mild day, without even any wind. There are delicate autumn crocuses under the beeches in the avenue. They liked what they saw in the Shoppe too, and bought a lot of nunpegs and plenty of cakes, with Nesbitt's farmhouse fruitcake a particular favourite. They were happily bundling themselves and their purchases into the volunteer drivers' cars when Sister Joy drove up. I watched from the Shoppe as she glared around her before striding in my direction. There was no time to hide in the stockroom.

"It's like Piccadilly Circus out there!" she declared, pulling the door behind her so hard that it banged and the poor open/closed sign crashed to the floor. "It'll be lorries and coach parties next! Who are all those people?"

I decided that was a rhetorical question and busied myself arranging chocolate brownies into a pyramid. Nesbitt is very keen on presentation, and is trying to train me. Brownie pyramids are not as easy as they look.

"I see you're not very busy, so could I have a word, Boniface?"

"Of course," I said.

"Can you make coffee? If you can, I'll have a coffee and one of those brownies, please. Can you bring it to the table over there? I've got more paperwork than you'd believe. When you're ready." She sat at one of the tables and opened her laptop, ready to be waited on.

We have only old instant coffee and a slow kettle in the back room at the Shoppe but I did my best.

"Ugh! Instant! Still I expect it's all you can manage," Sister Joy said, making a face. "Now, I need to talk to you about your employee. Who gave permission for you to take on an employee? Who signed the paperwork? What's her National Insurance situation? Who interviewed her?"

"Well," I said, "Nesbitt was a volunteer at first..."

"Nesbitt? What sort of name is that?"

"It's her preferred name."

"And what is her baptismal name?"

I hated telling her. It felt like giving a secret away.

"Bluebell," I said.

"*Bluebell!* Well, I'm hardly surprised she wants to keep that to herself. It makes you wonder what some parents are thinking. Anyway, who interviewed this Bluebell Nesbitt and decided she was suitable as an employee? I see no record of formal approval from the Diocese, even if she is an apprentice."

"There is no expense to us," I said, "she is sponsored by Intermediax, a company up the road."

"Sponsored? I know nothing of this. Is Intermediax an approved organisation?"

"Approved? In what way?"

"I mean has it been vetted by the Bishop's office?

There's a procedure. You can't just go about setting up connections with businesses ad hoc. There is a massive risk of bad publicity. Think about it, Boniface! They've only got to be producing something unsuitable, or be caught in some sort of sharp practice, and the whole world will be straight down on the Bishop's head. You people just never seem to think things through!"

She rolled her eyes and, spotting the chocolate brownie I had carried over, picked it up and turned it over, examining it. She then broke off a small corner and moved it across the plate with her fork, but did not eat it. "And then there are the piercings," she continued, "it's a hygiene issue, as you know."

"No," I said, "I checked. Piercings are nothing to worry about. The Environmental Health inspector met both of us, and we have the right certificate."

"Well, if you say so. But I was thinking more of the image it projects to the public." She took up her fork again and began cutting chunks off the brownie with the side of it. She still did not eat any. "Do we really want a teenager with a ring in her eyebrow and several other bits of metal inserted elsewhere to be the public face of St Win's?"

"The Bishop has met Nesbitt," I said, remembering.

"Really?" Sister Joy was suddenly more alert. She stopped bullying the brownie.

"Yes. He admired her lemon drizzle cake," I told her. I left out the bit about one accidentally hitting him that time and spoiling his suit. That was my doing, not Nesbitt's.

"Our Bishop is very kind, and willing to meet people from all walks of life," said Sister Joy, "but I'm afraid Nesbitt's position here must remain under review, Boniface. You are not in any position to offer someone employment. Nobody wants to disappoint the girl, but we have to be realistic. There are no funds to pay for employees, and that's all there is to it."

Sister Joy readied herself to leave. She wandered over to the vegetable display and picked up a carrot. It was not a very beautiful specimen, I admit. "I hope you won't take this the wrong way, Boniface, but it is a little difficult to see what benefit this shop actually brings to St Win's. I've studied the figures. Of course it gives you a nice little occupation, but you must know how low the profit margins are. It almost amounts to a vanity project. Shops are not what a convent should be about, anyway, are they? Trading...business...it lowers the tone, I always think. It's frankly a bit grubby and not in keeping with the serious philosophical and theological work we should be showcasing to the public. Don't you agree? Now, where can I find that novice of yours – Hermione?" !!!!!!!

She trod on the fallen open/closed sign on her way out, her heel making a dent and taking off the top of the letter 'l' in closed. She left a full cup of coffee and a smashed but untasted brownie.

Sister Doris has been training us in deep breathing for relaxation. I'd like to tell you that I inhaled deeply, using my diaphragm, and visualised a beautiful place of calm serenity before exhaling to the count of ten. I'd like to tell you that, but it wouldn't be true.

Pray for my patience.

Best wishes,

Sister B

17

St Win's
October 15th

Dear Wild Mountain Trekker,

Another documentary about loggers and narcotics crime lords on TV this week. I avoid them, usually, but it was my turn to keep the retired sisters company in the TV room. I had hoped to distract them with something about cooking or ballroom dancing, but they overruled me. Half of them knew the Amazon through personal experience and the other half had been to remote jungles elsewhere.

"Was it Dengue Fever they worried about where you were?" I heard Mother Martha ask her neighbour.

"No, Chagas Disease," she replied, dipping an armadillo biscuit in her tea, "spread by assassin bugs."

The only one who was still cheerful when the programme was over was Mother Deirdre, aged 102, who was too busy doing yoga in the corner to watch. We said a few prayers for you. There is a little comfort in the fact that, even though the terrifyingly tattooed narcos use powerful drugs and daily commit crimes we can hardly imagine, a lot of them are also religious at heart, and apparently sentimental about their mothers, so there must be a little spark of goodness in them somewhere.

I couldn't sleep afterwards. Partly because of the narcos and partly because I keep thinking I hear footsteps in the hall outside my room. They seem to move slowly up and down several times before the door at the end of the passage opens and closes.

It has happened once or twice before that one of the sisters sleepwalks. A novice years ago famously walked across the lawn and stood at the edge of the pond. Mother Mary Martyr remembers the incident well. She looked out of her window and could see the girl in her white nightdress standing like a ghost looking down into the waters. Mary woke her neighbours and they rushed down to the pond in case the girl fell in, but she only looked at the water for a few minutes and then turned and walked calmly back to her room. Even so, the event was alarming and they moved her into a different room. She didn't stay at the convent long.

So when I heard the sound I imagined something similar was the explanation. A sister who couldn't sleep or wasn't well. But it kept on happening. Four nights in a row I was woken by the footsteps. They seemed to pause outside my door. I imagined I heard breathing. On the fifth day I mentioned the sounds to Sister Doris. I happened to sit beside her at breakfast.

Sister Doris didn't react as I'd expected. "I wonder if it could be the stress of running the Shoppe," she said, "you've taken on a lot there."

"Stress? No, I think it's real."

"Real to you, yes."

"No, no, I don't think it's a dream. It happens every night."

"Surely the convent is locked at night."

"Well yes," I said. "I lock all the doors myself. I keep all the keys."

"Perhaps you feel insecure in other ways?"

"No. I feel fine. I just keep hearing this noise."

"Would you like a group of us to come over to your corridor tonight?"

I felt like saying yes, but was embarrassed, the Sisters get little enough sleep as it is.

"No," I said, "you're right. It probably was a dream."

I don't believe in ghosts. Do you? Do the tribal people you live with? I know different cultures have a different attitude to the question because ghosts were one of the topics in a textbook I once used. It was a good one for starting discussions, because everyone had strong enough opinions to overcome their deficiencies in English and join in. I like a ghost story as much as anyone else, but I don't believe they actually exist.

"They're not incompatible with the faith, you know,"

Mary Martyr remarked, "ghosts. Miracles and mysteries are all around us."

Which, whilst true, wasn't very helpful, really.

The footsteps came again the following night. This time they stopped outside my door. I held my breath and watched in horror as the handle turned and the door inched open. Through half-closed eyes I saw a beam of light sweep the room. It lingered on the desk and again on the bedside locker, where I keep the big ring of all the convent's keys, then flicked off. The door closed again.

I crept out of bed and listened at the door. Once the footsteps seemed to have passed and be moving away, I opened it by a crack and peered round. There in the moonlight was a dark figure. It moved stealthily along the passage.

My heart was hammering in my chest. I could only think that, if it followed the pattern of the previous nights it would soon go out through the door at the end and be gone. Which is what it did. A prowler? A thief? I had no idea. Wanting to make sure it left the dormitories, I followed, opening the staircase door very quietly to see the figure slip down the turret stairs leading to the back door and the garden.

"Was he carrying anything?" Constable Carl asked the next day, frowning with the effort of writing in the notebook he had produced from inside his stab-proof vest.

"Only a torch," I said.

"No bag? No weapon?"

"Not as far as I could see."

"Young or old?"

"I couldn't say."

"And his ethnic origin?"

"Sorry?"

"Was he black or white?"

"What's that got to do with it?"

"It's for the description. We might want to make an e-fit. You know, one of those pictures."

"It was dark, Carl, I couldn't see."

"Only asking. It's one of the questions on my list. What about clothes, what was he wearing?"

"Black, I said, "a sort of tracksuit. And training shoes. There was something a bit funny, though."

"Funny?"

"It was a very neat and tidy outfit. I mean, if you were a wardrobe lady and someone wanted a 'prowler' outfit, that's what they'd be given."

"Not sure I follow," Carl said.

"It was smart, clean, co-ordinated."

"Designer prowler sort of thing?"

"Exactly," I said.

My dear Sisters were very supportive, but I also had the strange experience of hearing how quickly stories alter in the telling.

By lunchtime, Sister Bernard said, "I hear you chased a burglar off the premises last night, Boniface. You're very brave."

"Chased?" I said. "Burglar? Where did all that come from?"

"Gertrude was saying in the kitchen. You should see the *pains au chocolat* they're making this morning!"

"It isn't true, dear," I said. "I just saw something. I certainly didn't chase anyone."

"Have-a-go-hero, that's what they call people like you in the local paper."

Perhaps it's because life in Three Fens is usually pretty calm, but by tea time villagers were coming into the Shoppe and saying, "I heard about your break-in."

"You're not safe anywhere these days."

"You need an alarm, Sister. There are a lot of funny people around."

"They had Jim's ride-on mower away last autumn didn't they, Jim?"

And so on. But how on earth did everyone know about it?

"E-Pol," said Constable Carl, when I managed to ask him. "Anything like that goes straight onto our email alerts. 4,000-odd subscribers. You don't have to worry, it's all anonymised. Data protection and so forth."

"What did it say?" I asked him.

"I'll show you on my phone," he said. And there it was, listed among Alerts! *'Intruder in private residential accommodation. Spotted by resident 2 am. Male, 18–50.'*

"Everybody knows now. Brilliant little system, that is," said Carl. "Have you got a lot of valuables?"

"We haven't got any at all." I said. "As far as I know the convent's plate and silverware was all taken off to the cathedral for safe keeping during the Second World War and never came back."

"What about electrical equipment, jewellery, paintings?"

"Well we have some computers, but all second hand, we have some garden tools and some kitchen machines. There are a few old paintings, holy pictures, most of them are 20th century prints. Nothing of any value."

"He's not to know that, though, is he? Probably imagines you've got gold things, church stuff, precious icons and whatnot."

I said, "There's something else, Carl, it's been worrying me."

"What? Did you remember something?"

"I'm not sure..."

"Anything you can remember. It's all useful."

"It's just...I think it might have been a woman," I said.

"Ooh, that's a bit weird," he said, the professional manner slipping for a moment. "You're sure it wasn't one of the other, um, nuns? Lost or something."

"Almost sure," I said.

Carl sighed. "Look, whatever's going on, Sister, you need some better security and the locks are all a bit antique, aren't they? You've no alarm or anything. You'd be classified as vulnerable. There are a lot of funny people around."

Everybody seems to be agreed on that, anyway.

So that will be another expense. At convocation we tried to decide what to do.

Sister Eustacia was all for shooting the prowler on sight, but that seemed excessive since there hadn't been any crime committed as far as we could tell.

"That is certainly what would happen in parts of Africa, I'm afraid," Sister Prudence remarked, "but here there is a more formal process to be followed. Besides we have no gun."

"We could borrow one of Odge's," Eustacia said.

"No, Eustacia, you have to have a licence. You can't just borrow a gun," we all told her.

"Stuff and nonsense," she muttered.

Although everyone was now persuaded the intruder

did actually exist, I was still the only witness. I didn't for a moment believe I was seeing things – whatever Doris's thoughts on the issue – but I was painfully aware that the e-pol and local paper publicity, as well as several convocations' worth of anxious discussion, all hinged on my word alone.

Constable Carl was right about the locks. They really are antique. I know every lock in the convent well and we have some very fine specimens indeed. Some are collectors' items and in my opinion they are all well-made, well-maintained, and perfectly secure. The keys alone are of great beauty. If I have anything to do with it, we will not be replacing our locks.

Meanwhile interest came in the unlikely person of Baz, the community service worker.

"I seen that story in the paper, Sister," he remarked, while he was buying pizza slices for lunch a few days later. "I don't like the sound of it."

"Well, Baz, there hasn't been any harm done," I said, cutting him a nice big piece. Baz is as thin as a blade.

"Yeah, but you can't be too careful with prowler weirdos," Baz said. "I'll have three of them custard tart things. What I don't like, *really* don't like, is something like this happening to you Sisters. That's wrong. All wrong. I got good contacts in these parts. Usually I know what's going on, like. I'll ask around. Animal and me, we'll keep an eye on things."

I found this oddly comforting, even though Animal and Baz are, strictly speaking, offenders themselves.

As usual, we'll just pray (and try to get some sleep).

Best wishes,

Sister B.

18

St Win's
October 18th

Dear Mountain Voyager,

Two police officers came to talk to us today. They stopped in to the Shoppe on their way, so I spoke to them beforehand. These were police officers way beyond the rank of Constable Carl, our local man. They wore plain clothes and drove an unmarked car. Detectives. I thought it was about the prowler, of course.

"Want a cake, Sylvia? I'm having one, they look pretty good. Chelsea bun for me and..."

"Not for me, Ron, you know I'm having a fasting day."

"Fasting!" he said, raising his eyebrows at me.

"We do quite a lot of fasting round here," I pointed out.

"Yeah, but not because you think your bum looks too big in your jeggings," said Ron, cheerfully.

"Ron!" said Sylvia, making an eyebrow gesture at him that meant *look out, nuns present!*

"So, cake or no cake?" he asked, oblivious.

"Oh go on then, just a small one – one of those *natas*, they can't have many calories."

Two of them would be enough to fuel a human body for a day in a tight corner, but I didn't like to say.

This was my introduction to Detective Inspector Sylvia Russell and Detective Sergeant Ronald Mills of the Fraud Squad.

"It looks," Sylvia told us, when we were all together, "it looks, at this early stage, as if someone had planned this for some time."

"Planned what?" Eustacia asked.

The officers looked at one another in surprise.

"Has nobody...?"

"Haven't you been told about...?

"Oh," said Sylvia, "Sorry ladies, we thought you'd been told."

"Don't say Wooler's made off with our money?" Eustacia said it light-heartedly – she was joking – but the question hung in the air, and as it did, it became serious. "He has, hasn't he?"

"Obviously nothing is certain..." said Detective Sylvia.

"...but after he'd gone they found the money wasn't there?" Sister Bernard asked.

"Exactly."

"What? But that's awful!" we all said at once.

"So far," Sylvia said, after we had taken the news in, "so far we can track the money to an account opened recently by Mr Wooler in your name. Did you authorise him to open a bank account? He would have needed signatures and documentation, proof of identity and so on."

"We all gave him a specimen signature. He said it was needed for security."

The officers winced.

"And other documents, like bank statements, letters with the address on them, passports? Did he ask for them?"

"Yes. He was always asking for documents like that," Hermione said.

"Oh dear, oh dear," said Sergeant Ron, "did you ask him why he wanted them?"

"Is this my fault? Because I gave him all those papers?" Hermione looked stricken.

"Let's start at the beginning," said Inspector Sylvia, "you've got this money coming – rent from a piece of land, is it? And Wooler knows about this, so he gets the paperwork from Hermione here and opens a bank account in the name of the convent using your documentation. He arranges for the money to be paid straight into it. Then, because he's set himself up as the main signatory, he can withdraw the money himself."

"So he's been planning this for months?" said Eustacia, "the worm!"

"He seemed disagreeable, but he didn't seem like a criminal," Sister Bernard remarked.

"Fraudsters often aren't like ordinary criminals," Sylvia said, "but he does fit the profile in some ways. Someone with a retirement plan who spends time setting everything up because they're only going to break the law once and then they're going to disappear and live off the proceeds. They sometimes devote years to putting everything carefully in place."

"They're often the methodical type," added Sergeant Ron, "would you say Mr Wooler was the methodical type?"

"Definitely!" we all said at once.

We told him about Mr Wooler's stringent demands for exactly the right biscuits and his tea and coffee timetable.

"All those Garibaldis," I said, "what a waste!"

"Yes, that would be the type of thing we'd expect," Sylvia said. "Well, not that only criminals eat Garibaldis, obviously, but the precision, the insistence on everything being just so. It fits the profile."

"So do you think the toad's made off with it and is sitting somewhere on a tropical beach?" asked Eustacia.

"Well not quite. He doesn't seem to have left the country. He left his passport at home. His wife found it."

"His wife?" we all said. "He was *married*?"

"Why is that surprising?" Sylvia asked.

Nobody could really say.

"We found a clerical collar at his house. He seems to have worn one sometimes," said Sylvia, "useful as a disguise now and then, probably."

"Did he say anything about a wife to you, Hermione?" I asked.

"No. He didn't really talk to me at all. Except to give me orders and tell me how disappointed he was."

"Disappointed?" Ron said, "Why was he disappointed?"

"He always found fault with our book-keeping and he seemed to be searching for something in the archives. He kept sending me off for boxes and files."

"He didn't say what he was looking for?"

"No. But he was irritated about it. He was quite sharp with me, as if I was hiding things he wanted. Did he just go off without his wife, then?"

"Yes," Sylvia said, "disappeared overnight. No note. Of course, we're watching her too. She appears to be as shocked as everyone else. She reported him as a missing person."

"Oh dear," said Hermione, "the poor woman. He goes missing without a word and then she's implicated in a fraud she's probably never even heard of. How dreadful."

"Well, as I say, we can't be sure at present. It's been known for a relative or partner to be a sort of sleeper –

you know, they're left behind seeming innocent, but in reality they're part of the plan, and may be handling the funds in some way, so we need to watch her."

"Did he not leave her a note?" asked Hermione.

"Just didn't come back from work one Wednesday," said Sylvia.

"Oh that's awful!"

"Yes, well. Moving on," said Ron.

"Of course the fact that he didn't take his passport needn't mean that he is still in the country," Sister Bernard said. "He might have a fake one."

"Yes," Ron said, "we'd actually considered that possibility."

"He's not the sort, though, is he?" Eustacia said. "I can't imagine Wooler, Mr Bring-my-tea-at 10.30 am..."

"...Coffee," said Hermione, "it was coffee at 10.30 – tea was at 3 pm. One sugar..."

"...Well, anyway, he doesn't seem the sort to be buying fake passports in seedy pubs."

The detectives looked a bit surprised.

"You can get them online these days," Hermione said, "I saw it on Crimewatch."

"A lot's traceable, though," said Sylvia. "He seems to have left in a hurry. It looks as if he planned things very carefully, but had to rush a bit at the end."

"Perhaps someone was on to him," Eustacia said.

"They appointed a new accountant. We believe that spooked him."

"And what about the money – our money?" asked Prudence. "Can it be traced through the bank?"

"The funds were paid into the account he'd opened in the convent's name, but then quickly paid out. We're guessing he paid it to himself. The obvious thing would be to get it out of the country. What they often do is find somewhere to deposit it overseas then travel out and either stay abroad or bring it back in cash. Fraudsters love a bit of cash."

"He's an older man," said Sylvia, "they're slower to give themselves away than the young ones, but they usually do something sooner or later that leads us to them. Someone like Wooler probably isn't your natural criminal. He's a tidy-minded sort who got greedy or had a grudge. We'll watch everything very carefully and he'll turn up. But it won't necessarily be soon, I'm afraid. Fraud's a long game."

"And meanwhile the chapel puddle is getting bigger by the day," said Eustacia.

"The suffering these people leave behind is awful, isn't it Ron?" Sylvia said. "We've seen families left high and dry – absolutely abandoned – old ladies robbed of their life-savings; charities cleaned out overnight. It's a nasty business."

"But there's nothing we can do but wait?" I said.

"Not really. DS Mills and I will keep you informed, and you can let us know if you hear anything that might be useful, but apart from that, it's just us and the team doing the backroom stuff. We will get him. We usually get this sort."

"We'll pray for your work," said Prudence.

"Right. Er, thanks," said Ron, looking embarrassed. "I'm not actually... you know... a believer myself."

"Don't worry, Sergeant," said Eustacia, "we have extra strong prayers for that."

He went quite pink.

So, Emelda, that's where we are now. We offer up the finding of Wooler twice a day and have an extra rosary whenever we can fit one in, and we wait for Detectives Sylvia and Ron to do their stuff. It's very frustrating, watching the repairs mount up all around us without being able to do anything about them, but if there's one thing we are very good at here at St Winifreda's, it's waiting hopefully, so we're playing to our strengths.

Now I must post this as well as our biggest order yet of nunpegs – 140 assorted – to Amsterdam. Who knew the level-headed Dutch would fall for nunpegs?

Take care in the high passes.

Best wishes,

Sister B.

19

St Win's
October 21st

Dear Mountaineer,

Do you remember the photograph you sent us last year? I have it on the Shoppe noticeboard. The steepness of those mountain paths make our eyes water here in the horizontal Fens. A mule is carrying an enormous load, picking its way along a road that seems to be about a foot wide cut into mountainous jungle. Thankfully trees cover the vertical drop of several hundred feet you described on its left. There are ruts in the path, it is slippery. One step wrong and... but this is the *main* road to your settlement. It puts our problems with the drive into perspective.

The drive is getting very rutted. It has never been a surfaced road, in the sense of tarmac or anything solid. It is a loose stony surface with grass. Delivery trucks and customers' cars churn it up. The more business we do, the more they churn it, so it's a sign of our success. But the result is a sticky mess and this winter being wet, the problem has been getting worse. Cars sometimes struggle, and not only that, but people walking down the lane from the offices get very muddy. I hadn't thought how seriously they might take this – I suppose living here has given us a high tolerance for mud – we just wear wellies and don't really take any notice of it, but neatly shod office workers are horrified. Their stylish footwear can't cope. They are tempted to get into their cars and buy their biscuits in the supermarket – and we can't have that! Something must be done. But funds being tight we need an inventive solution. Enter Farmer Odge.

"That drive of yours needs something doing," he remarked, as he came in for his usual supplies: Battenburg and dog biscuits.

"Nesbitt has made some Battenburg," I said. I had been looking forward to mentioning this. We thought we should encourage him to try it, him being a bit of an expert – if always eating the same cake makes you an expert. "We would welcome your opinion."

"*Made* some?" he said, with a hint of suspicion, leaning forward and examining the display of cakes on the counter. He spotted it nestling between the coffee and walnut and the Sachertorte. "It certainly looks the proper thing."

I reached it out and wrapped it. "It's on the house. If you have any comments, please let us know."

Odge was surprised. He didn't know how to react. "Well... I... You should probably not give your profits away like this," he said, "this is too much."

"This is market research," I told him. "We need to test the Battenburg market."

"Well then," he said, "I will give you a full report. And say thank you to Nesbitt too. Good worker."

He left. I swear he was blushing.

Two days later there was the usual sound of dogs barking in his huge tractor-car and he returned.

"Not making any purchase," he said. "Just thought I'd give you the, er, the feedback report, so to speak, on that cake."

"Oh yes," I said. "What did you make of it?"

"Superb! Quite excellent," said Odge. He squared his shoulders and looked over to the right, vaguely towards the handmade goods shelves. "I've eaten a lot of Battenburg, as you know. Various brands. I like a Battenburg. Not too sweet. Marzipan. You like them or you don't. I do. Now this one. This one, I would describe this as excellent. Delicious. The right amount of everything and all... balanced. Yes, balanced. Tell Nesbitt. Five stars. Five stars without a doubt. And I'm not just saying that. I know you want serious opinions. Genuinely, I think it is the best I have tasted, and I've eaten it all over Europe and once in the Ritz Hotel in London. Long story, but this beats that into a cocked hat. I'll have one whenever she makes one, please tell Nesbitt that."

"I will, certainly," I said, "and thank you."

"My men will do your drive next week," he added.

"Do what," I said, "sorry?"

"Your drive. I'll send them over to put some farings on your drive. It won't take long. They'll have to do it in the daytime, so it might hold up your customers for a while, but not too long. They'll roll it and it'll be a lot better. Not perfect, but a lot better for the office people's shoes. I know they worry about that sort of thing. Probably Thursday."

And he left.

When Nesbitt came in the next day – she had been at college – I told her about her five-star review. "Odge says your Battenburg cake is better than the Ritz Hotel's."

"I can't really see Odge in the Ritz, can you?"

"Well, no," I said, "it isn't very easy to picture."

"Probably in the Blitz," Sister Bernard guessed that evening. "People did all sorts of unusual things in the air raids, you know. Ducked into the nearest place, all boarded up, and found to their amazement that it was the Ritz or the Café de Paris; drank a cocktail; danced with a member of the aristocracy."

She's either been reading the Mitfords again, or caught one of the Sunday evening TV programmes which sort of mash history into one picturesque costume drama – all foggy London town and fox furs and men in uniform. Odge, whilst weather-beaten, is not actually old enough to have ducked accidentally into anywhere during the war, but I didn't like to disillusion her.

And so a few days later Odge's men repaired the drive by dropping piles of loose material – odd knuckly stuff, don't know what it is – and then driving the most amazing miniature roller up and down over it. It was a dear little thing, puffing exhaust out of a little upright chimney. Its roller was about four feet in diameter. I couldn't help going to watch. I love a vintage machine.

Odge's man saw me admiring it. "She's an Aveling-Barford, made in 1937," he said. "Lovely job. I did the renovations. One of the boss's little projects, she was. He'd paint her, but he doesn't want to lose the badges. Want a go? She's easy enough to control."

Of course I did! I couldn't get into the seat fast enough. I chugged her up and down the drive a few times, enjoying myself – and incidentally rolling the surface smooth at the same time. So the drive, whilst still not in any way perfect, is vastly improved. Smart cars can arrive at our door with fewer mud smears around their wheel arches. *And* I got to drive a roller. It's the first thing I've driven in months!

Oh, the irresistible power of cake!

But back to reality; now I must go and clean freezing water from the chapel floor. I saw a rat in there yesterday, I think.

Best wishes,

Sister B.

20

St Win's
October 24th

Dear Emelda,

The famously sharp East Anglian wind is stripping leaves from the trees as I write. We have a row of ash trees along our boundary and their leaves in shades of orange and yellow blow over Odge's bare ploughed field on the other side. They fall so that each tree briefly has a neat oval of autumn colour to one side, like a colourful shadow.

"The Bishop thinks convents may not be doing enough for the local community," Sister Joy declared last night at convocation. "You raise money for Sisters working in South America, Sudan, Kenya and Sierra Leone, you market goods made by convents all round the country, but are you doing enough for the people of Three Fens? This may be why you have been given the test of your money being stolen. There must be a reason, after all."

"I think someone's talking out of their elbow," Eustacia said. "If you ask me they're trying to cover their tracks. Our money's missing because they didn't keep a proper eye on their accountant, not because we're neglecting the neighbours."

Sister Joy pretended not to hear that.

"I shall be speaking to each one of you individually and I look forward to hearing your local plans. We can't all be glory-seekers in the jungle, after all!" And with that she left for a meeting in Bury St Edmunds, or perhaps it was Ely – it was *very important* anyway.

"It's certainly true that people nearby have supported the convent in good times and bad for centuries," Hermione said, after we'd heard Sister Joy's car leave, "the records show that clearly. Our neighbours were mostly poor themselves, but they have always been generous to St Win's."

"I am only a guest, but maybe I could make a suggestion?" Sister Doris said. "You see, where I come from we often get this kind of... direction I guess the word is, from our diocese. We long ago realised that they probably didn't know or understand our work, so what we generally do is..."

We all leaned forward to catch Sister Doris's advice.

"...make a banner. A good, big banner, with a slogan that is right on target. We hang it up somewhere very public, and then we we go right ahead exactly as before."

The beautiful wisdom of this was clear to us all, so that is what we did. Mother Martha and her needlework team made a splendid banner, it is at least twelve feet

THE POWER OF CAKE

long, the handiwork is superb, and it reads *Our Focus is Local*. I'm looking at it now.

You, as a Suffolk native, count as local in our eyes, even if you do happen to be in the Andes. We are used to this idea, but I had to explain it to Farmer Odge, the other day.

He said, "Where is this convent of St Anne's you send the profits from these things to? Is it the one over Norwich way?"

"No it's over North Peru way, actually."

"Northbrew?"

"Peru, South America," I said.

"Oh *Peru!* I thought you said Northbrew. Why do you send things to South America, then? Export is it?"

"No, they send their products here and we sell them."

"Oh! Imports!"

"Fundraising. We send the profits back."

"You're very international."

"We are! And proud of it."

"Farming's very international now, you know. I bought my last cattle from Belgium and sold them to someone in France."

So we put the banner up in the Shoppe, to remind us, and then made a list of all the local projects we are already involved in. Mother Hilda rides off on her motorbike every day and helps out at Beech House, a

Rehab Centre. Sister Mary of Light volunteers at the nursery in Widdy Fen, Sister Bernard has several local music students, and I have the Shoppe and the English lessons, but we all agreed we wanted something more and the something should be.... St Winifreda's Community Café!

Once this was decided I said, "The funny thing is, tables and chairs have been arriving in the Shoppe for weeks. Every time I look, there seem to be more of them."

Several sisters in the meeting looked at their shoes for a while. Eventually Sister Bernard said, "They were being given away. It was a leap of faith."

"We thought if we just sneaked them into the Shoppe a few at a time, the café would just grow by itself," Hermione said, "and it did, more or less."

I'm sure you know how this works, Emelda. I began wondering how one of those big coffee machines could be found – on a budget of £30 it didn't seem very easy – when Sister Patrick handed me a phone message: "Please ring Carla Dacosta asap."

When I rang, Carla said, "Sorry, Sister, I have to cancel Antonio's lesson for Tuesday. Something came up."

"He's well, I hope."

"He's fine, but his team is, you know, under a bit of

pressure."

"Well, I hope it is not too serious," I said. "Ms Dacosta, can I pick your brains on the subject of coffee machines?"

"Of course!"

So I explained, and she said she'd call back. Three days later two men carried in our new coffee machine. It is vast. It is assertively hissy. It is Italian and it is red. Its brand name is Razzo – which Carla translates as Rocket. The Rocket is a machine with personality to spare. Its presence has changed the whole character of our little enterprise from slightly timid and apologetic, to bold, welcoming, and possibly even slightly *Italian*. Nesbitt, Hermione and I spend two evenings watching instructional films on the computer, and now we are qualified Rocket controllers.

Most other things we needed were found by putting up a little sign on the Shoppe notice board – I'd scarcely had time to find a drawing pin before cups, saucers and plates began arriving. The office workers saw the sign and Intermediax donated a set of gingham tablecloths in their corporate yellow and white.

Sister Doris wandered in just as Nesbitt and I were finishing setting up the tables. "It's not just that He moves in mysterious ways. It's that He does it *fast* when you point yourself in the right direction. Don't you agree, Boniface?" she said. "A café! What's not to like?"

"Sister Joy won't like it, though, will she?" I said, watching Nesbitt, who was happily setting a jar of chrysanthemums on every table, turning them this way and that until they looked just right.

"I guess not," said Doris, "but that would be her problem, dear, not ours."

Our first official café customers were Wal and Wil, two good old boys from Water Lode, best friends and neighbouring smallholders. They are a giggly pair in their eighties. They came to the Shoppe for a tin of beans; the sort of errand wives send their retired husbands out on quite often in Three Fens.

"Come on Wal, let's push the boat out and have us a coffee while we're about it. The ladies wanted us out of the house. Might as well."

"Might as well. Go on then." Wil agreed.

"Two coffees Sister. Whatcha want, Wal? Cappuccino?"

"Whassat?"

"Cappuccino. You know, cappuccino," said Wal. Not having a definition to hand, all he could do was repeat the word: "*Cappuccino.*"

"I just want a coffee with milk in it," said Wil, who wasn't having any of that fancy nonsense.

"A coffee with milk in it is more or less an

Americano," I told them.

"Two Americanos then please," he said, and to Wal, "Americanos, we're going in for Americanos Wal, alright?"

"Right you are," said Wal, "two sugars, and we'll have some of them convent biscuits.

"I'll pay."

"You won't," Wil told him.

"I will. It was my idea."

"Don't be daft," Wil said, attempting to shoulder him aside at the till.

This went on for a few minutes before one or other of them managed to hand me the money and they sat down.

"You want to watch your manners," Wal said.

"You want to watch yours."

Both chuckling away, they carried their coffees over to the table in the corner with the armchairs.

And that was it. No fuss, no publicity, no razzmatazz, just a little café serving its first customers. And although it hissed and sputtered, I even mastered the Rocket. It's a bit of a character, but it responds to prayer and firm handling, like the photocopier.

The only small problem is that I am quite possibly the slowest *barista* in East Anglia. I enjoy the whole coffee machine process, but I haven't worked out how to do it fast. Nesbitt, on the other hand, can have a perfect latte in front of a customer before they've finished asking.

We haven't had a letter from you for some weeks, Emelda. I was reminded of this yesterday, when a funny little boy called Elvis was buying a cake (in small coin, the counting was very laborious). Elvis endears himself to us by solemnly putting his spare change, usually a single penny, into the Convent Restoration Fund collection box every time he comes. We were alone in the Shoppe and after he'd paid he clearly wanted to make conversation, but being about nine, he was up against his social limits when dealing with a nun, so I said, "That looks like a good book."

He was carrying a large book called *Giant ... of the World* under his arm. I couldn't read one of the words, his arm was over it.

"It *is* good," he said. "There's a picture of the biggest beetle in the whole world. Do you want to see it?"

Insects, the missing word was *insects*.

"Yes, please," I said, steeling myself. And he showed me a photograph of a small child holding up a beetle the size of a man's shoe. If you didn't know better you'd assume it was a prop from a horror film, frankly. The only thing I could find to like about it was its name: *Titanus giganteus*. "Wow," I said, trying not to wince, "where does it live?"

"The Amazon rainforest," said Elvis matter-of-factly, "its mandibles can rip into human flesh. Do you want to see the giant burrowing cockroach? They can live for ten years!"

"Thank you, Elvis, but I'd better get on now," I said, "we'll save that one for next time."

There isn't much chance of *Titanus giganteus* creeping up on you, Emelda, you'd hear it coming, it's so big its footsteps would echo through the jungle, but keep an eye out all the same. Luckily the giant burrowing cockroach lives in Australia. I tried not to, but I did glimpse it. It reminded me of a holy relic I once saw in Belgium.

Best wishes,

Sister B.

21

St Win's Community Café
October 27th

Dear Emelda,

We were very relieved to receive your letter. You seem to have trekked a huge distance, but at least the loggers are making you welcome. Yes, in answer to your query, we do have a Kidnap Policy. We drew it up some years ago after Mother Deirdre went to Bosnia that time. Thanks for the reminder. We will keep it up-to-date, but we very much hope and pray it won't be needed.

I wish I could answer your question about the strange fruit. I've looked it up on the internet and it seems to be a *camu camu*, which tastes rather sour, apparently, and is high in vitamin C. Peruvian fruits are extraordinary. There are several I can hardly imagine: have you seen a *tumbo* or an *aguage*?

Wind has blown all our customers home today. It's the tail end of a vicious storm that has frozen parts of the US solid and blown a force 12 all through the West Country. What we have of it here in East Anglia is a howling gusty wind. It's definitely a No Poncho Day for Carmella and the cockerels are so busy trying to avoid their feathers being blown inside out that it's even silenced them.

A few doughty office workers still brave the elements for biscuits and birthday cakes. They're young and energetic but they look like tornado survivors by the time they arrive. I give them free marshmallows in their hot chocolate.

No *aguage* or *tumbo* here in the Shoppe, but we have plenty of apples and lots of pears as well as our own walnuts, which are selling well, thanks to my hand-dying labours. We priced them through guesswork and then were astonished when we looked up their supermarket price – about four times as much. Sister Clementine and Nesbitt have used a lot in cakes. Fresh walnuts in cakes are particularly delicious and they have cake fans devoted enough to sweep their favourites off the shelves within minutes and brave any weather to do so.

Being without transport remains a trial. There are various options: the buses are very limited and taxis cost a huge amount because they have to come all the way out here first and then go all the way back once the journey is over. There is a community car service, which we use occasionally. You book a volunteer driver and they collect and deliver you. They come from the next village and in theory it's a good service, but in practice the only volunteer driver they ever send us is

Albert Miles, who's not in the first flush of his youth. Sisters stagger trembling up the drive after a trip to the chiropodist or the GP and usually reckon it would be better to suffer their ailments than drive straight over another mini roundabout with Albert, who apparently talks non-stop with his eyes behind his thick-lensed spectacles directed at his passenger and away from the road. Mother Martha can hardly bear to talk about her experience at the level crossing. She has, of course, no difficulty facing death herself, but she didn't fancy becoming a YouTube sensation whilst meeting her Maker, or taking any of the passengers on the 7.43 to King's Cross with her. Albert, she didn't mind about taking at all.

With transport options limited to walking; waiting a very long time for a bus; braving Albert's community transport, or hitching a ride with a visitor, we have started pinning Lift Wanted cards on the Shoppe noticeboard. Today's said "Railway Station. One passenger by 2 pm."

When Alphonsus arrived in his little sports car to talk to Sister Bernard about the website, he immediately offered his services.

"I can take someone," he said, "still no luck with the replacement van then?"

"Not yet, no." I told him. "We manage."

"I'm happy to help any time," he said, "only my car is on the small side..."

"Yes. Unless we put one or two sisters in the boot it wouldn't do for the hospital run," I said, "the retired Sisters would enjoy going in a sports car, though! Especially Mother Roberta, she used to be a racing driver in the old days."

"You're not serious?"

"Oh yes," I said, "Le Mans, Montecarlo... she was a contender, as they say!"

"Amazing!" said Alphonsus.

"She gave it up when she took up stunt flying," I told him. He raised an eyebrow. "Seriously, she was a wing walker. I've seen photographs."

He laughed. "I haven't said hello to you, Nesbitt," he said, "How are you getting on with your apprenticeship?"

"Yeah. Continental pastries at the moment."

"You should try her Portuguese custard tarts," I told him. "They drive from Diss for them. People order in advance and we have to hide their orders round the corner. Customers offer us extra for the reserved ones!"

"It's Nesbitt's Lemon Drizzle I pine for," he said.

I gave him a slice immediately and showed off by producing a cappuccino with chocolate sprinkles in a cross on the top – our unique selling point. The Rocket hissed, doing its authentic Milanese café impersonation.

"How are you getting on, Alphonsus?" I asked. He paused and looked down at his coffee.

"Well, I have temporary work, but times are quite hard," he said. "Having a criminal record doesn't exactly help when you're looking for a job in IT. I'm a notorious criminal. I am the Hacker with a Heart – the Daily Mail said so – and employers only remember the first part. My name rings a bell, they Google it, and that's me off the shortlist. So I'm glad of a little freelance work here on the website. Anyway, how is St Win's? The café's a great idea. I must visit Carmella and the greenhouses. I planted an awful lot of Pak Choi. I'd like to see how it grew."

"She'll be pleased to see you, Alphonsus," I said. "So will Hermione."

He sipped his coffee. "How is Hermione?" he asked eventually.

"She seems quiet," I said, "she buries herself in her work. None of us has seen very much of her lately."

He frowned and looked away. "I miss the old place," he said. "I even miss Animal and Baz telling me how useless I was."

Shortly afterwards he stepped out into the wild wind to find Carmella.

Sister Doris hurried in.

"Is the young man here?" she asked.

I explained he was in the garden.

"I'm going to suggest something," she said, "after he's finished the meeting about the website, I'll walk him back here, and you keep him talking while I bring Hermione over."

"Why are we whispering?" I asked her. "Are we conspiring?"

"Conspiring? Not at all!" said Sister Doris loudly. "Why that would be ridiculous! No, it's just that if Hermione finds out who is offering her a ride to the station, she might..."

"Avoid it?" I suggested, "Run a mile? Have an attack of nerves?"

"Exactly," said Sister Doris, "My view would be that this young woman needs to meet and have the opportunity to speak with this young man. She is depressed. Everyone tells me she used to be full of life and laughter and now she is quite clearly depressed on the rare occasions that we see her at all. There is clearly something she needs to deal with here – something they both need to discuss. I truly believe it will help her see things more clearly."

I agreed.

So after their website meeting Sister Doris walked Alphonsus back to the cafe.

"Who am I giving a lift to? Is it a run to the doctor's?" he asked, slightly surprised to be shepherded into a seat.

"It's Hermione," Sister Doris said. "Maybe you remember her? She is going to Norwich for an archivists' conference."

"Yes, of course I remember…"

"It wouldn't be everyone's choice, an archivists' conference, but there we are," Sister Doris went on. "Can you give her a ride to the station? She's staying with the Benedictines tonight. I'll go and fetch her now. Boniface will give you some more cake while you wait."

I took Alphonsus a slice of our finest walnut special. The Rocket started to splutter. I went over, gave it a fierce look and twiddled a few knobs. It subsided into a low hiss.

Hermione burst through the door carrying her briefcase and wearing a coat. "They said to hurry because there was a lift… *oh!*" She had spotted Alphonsus mid-sentence.

He rose from his seat to greet her.

"Alphonsus! I didn't know you were…I mean, I wasn't expecting…"

"They said someone needed a lift. I didn't know it would be you."

She dropped her suitcase in surprise. It fell over, and propelled forward by her own momentum, she caught a foot on its corner and began to lose her balance. I thought she was going to fall, she certainly began to, but Alph, with the reflex of a cricketer going in for a catch, darted forward and caught her elbow in one hand and her glasses, which had flown off her nose, in the other. Everything froze for a second and then he grinned, and presented the spectacles back to her.

"How are you, Hermione?" Alphonsus asked her.

"As clumsy as ever, by the look of it," she said, "but otherwise I'm fine, thank you," she said, "yes, fine. How are you?"

"Rather full of cake at the moment, but generally well, yes, thank you. If you're ready to go, I could carry the suitcase."

"No!" said Hermione, suddenly.

"Oh, sorry, I..."

"No. I mean I've changed my mind. I don't need a lift now. I'm not going."

"Oh, but they said there was a conference."

"I'm not going. I can't. Sorry. I know they meant to do the right thing, but I can't go with you, Alphonsus. Sorry. Sorry." Hermione grabbed the suitcase and fled. The door crashing behind her.

There then ensued a silence until the Rocket hissed and the clink of cups was heard over the hum of resumed conversation. Nesbitt and I made ourselves busy behind the counter.

Alphonsus looked at the door for a moment, then turned and went back to his table. He picked up his cup and brought it to the counter. "Obviously a change of plan," he said, "I'll be off then. Thanks very much for the coffee, and all the cake."

Nobody could fault that boy's manners.

Emelda, we've probably both known Sisters who shut themselves away too early. They don't usually last long. These days we understand human psychology a little better and try to avoid it. If Hermione is to join us, she needs to do it in the fullest understanding of all the implications of her choice. Sad, lonely recruits are no good; we need Sisters who rejoice every day in the freedom of their calling.

You can't become a nun to escape a broken heart or avoid your sexuality these days, as I explained to Nesbitt when we were sweeping up later.

"Blimey," she said.

Best wishes,

Sister B.

PS It's true about Roberta and the wing-walking. She won prizes.

22

St Win's
October 30th

Dear Emelda,

I told you, I think, that of the five eggs we hatched last summer, four turned out to be cockerels. Very handsome chaps they are, too. We feel rather proud of them, but they are four cockerels too many, as we already have Jean-Paul, their father, crowing. And they fight. Almost every time we pass the run there is a battle going on. Chicken politics are ruthless. They gang up on a single bird and several of them attack him; then they all change allegiance and attack a different one. It reminds us of the Referendum.

We call one particularly ambitious bird The Dictator. He likes to launch his attack from behind and his persecutions last days on end. Last week, after injuring one of his brothers, he stood still in the middle of the chicken run all afternoon. None of us had ever seen anything like it. He stood like a statue, not eating or scratching or doing any of the normal chicken things, simply glaring ferociously around him, intimidating the rest by death stare alone. The cockerels were definitely made uncomfortable by this and kept their distance. The hens completely ignored him. Hens have a lovely way of ignoring the fierce machinations of male birds. *Oh for Heaven's sake*, is the message they somehow convey.

It can't go on. The surplus cockerels will have to go. If we can't give them away, they will have to be dispatched. It's just that we haven't, so far, found anyone to do it. Quite a few of the sisters say they used to do it in the old days, but none feels much like strangling a cockerel any more – and they're sizeable creatures with argumentative natures, so they probably won't go gentle into that good night. I've been offering up this little problem in my prayers for some time now. Farmer Odge may be our only recourse. We hesitate to mention it to him out of pride, I think. We don't want to seem like feeble lady chicken keepers who can't even dispatch sensibly when it is required. A convent of wimps and chickeners-out.

No doubt in Peru chickens are dealt with without much fuss. I so enjoyed the description of the topping-out ceremony for the new school hall building you sent before you went on your trek. How the whole tribe came and all the elders made speeches that went on for a very long time and then all the young men and women danced and all the children sang a special song they had prepared about school.

THE POWER OF CAKE

Your translation:

> *School you are the love of our hearts*
> *We eat you like a ripe melon.*
> *School your learning is a gift for us*
> *Your teaching is as splendid as an Osfarra bird's*
> feather
>
> *Beautiful, radiant, beautiful, sunshining school!*

is pinned up in the Shoppe as an example of a wonderful attitude to education. The local schoolchildren are supposed to read it as they queue for their cakes and sandwiches. Perhaps a few do, though on the whole the cakes win their attention rather more than the instructive written word, if I'm honest. Perhaps they absorb it subliminally, associating it with the taste of cake. Poetry and cake; a powerful combination if ever there was one.

Returning to the matter of extreme country noise, I have been delegated to raise the issue of bird-scarers with Farmer Odge the very next time he comes into the Shoppe for Battenburg and dog biscuits. His men have placed one of these wretched cannon-like bird scarers just over our hedge. It's on a timer and lets off a double blast of noise that probably shakes ornaments as far away as Lowestoft every half hour all through the day. I have seen elderly sisters run for cover at the sound, and why shouldn't they? It's as loud as the Blitz. Wol and Wil, our regulars, nearly dropped their Dundee cake when the almighty booms rang out. Even Bob Fairbrother, whom I wouldn't normally consider the nervous sort, spilled his coffee when the cannon went off yesterday, but he was too engrossed in testing out new book titles on me to do anything other than pour the spillage from the saucer back into the cup.

"How about this: *Niche Marketing Explained*?" he said.

"Well..." I said, I had my hands full with the Rocket, which was being temperamental that day.

"You think it's dull, schoolmarmy, a bit 80s, don't you?"

"No, no. Just not very exciting," I told him, "I don't think it would make me buy it."

"No. I take the point," he said, sighing. "A couple of bakewell slices and a sausage roll too, please."

The irony, of course, is that while the terrible explosions of the bird scarer terrify all the rest of us, the pigeons land on Odge's fields in vast, cheerfully oblivious flocks and just keep eating.

It has been a beautiful, crisp wintry day here today, not a cloud in the sky and for once the wind was having a rest. I was admiring the sunshine on the bare poplars when my eye was caught by Sister Prudence strolling in the garden with someone I didn't recognise. They walked and talked for a long time before sitting on the bench by the pond. It looked a very serious discussion.

At convocation Sister Prudence said, "I had an unusual visitor today. It was Mrs Wooler."

"Oh, that's who it was," I said. "You talked for a long time."

"The poor lady is distraught. She came to ask our forgiveness for the behaviour of her husband."

"Well, *if* he did it," said Eustacia, "I mean I've no time for the man, but he hasn't even been charged with anything yet. There's such a thing as *due process*. We can't assume he's guilty, even if we are pretty sure of it."

The rest of us were surprised by this moderation.

"Wendy Wooler believes that he did take the money," said Sister Prudence. "He was furious before he left. He repeatedly complained about being passed over for promotion. A younger man was put in charge of his department. Mr Wooler could not stand it. He told her he had given the Church more than thirty years of loyal service and now it was publicly humiliating him."

"That poor woman," said Hermione.

"I invited her to stay," Sister Prudence said. "I felt it my duty. The press is hounding her. She came close to asking me for sanctuary."

"Well, I don't want to sound uncharitable, but what if Wooler is guilty and she *is* implicated?" Sister Bernard said.

"Why would she come here, if she had something to hide?" I asked.

"I don't know, but I think we should let the police know, anyway."

So that was agreed. Wendy Wooler is in Pigpen 2, slightly under observation, but otherwise welcome. I see her in the Shoppe now and then. She is a neat, unsmiling woman who always looks piercingly around as if carrying out some sort of inspection. She buys only water and (perhaps you guessed) Garibaldi biscuits.

It's chilly here now. The chapel pond has ice on it some mornings, which makes clearing it very cold work. Sister Bernard wears fingerless gloves to play the organ, so the music keeps us going, but after three sisters went down with bad colds in as many days, we decided last week that the thermal underwear renewal fund needed to be raided for some more layers and I was sent to town to buy them.

On Sister Bernard's recommendation, I went to a specialist outdoor gear shop. It was a little place, down a side alley, and filled with goosedown coats for the Arctic, colourful ropes for rock climbing, and helmets with torches in them for potholing. You would have been completely at home in it, Emelda, but I hardly qualified to shop there at all – the most outdoorsy thing I do is to feed the chickens. Still, they had a special offer, and we were keen to take advantage, so I had fun talking the choices of long-johns and thermal vests over with Lew and Maisie, the friendly assistants, who had both used the climbing equipment in the Alps and were heading for Nepal next. I came away with a pile of far more colourful, and, I suspect, far more efficient underwear then we have tried before. Our thermal vests are built for adventure, even if we're not. It's oddly inspiring.

We haven't had a letter from Peru for many weeks now, Emelda. I keep on writing, as we agreed, but sometimes I'm aware I am scribbling away about our goings-on here while you are in very dangerous territory. There was another documentary about logging cartels and land-grabs and drug dealing in your part of the world. I didn't have the nerve to watch it. Several sisters who did have patted my shoulder in a particularly meaningful way since and told me you need all the encouragement you can get. Write if you can, and stay safe.

I'm hurrying to finish this in time for the bread van. Dan the driver posts letters, if we ask. I've just opened the Shoppe and it would be peaceful if it wasn't for the competitive crowing. One cockerel starts and then the others all have to out-do him. I often wonder what the hens make of it. Do they savour each crow like a Pavarotti aria, or do they long for silence? It's a shame the cockerel problem and the bird scarer problems couldn't be made to cancel each other out. Excuse the unworthy thought, but if only cockerels were more sensitive to loud booms I could just move their run a bit closer to the hedge and they'd all expire from the shock.

One of the Pigpen guests has written: *"too much loud bird noise in the am from 6"* in the Visitors' Book.

"Oh dear, it'll be Tripadvisor next," Sister Bernard said, when she saw it.

Pavel pointed out that someone with my walnut-cracking experience would need to adapt their technique only slightly to dispatch a bird, but that was only a joke (I hope).

I can't leave you with that image. Picture instead an empty Shoppe and coming from the borrowed laptop, the lively rhythms of Salsa. Then picture a colourfully-clad figure "casting her legges to and fro" (as Chaucer puts it). It's me; I'm practising! I'll never pass as South American, but I *feel* it, a little bit, now and then. It's an excellent way of warming up on a frosty morning. *Cha cha cha*!

Best wishes,

Sister B.

23

St Win's
November 1st

Dear Wanderer,

This morning I was weighing out sprouts in the Shoppe when I noticed a little hand – a child's hand – reach up from behind one of the potato sacks and take hold of a nunpeg. The hand and the nunpeg then disappeared. I served the customer, not being quite sure my eyes weren't deceiving me, and then looked towards the potatoes again. A little face peeped round. It was a girl of about three.

"Hello," she said. "I found this dolly. It was in the potatoes. It's funny. Is it yours?"

"I sell them in the shop. It isn't really a dolly, it's a peg, for putting the washing on the line," I told her.

"That's a funny idea," she said. "It's like a dolly, but it goes on your washing! That's funny."

"Is your mummy here?" I asked." Is she outside?" I couldn't see many cars now that the sprout lady had left.

"She works in this shop."

"Who does?"

"My mummy."

"Does she?" I was confused by this.

"Yes. Sometimes she makes cakes. Sometimes she

comes here in the shop."

"Does she?"

"Yes!" She looked at me as I came round the counter and bent down to talk to her. "And I do know what your name is," she said.

"Do you?"

"Yes. It is Sturbee."

I said, "Well, you're right! How did you know?"

She was very pleased with this. "I knew that for ages! My mummy said."

"And what is your name?"

"Roselily," she said, "Roselily Nesbitt."

Very soon afterwards Nesbitt came running across the yard into the shop from the kitchen, where she'd been cooking with Sister Clementine. She threw open the door in a rush and a panic and stopped in her tracks when she saw me sitting on the stool talking to little Roselily, who was telling me about her new kitten. She stopped and smiled at Nesbitt happily.

"Where's Gran?" Nebitt asked her in some alarm.

"She's in the car," Roselily said. "She's asleep." Nesbitt looked distraught. "Stay here with Sister B.," she said and rushed outside again.

Roselily looked after her mother. "Is she coming back?" she asked me.

I said, "Yes, she'll be back in a minute."

I heard a car door slam and Nesbitt's rushing footsteps. She burst ashen-faced back into the shop and said, "She's ill. She's collapsed. She must have got Roselily out of the child seat somehow."

I said. "Nesbitt, you stay with Roselily and I'll go and get Eustacia. She's a nurse. I'll call an ambulance on the way."

"She has these turns," said Nesbitt.

"What sort?"

"Strokes, attacks. She's been alright lately, but it might be that again."

Eustacia hardly had time to put the patient into the recovery position before the ambulance arrived. They had Mrs. Nesbitt packed off to hospital in short order. Nesbitt wanted to go too, but they wouldn't let the little girl travel with them.

"My cousin can look after her," Nesbitt said. "I'll ring and ask her to come."

"Where is she?"

"In Fen Drove. She might not be home from work yet. I wish I could drive."

Nesbitt looked helplessly at her mother's car. Its doors were still open.

"I could drive you both to your cousin's in your mum's car," I said. "I'd be happy to take you to the hospital afterwards, too."

"Could you?"

"I'll just lock up." I said.

"Where's Granny?" Roselily asked. "Mummy, where's Granny gone?"

"She's not very well. She's gone to the hospital. The doctors can make her better there," Nesbitt told her.

Roselily, so calm so far, suddenly started to cry loudly, her mouth wide and tears pouring down her little cheeks.

It was terribly hard to watch, even for a second.

Nesbitt knelt and hugged her. "I'm taking you to Sal's and then I'm going to the hospital, Rosie. You can have your tea with Sal and Uncle Jim and I'll be back to get you soon."

The girl howled louder at this. She shook her head.

"I don't want to go to Sal's. I want to go with you. I want... to... go... with you and Nana, Mummy."

Nesbitt picked her up and said to me, "I always take her with me if she asks me to. I just always do."

I could see it was a sort of pact. It wasn't to be argued with.

So I drove Mrs Nesbitt's car to the hospital after the ambulance and Roselily, Nesbitt and I waited in A and E while Mrs. Nesbitt was seen, examined, scanned and admitted. It all took hours. At one point Nesbitt was called in to see her mother.

"I'm sorry but it would be better if your little girl

waited here," the nurse said.

I said, "She can stay with me if you like," but I wasn't sure whether Roselily would be happy to be left.

Nesbitt explained it to her, and she was brave. Just nodding and waving goodbye. We sat for a while side by side, Roselily sucking her thumb, thoughtfully. After a while she turned to me and, pulling her thumb out, said, "Will the nurse make my Nana better soon?"

I said yes, but sometimes you had to wait a while in a hospital.

She put her thumb back in and considered this. Then (thumb out), "Why you have to wait?" (thumb back in).

"All these other people," I said. "They want to get better too."

(Thumb out, loud stage whisper) "Are these people poorly too?"

"Yes," I said "they're waiting to see the doctor or the nurse."

"Is that man poorly?" She pointed to a man sitting opposite.

"He might just be waiting." I said, aside, hoping not to embarrass the man.

"He doesn't look poorly," she said. "That boy's got a bandage on his arm. He might need a plaster. I've got a plaster, look!" After a struggle with her sleeve, she

185

managed to pull it up and show me her arm, where there was indeed a pink plaster with a cartoon on it.

"That's a nice plaster," I said. "Did you hurt yourself?"

"It is nice," Roselily told me. "I didn't hurt myself. I'm allowed to have a plaster sometimes, even if I don't have a hurt. But not too often. If I put too many plasters on I would be all sticked up and that would be silly."

"It would," I said, "very silly. You might have a plaster on your finger and not be able to bend it."

"Or a plaster on my thumb and not be able to suck it!" she said, giggling.

"Or a plaster on your toes and not be able to wiggle them!"

"Or a plaster on my nose and not be able to smell! Or one on my hair! Yow! That would really hurt. It hurts to take a plaster off."

"You have to do it quickly," I said. "Then it's not so bad."

"My Mummy says that, but I think very slow is better. Very, very slow. Then it doesn't even hurt at all. My Nana can do it."

The thumb went back in as the dear creature remembered her Nana.

A couple of times Roselily and I went off for a walk. I remembered Rev Tim's gerbils in the Chapel office, and we visited to see if they were still there. They were, and

Roselily gave them sunflower seeds through the bars of their cage. Their bounciness made her laugh aloud.

She held my hand some of the time as we walked down the corridors, which I liked very much, but she also had a lot of fun running ahead – the corridors are enormously long – and jumping out at me – *boo!* At one point she looked up and said, "You like black dresses a lot, don't you, Sturbee? I like pink best, or yellow, but black is *quite* nice too."

Back in A and E she was bored and a bit upset, but she did very well, playing with a little figure she found in her pocket and reading some books they had in a pile until she fell asleep on Nesbitt's lap.

Nesbitt said. "You should go, Sister, you don't need to wait."

"But how will you get home?" I asked.

"We can get a taxi."

"It'll cost a fortune. I'm happy to stay."

In the end Sal and Jim arrived at about 10 pm and carried the sleeping Roselily home with them. Nesbitt stayed with her mother – they offered her a camp bed, and I drove home alone, rather overpowered by the whole episode.

I had worked with Nesbitt for almost a year and she had never mentioned a child. Never once. How could we not have known? Childcare worries and all sorts of other things and she never said a thing. Nineteen now, so she must have had Roselily at 16. Everyone must have known in the village, but nobody had ever mentioned it.

When I told them at convocation, Sister Bernard sighed. "They probably thought we would be judgmental. People assume we will be harsh and there are all sorts of TV dramas and films now about horrible convents where they punish and imprison single mothers and steal their babies to have them adopted. Very well-acted some of them are. Frightful things were done, Sisters, we have to admit it."

"But not here, surely?" I asked, suddenly anxious about St Win's past and hoping to goodness it wasn't filled with single mothers toiling over boiling cauldrons while evil sisters sold their babies at the back gate to the highest bidder.

Hermione was consulted, as historian we figured she should know the full facts.

"Did we, Hermione? Did we have an orphanage here? A laundry? Did we take people's babies away? Tell us the worst!"

"As far as I can tell from the convent's papers we never did anything like that." A collective sigh of relief here. "The sisters accepted money for prayers and benedictions, they sold their garden produce and they rented the Poore Pasture in King's Hedges – but they don't seem to have run an orphanage. I've just got as far as the early 20th century in the papers now. During the First World War they knitted scarves; there is a terrifically grateful letter from the Red Cross thanking them for a huge number of scarves and socks and they also seem to have hidden some prisoners of war, but I haven't got through all those papers yet."

"Why would the convent hide prisoners of war?" asked Sister Bernard. "Seems an odd detail."

Eustacia was still thinking about Nesbitt. "It's come to a pretty pass if someone like Nesbitt can't even dare mention her baby for fear that we would sack her or condemn her to work as a slave labourer or something."

We all agreed.

I looked around the Shoppe as I went to settle it down for the night, and realised how much we owe our apprentice. Nesbitt's ideas are what changed it from my vision of a convent shop – a place that sold sprouts and spuds to a very few customers – to the place we have today, but she didn't feel able to tell us about her little girl. I shudder with shame to think of it.

I keep looking at the nunpeg that first attracted Roselily's attention and picturing her little hand reaching up to take it.

Yours, still astonished,

Sister B.

24

St Win's
November 4th

Dear Emelda,

Still no news from Peru. We have spoken to the convent in Santa Anna, and they've heard nothing from you either, so we're working on the principle that you are far up country and too busy helping the loggers to want to leave or be able to send letters. Or perhaps it is Raulito who has given in to the temptation of strong drink, or had difficulty with his canoe, or one of his many river-port wives. Our local postman sometimes has one of those problems – I'd better not say which

Nesbitt came to talk about her working arrangements today. She has her mother to care for now, as well as Roselily. She's only been away a week, but the customers in the Shoppe and café are already up in arms.

"Where's that girl Nesbitt? We en't seen her for days. Don't tell me Nesbitt's left," Baz said on Monday, "her sausage rolls are the best!"

"Yeah!" Animal agreed, "the best! Lovely and tasty, they are. And big, really big!"

Bob Fairbrother had to manage with only one Sachertorte and no Danish pastries, and Odge's face fell when there was no Battenburg.

"Perhaps you could try a lemon drizzle, or a piece of fruit cake," I suggested.

"I'll just take the dog biscuits."

Then there was the matter of my slow coffee service. Queues formed. People started abandoning hope and asking for tea instead. I confessed at convocation how difficult it was to run the café and the Shoppe without Nesbitt. Sister Clara offered to help, but the Rocket took against her last time.

"Let us say a prayer for Nesbitt and how we can best help her to flourish in her future life," Sister Prudence declared. We all bowed our heads and Prudence called out, "Dear God, we all know that Nesbitt is a wonderful young woman with mighty challenges before her. Please tell us how we can help her immediately. Amen."

"I could look after Roselily while Nesbitt is working here," Sister Mary of Light said, "I'm qualified. I can easily look after one little girl for a few hours."

"But where would you do this? Do we have the correct facilities?" asked Prudence.

"I could use the parlour for quiet play. The nursery would lend me a few toys. We don't use the parlour very often. We could have a little play corner in the café too, perhaps, so Roselily could visit her mum. Customers' children would be able to use it too."

"I could lend a hand," Sister Bernard offered.

"Put my name on the list." "Me too, I can help," about a dozen other sisters called.

Sister Prudence smiled widely and put her hands together in prayer again. "Thank you, dear Lord. We can always rely on you!"

So when poor Nesbitt arrived, looking tired and a bit sad, I was nearly jumping with secret excitement. Practically every sister in the convent made an excuse to drop into the Shoppe and have a few words with Roselily. I don't think so many sisters have been in the Shoppe at once before. If they hadn't been so gentle, I might have called it a scrum. Roselily is used to ladies in black dresses now. She showed them all her new shoes, which twinkle magically when you dance in them. Mary of Light took her for a walk, so Nesbitt and I could talk. I'd planned this part carefully. We talk best side-by-side, working, so I said, "I need to cut some fruit cake."

"I'll do it," she said, fetching her apron and washing her hands.

"How is your mother?" I started laying out bread for sandwiches.

"Not too bad. Walking on her own now. But she can't look after Rosie yet."

"No. We thought perhaps we could do something here," I said, starting to butter. I was nervous about putting it to her in the right way. She'd hate any favours. "Sister Mary is a nursery teacher. She could look after Roselily for a few hours here. I know your family will help, but, just in case you needed anything more. Even if you couldn't work here, we could care for Roselily on your college days, so you could complete the training, if it would help."

There was a long pause, during which Nesbitt sliced and wrapped five perfectly identical slices of fruit cake without looking up.

"I can't pay," she said, finally, "and it's no good just going to college, I need to be working here with Sister Clem to do it properly."

"Sister Mary already has a team. They will cover as many hours as you need. She's been working at a nursery. She knows what's involved. We can borrow equipment from the nursery in Withy Fen and we thought of putting a little play corner over there, in the café."

"Why would you do all that?" She fanned her cake slices evenly around the edge of the circular display stand.

"Takings have plummeted with you away. There have been queues. The Rocket's being difficult. This place will never succeed without you. We'll go out of business. I mean it. We need you here. Please come back if you can. At least until you finish the apprenticeship."

She finished the fruit cake display, washed the chopping board and wiped down the surfaces.

"People ask about you all the time. They're disappointed when you're not here. The place stops looking – it just stops looking right when you can't come. It stops looking its best and begins to look sad, and a bit untidy. I do my best, but I haven't got your touch, your talent for it. Please, Nesbitt, if you can manage it, the customers would all be grateful. So would I."

"You just put mayonnaise on that instead of mustard," she said.

"Is that a yes?"

"Yes. Could you not tell Mrs Dunbar from the college? It'll just be complicated."

"Not a word," I said.

Sister Joy wasn't at convocation to hear the news. She sent an email to say she was writing up her report.

Pavel was working on something in the woodshed yesterday. It looked like a wendy house. News flies fast in the flatness of the Fens.

It seems to be getting stuck in the Peruvian Andes at the moment, though, sadly.

Let us know you're alright, if you can. We're all remembering you in prayers, of course. Perhaps I'll ask Sister Prudence to offer up one of her no-nonsense

Kenyan prayers for you. Something like: "Holy God in Heaven, send us news of Sister Emelda's well-being immediately!"

Best wishes,

Sturbee

25

St Win's
November 7th

Dear Emelda,

Sister Joy hadn't visited the café until this week. She usually only comes for meetings, sweeping in and out in her little car and never at a time that might be useful to give anyone a lift. But finally on Thursday she came to take notes for her report. It wasn't the best timing. For one thing the babysitting sub group had set up a water play trough for Roselily in one corner as well as the usual painting easel and beanbag reading nook. They always clear up, but you can't really have water play without water pistols and puddles.

Then there was the U3A art group, routine Thursday visitors now, which had commandeered half a dozen tables and were life drawing Mr Robins. He was wearing a toga and sitting on the stepladder.

Several of our regular homeworkers were plugged in and typing away, including Alph, who was working with Hermione on the website.

Then there was the business of the fancy dress.

On Monday Nesbitt had shown me a college practical assignment, which was *"create a seasonal menu* and a fitting ambiance in which to serve it".

"I can't do it. I missed a week. Now there isn't time. It's a lot of marks. She'll fail me," she said, in instant despair.

Tilly Matthews of *Beautiful Homes and Lovely Country Gardens* (or it might be the other way round) happened to be buying a Tarte au Pommes, and overheard. "I'd go Hallowe'en," she said, "easy peasy. A few pumpkins, a few cobwebby things. We've got loads of that stuff in the office, we did a big Hallowe'en shoot back in August. We're always months ahead. I'd be glad to get rid of it. There are witches hats and everything."

"But Hallowe'en was a week ago, Tilly," I said.

"Does that matter?" she asked.

"One of the others is doing Easter, so I don't think they're bothered which season we go for," Nesbitt said.

Tilly pulled out her phone. "Zelda? Hi Honey. Can you pop those Hallowe'en boxes in your car and bring them over to St Win's?" She paused, then held the phone away and said, "She wants to know if you need the costumes too," but didn't wait for a reply and said into the phone, "oh yes, bring them along, love, why not?"

By Wednesday the whole café was full of cobwebs and spiders and silhouette witches. It was nothing but cardboard, sugar paper and poster paints, but it was very effective.

Nesbitt and Sister Clem gave a spooky look to the cakes by creating a range with blood red sponge and a set of very memorable iced severed finger biscuits. They made pumpkin soup and ghost-shaped loaves. Everything was ready for Mrs Dunbar and her clipboard.

Into this came Sister Joy, with her little laptop under her arm. It's fair to say that our Hallowe'en themed café was not what she was expecting.

She stood still at first, just inside the door, astonished. She took in the café, the decorations, the customers, the children's play corner, the elderly painters, the laptop workers, the cardboard decorations and all of us in our hats, and she blinked. The knuckles on the hand holding her laptop whitened before our eyes.

"Boniface, could you step outside for a moment?" she asked.

I followed her into the car park. She glared at the walnut tree, before closing her eyes and taking a deep breath.

"What in the name of the Lord is going on here?" she finally said, in a stage whisper. "This is exactly, *exactly* the kind of irreverent nonsense that would cause a sensation, an absolute sensation in the media. Don't you understand? What is it that you cannot grasp about keeping a low profile? I couldn't have made it clearer. I can't imagine what you were thinking! I turn my back for five minutes and what do I find? A novice chatting with her boyfriend, an illegitimate child being entertained, a nearly naked old man! The whole place swathed in disgusting images of ungodly witches and superstitious, commercial rubbish! This is too much!"

At this moment Tilly pulled up in her car. "Hi Sister B!" she called. "Alright if I get a few shots? It's looking fab!" She pulled a large camera out and started taking photos of the outside of the Shoppe and Café.

It was Sister Joy's worse nightmare. She went rigid and hissed at me between gritted teeth, "Get her out of here! We cannot allow her to…"

"Ooh!" said Tilly, "Look at you, all Hallowe'en! What fun!" And she took a photo of me in my pointy hat and another of Sister Joy whose face was a picture of horror without even needing a mask.

"NO! Stop! You can't… you haven't got permission… you can't just… I work directly for the Bishop…" Sister Joy was burbling in dismay.

"Oh, do you?" Tilly smiled, adjusting her camera and lining up a shot through the window with a pumpkin in the foreground, "how's his foot?"

"Sorry?"

"His foot. He's my uncle. I was playing football with him on Sunday. Somebody stomped on it. Fouled him."

Sister Joy blinked, trying to process this.

"It might have been my brother, actually, it was a needle match, Olds versus Youngs," Tilly said, "well, give him my best!" And she marched straight into the café and began taking photographs.

"What did she mean by that?" Sister Joy asked the walnut tree. The tree wasn't saying. "This will all have to be included in my report, and I shall deliver the draft next week. I'd like that added to the agenda."

"We don't have an..." I started to say, but she'd already slammed her car door.

Mrs Dunbar, on the other hand, absolutely loved what we'd done. Tick, tick, tick, tick, tick. Full marks Nesbitt (and team).

Best wishes,

Sister B.

26

St Win's
November 20th

Dear Brave Supporter of the Peruvian Poor,

I enclose with pleasure a portrait of Betty Duck by Pavel, a fine draftsman and sensitive watercolourist – which I am ashamed to say surprised me in a man built on such a giant scale; I should know better than to generalise.

A beautiful dawn sky this morning. Apricot around the horizon and dove grey above, with linear charcoal smears of cloud. Tremendous cacophony of crowing, as usual. The cockerels are still fighting. We hear shrieks and find them squaring up to each other. We'll have to do something.

Noise is louder than usual in the Shoppe at the moment because one of the side window panes was broken in the night. It's plugged with cardboard until Pavel can do the repair.

Nesbitt has been presented with a Peruvian cookbook by Mrs Odge. It was a raffle prize, but the Odge family felt Peruvian food was a bit out of their range. Nesbitt's reaction was a surprise. You know how guarded she normally is. She took it and said, "Oh wow!

For me?" and then suddenly hugged Delphine Odge before running into the back kitchen to begin cooking from it. Delphine was left blinking, but I could see she was pleased. I offered her a free cup of tea.

She was enjoying it when Lady Cottenham stomped in, in her wellies and headscarf. She wears headscarves like the Queen, but she probably swears more than Her Majesty.

"Bloody weather, eh? I want some ground coffee for my daughter-in-law. Fancy Londoners won't drink anything instant. Colombian, she liked that last time. Morning!" she greeted Delphine Odge.

"Oh! Morning."

Just then the birdscarer over the fence went off with a sound like a rifle shot.

"Oh Good God! Whose is that birdscarer? Is it one of your husband's?" she said to Delphine.

"Yes. Must be, I suppose." Mrs Odge shrugged as if there was nothing to be done about it.

"I nearly jumped out of my skin!" roared Lady Cottenham.

BANG! the thing went off again. It's set to fire pairs of blasts. Lady Cottenham's labradoodles, tied up outside, all jumped and started to bark furiously.

"Well, I'm not having that!" said Lady C. "That's plain antisocial! How long has that thing been blasting away for?"

"Several weeks now," I said.

"Well, he's pushing his luck, if you ask me. The cheek of it! I'm going to put an end to this. It's outrageous. Someone will have a heart attack!"

She pulled a mobile phone out of her poacher's pocket and pressed a single button.

"Odge? Is that you? Now listen. Your bloody bird-scarer is far too close to the convent. It sounds like the Battle of the Somme in here. (Short pause) Nonsense! (Short pause) Don't argue, Morris, there's a good man. Get it gone, will you? (Pause) No, not tomorrow! This is serious. Send him over today. Now, if possible! And get him to take it a decent distance away. There is an old people's home here, you know. Health and safety. You don't want to be responsible for the poor dears clocking off any earlier than they need to. I don't want to have to phone again. Is that clear? Right! I'll say goodbye then."

She banged another button on the phone and stuck it back inside her coat. "There we are. Bloody old fool. Saving your presence, Delphine, but he's absolutely in the wrong."

I wondered whether Mrs Odge would feel the need to defend her husband, but she sipped her tea serenely. Apparently not.

So at last we are free of the thunderous bird scarer

all day long. Our prayers and services are no longer interrupted every 23 minutes by an echoing double blast. I'd like to tell you that peace has returned to St Winifreda's, but it hasn't – the cockerels are all still crowing. At least the bird scarer was on an automatic timer and didn't start until dawn. The cockerels start well before. One of them starts solo and then the cockerel chorus all join in.

We are up for prayers, of course, so it doesn't wake us, but they must be able to hear them in the village. We've started leaving earplugs out for the B&B guests and Alph has added "guests are reminded that the convent keeps cockerels" to the website information, but somebody still gave us only three stars, "Cocks crow from 5.30 am. Gorgeous Danish pastries for breakfast, though."

Antonio Ferrara was here yesterday for a lesson. We are ploughing on, but I can't claim a great deal of success with his pronunciation so far. He is touchingly modest, "You know, Sister, I like very much English, but it forgets me very quickly. We must not abandonate our hope, eh? Even old dogs can learn new trips!"

I like teaching him. He applies himself with solemn seriousness to each task, with a little stream of bracing Italian self-talk under his breath. *"Alora, Antonio, conditionelle, avanti!"*

THE POWER OF CAKE

He sometimes takes a coffee on his way out, which is how he ran into Roger Collis. Collis is important enough to send minions for most of his shopping, but he was choosing his own cake for once. When he saw Antonio he stopped dead.

"Antonio?" he said. "It isn't Antonio Ferrara? It can't be!"

"Well..." Antonio said, with a smile and a shrug.

"It is! I can't believe it! What brings you here? I'll have to shake your hand," Collis said. He was delighted and pumped Antonio's hand for ages. "You're doing a brilliant job. Brilliant."

"Thanks," said Antonio, reclaiming his hand and sipping his coffee. He didn't seem to find this unusual.

"It's a pleasure, a real pleasure to meet you," said Collis, "amazing! Made my day!" He was smiling from ear to ear. They chatted for some time.

"I know that Antonio from somewhere too. What does he do?" Nesbitt said later.

"He is a manager, that's all I know," I told her.

"I've seen his face somewhere or other," she said, "I think he might be famous."

At about 4 o'clock Baz came into the Shoppe and said, "Can I have a word, Sister? Outside?"

It was getting dark, and I could already see Ted waiting in the community service bus.

Baz was being very confidential. "I seen that woman poking about in the Shoppe," he said. "I thought you should know, what with the other thing, you know, the prowler."

"Which woman?"

"That one staying in the Pigpens. The small one with the blue Ford."

He was describing Wendy Wooler.

"What did you see, Baz?" I asked him.

"Me and Animal was having a walk round last night, late. It's not a patrol, like, we just keep a look out."

I said, "Baz, I don't think that's a good idea. You might get into trouble."

"We're not doing anything wrong," he said, "anyway, we seen her in the shop. She was looking shifty. And you know you had that broken window? It might have been her, breaking in."

"What was she doing?"

Ted honked the horn of the bus.

"Looking through your little cupboard on the wall," Baz said, "where you got the keys. I reckon she's after your keys. Anyway, I'm just saying what we saw. I'd keep an eye on her and on your keys, if I was you."

I thanked him.

"And another thing," he said, "I seen another woman down there at night. Jiggling about in tights and whatnot to loud music. Trying to dance. Just thought you should know," and he loped off and climbed into the waiting bus.

At convocation Sister Bernard asked me about Antonio, she said, "Antonio Ferrara, did you say? Is he a tall man? Greying? Smartly dressed? Suit and tie?"

I said he was, exactly.

"I think that's the ex-manager of Lazio," she said, jumping a little in her chair, "Isn't he the one seconded to Norwich this season?"

"What kind of company is Lazio?" I asked, "Do they have an office in Norwich?"

To my amazement, the entire sisterhood stared at me and said in unison, "*YOU'VE NEVER HEARD OF LAZIO?*"

"Even I know that's an Italian football club," said Sister Doris, "and I'm American and more of a rugby league follower."

"That's a big team, then, is it?" I hardly dared to ask.

"Big enough to give him demigod status in the football world," Sister Bernard explained. "Imagine that! Antonio Ferrara, in our café! I wish I'd been passing. I wonder what he's doing here?"

"He'll be back," I said, "he's having more English lessons. But he's sworn us to secrecy, so we must not tell people."

"Well, that is something we can easily guarantee," said Sister Prudence. "Now I'm sorry to turn the discussion to more practical issues, but has anyone seen Hermione lately? She isn't coming to convocation or meals. What shall we do?"

"I can explain that," said Sister Doris. "I spoke to her yesterday, and she felt she needed to have a break."

"She said nothing to the rest of us," I said. "This seems very sudden."

"We needn't be concerned," Sister Doris told her, "she made the choice perfectly calmly, but she wanted to go immediately. She's gone to help with the refugees. The Ursulines have a house near a reception centre in Kent. I encouraged it. She needs to do some thinking. She said she'd be in touch soon."

I suppose it isn't entirely unexpected, but we all felt, as Antonio would say, a bit abandonated.

Best wishes,

Sister B.

27

St Win's
November 24th

Dear Teacher of Peru's Poor Children,

It is European Culture week. We are celebrating here in the café by offering a discount to anyone who places their order in a European language – well, that was the plan, but on the first day, about ten minutes after I put up the sign, Jonathan from Intermediax came in and asked very politely whether the discount applied to African languages.

"I could order in French or Spanish, but I would much prefer to do so in Swahili or my local Kenyan language," he said.

This was a perfectly fair point, so I changed the sign and now the discount is for anyone ordering in another language from anywhere. I'm sure the organisers of European Culture week will understand and not want us to be too parochial.

The result has been very entertaining. Of course, the Polish and Lithuanian field workers have taken full advantage, though they prefer ordering in English; they want the practice. We made a board to record all the languages people have used. Apart from Polish and Lithuanian, we've had Latvian and Russian and Mandarin Chinese (that was Mrs Yu, who came for her English lesson on Thursday); French, German, Italian and Spanish – these were all workers from the small business units; a couple in the Pigpen bed and breakfasts turned out to be Swedish, so we added that, and Wendy Wooler, who is staying with us in Pigpen 2, ordered in Latin. Between the visiting sisters (Dinka, Portuguese, Albanian, Malayalam, Hindi) and the pensioners coming for lunch (Welsh, Gallic and Afrikaans), we clocked up more than 20 languages in the cosmopolitan Shoppe in a single week.

Bob Fairbrother rose to the challenge by using a different language every day. He typed the words into his phone and somehow it told him how to say them.

"*En kop kaffee venligst,*" he said yesterday, "and what do you think of *101 Ninja Tricks for Niche Marketing Success?*"

Solemn little Elvis looked worried when he saw the sign. "I only started French in September," he said. "I can say 'please', but I don't know how to say 'cake'. Can I do sign language?"

I said sign language would be great, expecting him just to point to his usual cake, but no, he made a series of movements with his two hands together – proper sign language for the deaf.

"Where did you learn to do that?" I asked.

"Cubs," he said. "I can do semaphore too," and he asked for a chocolate brownie in semaphore – at least I think he did, I last did semaphore four decades ago. After paying he put the discount, as well as his usual 1p change, into the restoration fund collection box, bless his heart.

Antonio Ferrara, who dropped in for his lesson, naturally enjoyed ordering his espresso and orange cake not just in Italian, but in his regional Neapolitan dialect. He happened into the Shoppe at the same moment as Elvis was enjoying his cake. The boy seemed transfixed. He stared at Antonio in wonder. His mouth fell open.

But not everyone enjoyed the language challenge. One boy – he's about 25 – from Hog Fen said there were foreigners everywhere and he didn't see why they should be getting discounts. I said it was just a little community activity and harmless enough and if he knew two words of any language he had learnt at school the discount was his.

"What's wrong with good old English?" he wanted to know.

"Nothing at all, which is why we use it exclusively for 51 weeks of the year," I said.

"I can't ask for my coffee in no foreign language."

"Didn't you learn one at school? French or German?"

"No. Well, I went to lessons, but it didn't stick."

"Not even the numbers? I'd accept the numbers on their own."

"Can't remember."

I gave him the discount and a shortbread biscuit to cheer him up, but the blow had been dealt. He felt inadequate and underqualified for life in the modern world. And he's probably right to feel that way, I'm afraid. But I had contributed to his feelings of exclusion, which I wasn't happy about. I resolved to offer it up and see what ideas came.

Your thoughts on this are welcome. No letter from you still, but it's probably just the remoteness of the terrain. You could email, if the loggers have a connection. It seems unlikely, but we'd love to know you're well.

Happy International Culture Week to you and your hosts.

Matakwa bora (it's Swahili, I asked Jonathan),

Sister B.

28

St Win's
November 30th

Dear Emelda,

This morning there are arrow-straight cloud lines across a dusky pink dawn sky. Another storm is forecast and the fields around are already very wet. The rivers are high and there is flooding in all the river meadows, but, apart from the chapel floor, St Winifreda's is dry, thank the Lord. A working roof is something you never take for granted once you have lived with leaks for a while.

The ever-enlarging chapel puddle is now quite a problem. It laps onto the floor tiles and they are beginning to lift, and the whole chapel smells damp (and *is* damp). It's not healthy for us or the building. I keep thinking back to the old journals Hermione found in which the poor sisters kept dying of pneumonia and pleurisy.

We had not shown the problem to Pavel until this week, because he has been working very long hours on the bell tower, but finally yesterday we invited him in to see it. He was alarmed; so much so that he immediately called in Ollie, the tower engineer.

Ollie wore his hard hat and brought measures and damp meters, but didn't need them to see how serious it was. "I'm pretty sure it's subsidence," he said. "The north corner is falling away. Probably something to do with the clay you're on here. It shrinks in dry weather and expands when it's wet, and after hundreds of years of that, buildings just begin to crumble. Then you've got tree roots on the other side, which won't help. You need to get this looked at and soon. It won't get better; it will just get much worse the longer you leave it. And without a proper survey, it's hard to know how the rest of the building is affected. It might not be safe. I think you should close it off."

So for the second time in a year we can't use the chapel. Last time it was because the tower was about to fall on it. This time it's the puddle. Its door is criss-crossed with yellow tape saying KEEP OUT, which makes us very sad indeed. And although we should have enough money to do the work, we haven't because Mr Wooler has it in a Swiss bank account, or somewhere. (Forgive me, Emelda, I forgot *due process* for a moment there.)

The detectives were back again last week. They have a little routine now. They stop in the café for a coffee and something sustaining like a chocolate croissant or a Chelsea bun. DI Sylvia always has a skinny cappuccino to avoid the extra calories, but generally she does eat a cake. DS Ron seems to be aiming for as many calories as possible. They're always happy to chat. I asked them this time whether there had been any progress and they said the suspect was lying low. A younger fraudster might have been tempted to show off with a bit of spending by now, but it looks as if Wooler is the careful sort. No large sums spent on flashy cars as far as they can tell.

"Do you know where he is?" I asked.

"Well, there's been a tip-off," said DI Ron, "he could be on the Norfolk coast near Cley, birdwatching. He likes a bit of birdwatching, so it might be him. We've got a photograph. Do you think you could recognise him?"

I said I'd know him anywhere after the wasp incident in the Shoppe and peered at a grainy long-shot they produced; a man in an anorak with the hood pulled up.

"It's someone about his size," I said, "but I couldn't say much more than that."

"Yeah, they're not the best shots, but our source didn't want to get too close."

"Perhaps they could try taking a photograph when he has his hood down."

"But it might be him?" Ron urged. "It's rained for the past three weeks, he's never taken his hood down, nor have any of the other birdwatchers."

"It *might* be him," I said.

It wasn't easy. Mr Wooler has no distinguishing features at all, except a heart of stone, which unfortunately doesn't show up in photographs.

"We were wondering," said Ron, "whether any of you Sisters are allowed out, like."

"Yes, of course we are," I said, "we're not in a detention centre!"

"So someone might be able to come to Norfolk and see if they could identify this man?"

Rev Mother had wandered in by this time.

"Hermione's your best bet, she's the one who worked most with him, but I'm afraid she's away," she said. "It'll have to be you, Boniface".

"And it would be OK for her to... to not look like a nun?"

"Of course."

"Only someone looking like a nun would..."

"...attract attention?"

"Yes. Not many birdwatchers wear the black thingy..."

"The habit. No. Obviously."

So that was it arranged. There only remained the slight problem of my disguise. Or rather my civilian clothes.

I don't how it was in your old convent, Emelda,

but here we keep a little store of what Rev Mother calls 'civvies' or 'mufti'. (I looked that lovely word up. According to Burnell's *Hobson-Jobson: A Glossary of Colloquial Anglo-Indian Words and Phrases, and of Kindred Terms, Etymological, Historical, Geographical and Discursive* (1886), which is one of the jewels of our little library, it refers to "the attire of dressing-gown, smoking-cap, and slippers", which was like the Oriental dress of the "Mufti", the Mufti being Islamic scholars.)

I like the sound of dressing-gown, smoking cap and slippers, but our store of clothing certainly doesn't run to such things. It's more along the baggy cord jeans and bobbly sweater lines. I don't consider myself vain, but I must admit my heart sank rather at the charity shop smell of the stand-by wardrobe, especially since I distinctly remember the pair of trousers that fitted me being donated by Mr Frogshall very soon after Mrs Frogshall passed away. Very soon after indeed.

I mentioned this to Eustacia, who said, "What in the world has that got to do with it, Boniface? She didn't die of ugly clothes or something horribly contagious, did she?"

"No," I said, "I believe she was electrocuted on a spa holiday in Marbella."

"Well, I'm very sorry to hear that, but I can't see why it should put you off wearing her clothes. Brace up and get on with it, dear, I should."

So the following rainy Thursday we set off for Cley, and I wore Mrs Frognall's russett cords and chunky green cable knit sweater and Sister Bernard's old gaberdine school coat. I was no fashion plate but at least I was passable and waterproof.

The police officers, to their credit, managed not to register any sort of reaction to my appearance. They must have seen all sorts in the back of their unmarked car, an oddly dressed nun was at least not likely to give them any trouble. Sylvia and Ron chatted away up the front and listened to radio bulletins about all sorts of interesting criminal activity going on with comments like, "Hello! That sounds like one for Marco and his team," or "Blimey, don't tell me Denzel Pagett is out again. I thought he got two years last time."

I asked them why someone who had just run off with a lot of other people's money was hanging around the North Norfolk coast birdwatching instead of running away.

"We were wondering that ourselves," Sylvia said.

"He's got to be waiting for a reason. Maybe he's left something he needs behind. A passport or some other document," Ron suggested.

"I think he might be waiting for his wife," Sylvia was putting lipstick on, looking in a little hand mirror, "I reckon they're in it together."

"He's never rung her," Ron pointed out, "we're monitoring her calls."

"She seems genuinely upset," I said. "She's staying at the convent, did you know that?"

"Yes. Your boss told us," Sylvia said.

"Surely, though, it would be better for Mr Wooler to go ahead, get right away. He must know you're after him by now," I said.

"Not necessarily," Sylvia clicked her little mirror closed, "he probably spent a long time covering his tracks and a lot of frauds go unreported, especially charity and church frauds. Everyone just wants to pretend it never happened because it makes them look so inefficient. We've had cases where millions were taken and nobody wanted to press charges, haven't we, Ron?"

"Yeah. And those are just the ones we've heard of. There must be plenty we never even know about."

I could hardly believe it. "He thinks he's just got away with it then?" I asked. "He steals money from us, and two charities, and he thinks nobody's even going to bother to look for him?"

"They often kid themselves," said Sylvia, "they like to think they're so clever the slow old plods can't possibly catch up with them."

"Yeah," said Ron, pulling the car round a

roundabout. "We enjoy showing them who's slow, don't we, Inspector?"

"We certainly do, Sergeant."

The sky was a uniform grey of the kind that drives Prudence to pray for even the tiniest spot of blue, and the rain lay on the road surface and hissed beneath our tyres all the way up the A road. It was lovely.

Finally Ron turned and said, "Now, here's how we'll do it. We'll go for a nice walk along the headland, and across the dunes. We're told that this man goes to the hide at the end of the path near the café nearly every day. He watches the marshlands. He has a camera and he carries a tripod. We'll stroll along as near to him as we can get without attracting his attention and at some point we'll all stop and pretend to be looking around, admiring the view, so that you can give him a couple of hard looks, without being noticed, and see what you can see. You alright with that?"

"Does it need all of us?" Sylvia said. "I'm not sure it does. I could wait in the café."

"We'd look more like a family group, I reckon, if you came too." Ron said.

"What sort of family group?"

"Brother and sisters, I was thinking."

"Why would a brother and his two sisters go for a walk along the beach in the pouring rain?" Sylvia asked.

"I'm just interested in your back story here, Ron."

"They're nature lovers and they have always been to this same beach every year on this very day for the past twenty-five years because once, when they were all a lot younger, they saw this really fantastic bird. And they all love birds."

"What fantastic bird? Just so I know as I get soaking wet out there. A phoenix? A dodo?"

"I was thinking of a Two Barred Crossbill or a Common Crane, something like that," Ron told her.

A brief silence followed. "I never knew you knew about birds, Ron."

"You never asked. I know about all sorts," Ron said, parking the car in a huge car park which had only three other cars in it. "So do we go with the family outing idea then? All of us together?"

"All right, you win," she said, "as long as we can dry off in the café afterwards. But remember, it's crucial, if this is him, that he doesn't see us, or suspect. We can't arrest him until he's done something that connects him directly with the money. So far he thinks he's outwitted us; that suits us fine."

We weren't the only walkers. Norfolk visitors are a hardy breed. They bundle up and trundle along the shingle bank enjoying nature, despite anything the weather can throw at them. Sometimes they sit in the car with a Thermos, but mostly they're out in the elements, usually in pairs, often with a dog or two. And once you're out in it, you can see why they come. It was exhilarating, and gentle, watery colours were all around in the sky and sea and the few little weather-beaten plants.

"We're coming up to the hide now," Ron shouted over at us. "Sylvia and I will walk ahead to the best spot for getting a good view of him, and then when you catch us up it will look natural to stop for a minute and talk. We'll keep going a little way beyond..."

"Not too far, Ron, my shoes are leaking. This is a bit rugged for me."

"No, not too far, you can see there's a fencepost or something over there. We'll just head there and then turn back and make for the café. And keep smiling, people, we're supposed to be having a lovely time, don't forget."

"Ooh look!" said Sylvia, grinning maniacally and pointing to the sky, "Some sort of bird! How marvellous!"

Ron rolled his eyes.

As planned, we orchestrated a spontaneous-looking gathering and under cover of admiring the view and checking my wellies, I had a good look at the hide. The first time I could see very little, but the second time a man came out carrying a tripod over his shoulder. It certainly looked like Wooler.

At the fencepost Ron said "So? What do you think?"

I said, "It looks like him to me, but I can't be completely sure, he's too far away and the rain's so heavy."

We walked back along the headland, the rain in our faces. The figure we hadn't quite identified stayed just ahead. He was heading for the car park too.

"Sorry Sylvia, if he heads in the café, we'll have to go somewhere else for our tea. We can't risk him recognizing the Sister here," Ron said.

"That's very unlikely," I told him, "I look nothing like I would normally. I don't think he's ever really looked at me anyway. He's always been very offhand with all of us."

"I'd like to ask a few questions in there; it might be worth having a word with some of the other birdwatchers," Sylvia said.

"You wouldn't just be after the cake?"

"Did I mention cake? I was motivated by good investigative practice, not cake," said Sylvia, "if you don't mind, Sergeant."

"It would be much easier to see his face indoors; he'll probably take off his hood," I suggested.

Ron wasn't sure. "He has no idea at the moment that anyone has identified him. If we alarm him, there's every chance he'll cut and run."

The figure ahead of us trudged on. As well as the tripod over his shoulder he had a camera with a long lens around his neck and a long tubular carrying case over his shoulder.

"He's got a lot of gear," Sylvia said. "Any reason to think he might be armed?"

"Nothing in the information we have," replied Ron.

Armed! I pictured a scene in which Wooler pushed a hidden button on his tripod, turned it into a rifle and sprayed the foreshore with bullets before being winched into a passing helicopter. Too many James Bond films in my youth.

In real life he just battled on, leaning into the wind, burdened with his equipment. When he reached his car he put the tripod on the back seat before climbing in, but didn't start the engine. He was parked between our car and the café. We climbed into the police car and watched him from across the car park as he pulled out a flask and took a sip of tea. Rain hurled itself at all the windows.

Sylvia said. "Don't look too obviously, but can you identify him more clearly now?"

"It's Mr Wooler. I'm sure of it from here," I said, "and look, he's eating a biscuit. I bet it's a Garibaldi. And another thing, it's exactly 3 pm. He always drinks tea at

3 pm. He's a very punctual man."

"You'd think he'd lash out on a cup of tea in the café, considering he's got about a million stashed away somewhere. *Allegedly*," Ron remarked, climbing into the driving seat.

"I told you he was careful," Sylvia said. "He's not the sort to flash the cash. I reckon he's waiting for something."

"Can't say," Ron said. "No way of knowing what's running through his mind."

"He's not in any hurry now, anyway," Sylvia said with a sigh. "I'm desperate for a cup of tea."

I must admit I liked the idea myself.

"I'd like another photo, closer up," Sylvia said. "How about I walk past him to the café and take the hidden camera. I'll get us some tea while I'm there. White?" she said to me. "Sugar?"

"Yeah. We're done here, anyway. We've identified Wooler. Nothing else planned for today, is there?"

So Sylvia put her bag over her shoulder and adjusted it so that a tiny hidden camera in the strap would face Wooler as she walked past. With her head down and her hood up, she paused to pull a shoe back on close to Wooler's car, and then struggled on through the downpour towards the café.

A small blue car suddenly pulled into the car park

and stopped close to Mr Wooler's. A slight figure stepped out wearing an old-fashioned plastic raincoat with a transparent bonnet tied under the chin. She walked briskly towards Wooler's car, and climbed in.

"Oh hello, he's got a visitor," Ron said, ducking down and grabbing the camera. I tried to sink out of sight too, but I'd already recognized her.

"It's his wife," I said. "That's Wendy Wooler."

Ron was taking photographs, reaching the camera over the dashboard. I could just see the couple by peering through the headrest of the front seat. There was no greeting. Stiff and irritable, they spoke staring straight ahead, gradually becoming more animated until it was obvious they were shouting. She was back in her car and driving away within two minutes. Her husband carefully capped his Thermos flask and stowed it away before driving off in the other direction.

In the café, over a very welcome cup of tea, Sylvia said, "Did you get some shots? This must be how they communicate. He's doing the waiting while the Mrs does the running around. I think he's had to leave something behind and he's told her to get it."

"What, though?" Ron wondered, setting about his large slice of chocolate cake. "They haven't been near their bank accounts. We checked."

"Passports?" said Sylvia, "Bank papers? Something

they can't leave without, anyway. It might even be the cash."

"That would be quick. Surely he hasn't had time to get it laundered."

"He's well organized," Sylvia said. "He's had time to get to Switzerland or one of the Channel Islands and back. He'd use the Church's banking contacts, insiders usually do. He's probably spent years setting everything up."

"So why's he hanging around? What's he waiting for?"

"And what's Wendy Wooler up to?"

"Oh!" I said, realising, "there's a safe at the convent. He insisted on having a safe in a secure room. He said it was data protection, or something."

"Did he now?" said Silvia, looking pleased.

"We thought it was a bit odd, but he was very insistent," I explained.

"And didn't you say you'd had a prowler since the money went missing?" Ron said.

"It was Wendy Wooler, wasn't it?" I said, "I *thought* it was a woman! And she's been trying to get into the key cupboard too, someone saw her."

"So he's sent wifey to get whatever it is in that safe!" Silvia declared, sucking her teaspoon with an air of cheerful satisfaction.

But Ron frowned, "Then why didn't she just get the stuff and hand it over?" he asked.

"She couldn't open the Retreat Room door," I said.

Both detectives stopped eating and gave me searching looks.

"I didn't trust him. It was the wasp thing that did it." I explained about Wooler and his wasp frenzy.

"You concluded he was a criminal because he's afraid of wasps?" Ron said.

"No," I said, "well, yes, sort of. It was extreme and – it just made me think there was something wrong. I couldn't say what, I just didn't like the look of him. And I didn't like the idea of someone having the only key to a room in the convent. I look after all the keys. It just didn't seem right. Luckily the Retreat Room has a two-key lock. It's a lovely old thing, a collector's item. It looks like an ordinary lock, but it has a hidden second keyhole. You can only open it with two keys. When Mr Wooler went missing, I locked it with the second key."

"Those are good instincts," Sylvia said, raising an eyebrow, "good in a police officer, anyway."

"That must be why Wendy Wooler was prowling around at night and why she broke into the key cupboard," I said. "He must have sent her to stay with us so she could get access to the keys."

"But she didn't manage to get the key even then,"

Sylvia said. She was looking through the photos on Ron's camera. "Why not?"

I just reached into my pocket and showed them the huge keyring. "I like to carry them." I said, "just to be on the safe side."

"That's why they both look so angry," said Sylvia. "Look at those faces!"

"They're blaming each other, I imagine," Ron said. They chuckled. "It's time Mrs Wooler was asked a few questions. I'll send someone over to pick her up when she gets back to the convent."

"Can they be discreet?" I asked. "We don't want the other B&B guests to get the wrong impression. The cockerels are bad enough."

"No problem," said Ron, "discreet's more or less our middle name, isn't it, Inspector?"

Forgive the long letter, it was all rather exciting. A day at the seaside always is, even without the detective work.

The police officers agreed the chocolate cake at the National Trust café wasn't a patch on St Win's. And theirs was *three times* the price!

Cakes for the Constabulary: good title for a cookbook.

Best wishes,

Sister B.

29

St Win's
December 4th

Dear Wanderer,

The crows in these parts are commuters. Every morning loose flocks of them fly over, heading for whichever field offers the best *worms du jour*. There are always a few stragglers – the late risers, and some who call raucously to the others as they fly. Sometimes in the Fens I've seen what appears to be a regional meeting – hundreds or even thousands of birds crowding a single field in a noisy, fidgety parliament. Crows, jackdaws and rooks all together. Very mysterious.

I've become a safe cracker.

As soon as I mentioned the safe to the police officers, it seemed obvious that Mr Wooler had something important hidden there. He was the one who'd insisted on its installation; he'd spent hours in there, locked in, working on his computer. Wendy Wooler had tried very hard to reach it. Obviously, it contained something they needed.

I explained all this at convocation after I came back from Cley.

"So what's in it?" Eustacia asked.

"They're coming back tomorrow to see. They need all sorts of permissions and warrants first," I said.

"Stuff and nonsense," she said. "He's a criminal!"

"An *alleged* criminal," said Sister Bernard. "Who actually owns the safe?"

"Wooler himself, I guess," I said, "he brought it and had it installed. The diocese probably didn't know anything about it."

"I imagine criminal damage is the worst they could charge us with, if something were to happen to it," Sister Bernard said. They all looked at me.

"Can you open it?" asked Eustacia.

I said I didn't know, but I was very happy to try.

"Dare I ask where you learned to do this?" Sister Bernard said. We were working late at night, so that the other sisters could be asleep and not too far implicated.

I told her about my Dad's lock collection. "He used to bet me I couldn't open the difficult ones. That's how I paid for my first roller skates."

I showed her how the two keys worked on the Retreat Cell door. The first one looks ordinary, but the door won't open without the second one, which fits into a hidden keyhole at the bottom. "It's a beautiful mechanism, simple, but ingenious, and..."

"Yes, yes, can we see what's inside now, please?"

I forget that most people don't share my admiration

for locks.

We were surprised, when we let ourselves in, at how untidy everything was. Wooler had always seemed very neat, but the small turret room was scattered with papers and a shredder in the corner was overflowing. We left everything untouched, as evidence. The safe, when Sister Bernard and I examined it, was not very big. It was heavy steel, with an electronic keypad. We tried a few random combinations and it beeped angrily at us. I wish I could tell you that I then drew on my super-sensitive fingertips, my encyclopædic knowledge of locks, and all manner of electronic wizardry to tackle the problem, but I didn't. I used YouTube. Frankly, Emelda, they don't make safes the way they used to. Dozens of cheerful chaps on the internet are quite happy to show how to open a modern safe: a length of flattened wire, a bit of fiddling and beep! the green button lit up and the door opened. And inside there were two passports, a tablet computer and a folded piece of paper with numbers on it. The passports were in Mr and Mrs Wooler's names, but although Mr Wooler's photo looked as much like him as any passport photo ever does, his wife's looked nothing like Wendy Wooler. The photo was of a much younger woman.

"Oh hello, said Ron, when I showed the police officers the next day, "that explains why poor old Wendy was looking so grumpy."

"Looks like he was planning to retire with another woman entirely," Sylvia said.

"Would you believe it!" Eustacia remarked at convocation when I told everyone. "Not only was he married, he had another admirer as well! No accounting for taste."

"There are women who find bird watchers attractive, I believe," Sister Bernard said, "particularly if they have a few hundred thousand pounds to spare."

"We must pray for everyone concerned, Sisters," Prudence reminded us, "we are all miserable sinners, remember."

The police officers cheerfully photographed the contents of the safe before we put them back. They're hoping Mr Wooler will try to reach it again. If they can catch him in the act, the case against him will be much stronger.

"So you've got the card with the special numbers," Sylvia said. "Ring any time, night or day, and we'll have someone round fast to pick him up. I'll have two of those mince pies, while we're here, for the journey."

"Mince pies are OK on a fasting day, obviously," Ron said, winking in my direction.

I was yawning by the time Ben and Steven McFadean, hikers and tower enthusiasts, checked in to stay in the pigpens. They told me they were trying to visit every folly tower in the country and photograph it for their website, International Folly Towers. They also told me they were gay.

"I thought I should mention it," Ben said, "in case the convent had religious scruples about letting us stay."

Delphine Odge was in the Shoppe at the time; she edged closer to hear the reply.

I handed Ben our laminated Bed and Breakfast Policy. It took three meetings of the Diversity working party to get the wording right, but we're proud of it now.

"Yes. It's quite long, isn't it?" he said, holding the document at arm's length, "could you give us a quick summary?"

"All welcome, but be nice to other people and the fixtures and fittings – that's the short version," I said, "it's on the back."

When I came back from showing them their room, I found Delphine studying the policy in her reading glasses.

"Is this Church policy? It seems very different from what I've heard," she said.

"We couldn't find an official policy on Bed and Breakfasts, Delphine," I told her. "We had to come up with our own. It's worked very well so far."

"I'm not sure I even know what half these things

are," she continued, pointing half way down page two. "We had a talk on The New Diversity at the WI, but I don't think some of these were invented then."

"We may not be at the cutting edge of social change here at St Win's," I said, "but we do try to keep up."

"Speaking of the cutting edge, I'll have a slice of carrot cake while you're there. It just makes me feel old. I can remember when it was scandal if you were seen holding the wrong boy's hand at the bus stop, never mind marrying someone of the same sex or re-assigning your gender. It's another world."

"Better or worse?" I asked, wrapping her cakes.

"Mostly better, but a lot more complicated," she said, with a sigh, and then her phone beeped and reminded her she was late for Pilates.

The McFadeans' website is interesting. I had thought folly towers were a particularly British phenomenon, but no, apparently people all over the place have been inspired to build them. Germany has a particularly rich and eccentric collection – there were pictures. There was a very odd one in Poland with stairs you could ride a horse up, in case you felt the need. All of which made our tower seem quite modest and homely, which by normal standards it is not.

The McFadeans love it, even though it is partially dismantled. They've had long talks with the masons.

When they explained that an American benefactor was watching the renovation work via a webcam because he stayed with his wife last year and she fell in love with East Anglia, and especially St Win's, Ben and Steven went out, stood in front of the camera, and made a little speech of thanks. It was a comical sight, the pair of them side by side speaking to the little camera half way up a telegraph pole, but oddly touching. I have no idea whether Ira and Nancy Marciano will ever see it, but perhaps they will.

Now I must go and read aloud to Sister Margery, our visitor from Yorkshire. She is blind, but was once a very fine embroiderer as well as running a boarding school.

"Did I hear someone say that Joy Vernon was working with you, dear?" she asked me. "I used to teach her years ago."

"Yes, she's writing a report on us," I said as neutrally as I could.

"Funny girl, that one," Margery remarked.

"Watch your step. I won't say more."

I am reading to her, at her firm request, from the Shorter Oxford English Dictionary. She likes me to open it at random, pick any word and read the definition. Tonight it was:

"**Dodge** v. 1568. [Of unknown origin, Wedgwood

and Skeat compare an alleged dial. Sc. dodd to jog.]
1. To move to and fro, or backwards and forwards; to shuffle 1704; to use shifts with a person so as to baffle or catch him – 1816. 2. To play fast and loose with; to baffle by shifts; to trifle with; 1573. 3. Trans. To avoid or elude by changes of position, shifts etc. 1680. 5. To follow stealthily, 1727. 6. Trans and intr (dial) To jog 1802. 1. The King had been dodging with Essex eight or ten days DeFoe, Dodging behind the mizzen mast 1756. 2. With Fate's lean tipstaff none can dodge. 3. He dodged me with a long and loose account Tennyson. 5. I will dodge your steps from hence. Dodgy a. evasive, artful. Dodgily adv. Dodginess."

All of which seemed appropriate for Mr and Mrs Wooler. Whatever Fate's lean tipstaff might be, I'm pretty sure they can't dodge it for much longer.

After that we had a bit of *George's Marvellous Medicine,* her other favourite:

"Whenever I see a live slug on a piece of lettuce," Grandma said, "I gobble it up quick before it crawls away. Delicious."

It's fun reading to Margery.

Best wishes,

Sister B.

30

St Win's
13th December

Dear Emelda,

Somebody eccentric in Holland has invented the idea of using nunpegs as Christmas tree decorations. We were wondering why there had been a great surge in orders, and then one of the emailers attached a photograph from a Christmas decoration wholesaler's catalogue. People now order twenty or thirty at a time so they can do the same. The nunpeg-making team are flat out, and even the packing and posting needs three of us most evenings, so we were glad when Hermione came back and could lend a hand.

I was walking back from Salsa in the dark when she caught me up.

"Is that you, Sister B?" she called, making me jump.

"Hermione! Good to see you. Not on your bike?

"I gave it to someone who needed it," she said. "How are things at St Win's?"

I told her about the safe and what we'd found out about the Woolers.

"I heard about that," she said. "Aren't you worried they'll come back?"

"We hope they will," I said, "then the police will have enough evidence."

I asked her how she was.

"I'm well, but a bit sad. I've come back to say goodbye. I won't be able to stay."

We walked on a few more steps, treading carefully. It was icy underfoot and the nearest streetlight is nearly a mile further on.

"We'll miss you, Hermione. But you must make the right choice, of course."

"I was offered a job with the project and I accepted. I've never seen so much desperation, especially among the refugees. It's incredibly hard work, but a privilege to be able to help, it really is."

"Wonderful work," I said, "absolutely."

We walked a little further. An owl shrieked over Odge's barns.

"It means leaving St Win's completely, I suppose?"

"Yes. I won't be going any further with my vows. It was a hard decision, but I think it's the right one."

I had to say something else. "And Hermione, what about Alphonsus Dunn, will he be part of your future, do you think?"

In the dark I saw her shift her rucksack around on her shoulders. "I think he was just a prompt, really. Just a way of making me take a long look at things. We got on well, but that was all it was."

"I see," I said, but walking on, I was struck with a terrible feeling of sadness. I was glad it was dark because my eyes actually filled with tears.

By the time we reached Odge's big five-bar gate I was hurriedly praying for guidance.

"Are you alright, Sister B? I'm sorry if I've disappointed you."

"Oh no, it isn't that, dear. I know you must make the right choice about the convent, it's just, well, it's about Alphonsus. You will be kind to him, won't you? He's had a hard time."

"Of course!" She sounded surprised. "I don't think he'll be particularly upset. It's not as if we... have any sort of understanding between us or anything. We're friendly, we've chatted, but he's never said anything... or done anything to indicate that he is particularly... um interested in... you know, developing a relationship, or anything like that."

"Well, it would be natural for him to be reserved – a novice sister in holy orders, of course he would hesitate. He's not very confident."

"Has he said something to you?"

"No. He wouldn't do that. He's shy. I won't mention it again, dear, it isn't my business."

Hermione stopped walking. "Oh, Boniface! That's

what everybody says! Everyone's so thoughtful and tactful and sensitive! Actually I just wish there was someone who could tell me what to do! Just tell me clearly. What are the rules? How does this work? That's what I want: clear guidance! I need it now. The only straight-talking advice I've had is from my mother who said I was mad to think of the convent anyway, and if Alph was too slow there were plenty more fish in the sea. And please Sister B, don't tell me all I need to do is pray. I've prayed about this until I'm blue in the face."

She laughed bitterly, and strode off. She's tall and young, I was hard-put to keep up. I said, "Wait, Hermione, please! It's just that I know so little about relationships outside..."

She marched on, she was beginning to leave me behind. "It's not true, though, about the fish in the sea!" I called after her.

She paused. I prayed for the right words and blundered on, "I mean, there are plenty more, but from what I've heard there aren't many good ones. Also, the good ones aren't always easy to spot and don't come along at convenient times. I mean you're looking for a mackerel and along comes a flounder or a lobster instead. They blunder in at the wrong moment. That seems to be how it works. And it's a lot easier to ignore them, and go on with the plans you have made, but some chances only come once. Really. They never come again. Your life will probably be fine if you miss that flounder, it might be good, successful and so on, but it won't be the right life. It won't be the life you were meant to have."

I stopped then, being out of breath from hurrying and from the terrible jumble of words that was coming out as well.

Hermione's shoulders were shaking when I caught up. She appeared to be laughing and crying at the same time. She couldn't speak for a moment or two. Then she wiped her eyes and caught her breath and said, beginning to giggle again, "How did flounders get in there?"

"I'm sorry. I haven't had Doris's training. You get the drift, though?"

"I do get it, yes."

We walked on, we'd reached the convent drive by then. Beside the gargoyle with the scales and fangs she stopped again and said, "I feel a lot better, suddenly. Look! Your leggings actually glow in the dark. How's the salsa class?"

I showed her my newly-learnt lateral cross-over with jump. Or rather I tried. It was icy. I fell over a gargoyle and now have a bashed shin.

Flounders? What was I thinking?

Yours, still waiting for the gift of eloquence (and graceful dancing),

Best wishes to you and the loggers,

Sister B.

31

St Win's
18th December

Dear Emelda,

It's nearly 11 pm. I have just checked the Shoppe and I'm in the back room, being circled, as I write, by an enormous bluebottle. The light must have woken him from hibernation. I've dimmed it now. He has the deep buzz and body shape of a B52, which is very distracting. He hurls himself periodically at the window pane with a loud *thunk*, but if I let him out, he'd freeze. I've tried explaining, but it's difficult to reason with bluebottles.

It will be very mild for Christmas this year. Windy and wet, but well above freezing. The red rose near the parlour entrance still has a single flower. We've been busy. A week to go, but people have begun buying Christmas-dinner-style vegetables this week – sprouts above all. Quite a number have also taken a few nunpegs or pipecleaner priests as stocking fillers.

The ladies of Hog Fen are hard-pressed at this time of year. "Ooh!" one said to another, looking at the cakes yesterday, "those mince pies have a lovely home-made look. Could I pretend I'd made them myself, do you think? Only Pete's invited half the rugby club, his whole family and all the teachers at his school for drinks tonight and I've only just finished work. His mother would have a seizure if she thought I'd shop-bought a mince pie, but I reckon I could get one of these past her."

"Tell me about it," said her friend, "my brother-in-law's staying – the one who has to have three types of toilet paper – and my niece is allergic to all nuts, kiwi fruit, feather pillows, mothballs and – oh, what was it... something else I can't remember..."

"Every Christmas the same. She runs straight to the kitchen to see how she can catch me out. Last year it was packet bread sauce. Said it stuck to her tongue and ruined the whole turkey dinner. After second helpings, of course."

"...I remember; it's *quince*! She's allergic to quince. The tiniest whiff of it could kill her."

"Isn't quince quite easy to avoid?"

"God no, it sneaks in all over the place. I've spent the last week peering at labels in the supermarket. My worst nightmare, that is. Poor little Pippa blowing up like a balloon over something I've cooked. I'd never forgive myself."

"I usually just do shepherd's pie for allergic people. You can't go far wrong with a shepherd's pie. As long as you leave out the quince..."

"...and the mothballs! I love Christmas, though, don't you?"

"Oh yeah, can't beat it."

We put up our tree today. We keep it planted in a tub in the garden – this is apparently the most environmentally-friendly thing to do – even if it does mean someone (me, since you ask) has to dig tree and tub out of very cold wet earth in the dark, and lug it solo, soaking wet and shedding rainwater and pine sap (the stickiest substance known to nature) all the way in from the garden. Is it possible to carry a tree in a pot without your face being buried in it? If it is, please let me know how. Do I have it on my hands, veil, shoes, cuffs and chin? Yes I do. Does it scrub off? Not as far as I can tell. Nice smell, though.

I did it alone because Pavel's away for the holiday and nearly all the sisters were getting ready to go to the lovely candle-lit carol service at St Peter's. The Bridgettines very kindly sent their full-sized bus to collect everyone. The carol service is a great favourite and I was sorry to miss it this year, but there was paperwork to be done in the Shoppe, as well as the Christmas tree, and besides I'm slightly on guard duty.

A mystery package was delivered yesterday by a very nice Lithuanian driver. I nearly turned him away because we have certainly not ordered anything, but he said he would not be allowed to finish for the day until he'd dropped it and he'd already made 146 deliveries and needed to get back to Diss before his children went to bed, poor man. It was definitely addressed to the convent, so in the end I signed. It is a narrow cardboard case about the size of a tabletop and perhaps six inches deep. It's heavy. I helped him put it in the cold store. Writing on the side says *Wesołych Świąt*, but we have nobody by that name here.

The details have come through about my talk to the Sisters Worldwide Conference. It's not until early January, but I already go hot and cold just thinking about it. I picture a little room filled with earnest letter writers eagerly sitting there, notebooks at the ready, and me at the front with absolutely nothing to say. They look up smiling and eager, their pens atremble; I look back silent and panicked, and all my notes turn blank before me on the podium.

I've started having dreams. You know the sort of thing: I am in a huge building with endless empty corridors, running late for my talk. I ask receptionists the way to seminar room 21 and they give me very detailed instructions: up the escalator, three doors down on the left, then through the double doors and it's the last big door before you get to the lifts. I run there, but forget the directions and have to ask another receptionist who looks just like my old school friend Sylvia McCall, but seems also to be a penguin, which strikes me as odd even in the dream, then when I finally reach the seminar, all the delegates have turned into Lithuanian fieldworkers and only want me to give them cake, not to hear my speech, but I haven't brought any cake with me...

The solution might be to focus on the quantity rather than quality aspect and talk about how to scribble in spare moments, perhaps. I could mention my letter-writing locations, for example here beside the till; sitting on the stool in the storeroom; in the waiting areas at Outpatients.

Even as I write this, I can picture the disappointment in their faces...

Well, Emelda, there really is nothing like a little emergency to interrupt a bout of morbid introspection!

I looked up from the first part of this letter disturbed by a loud outburst of crowing and alarmed quacks. It must be a fox raid. When I hurried to the window I saw not a fox, but a human figure dart from the garden across the drive. The whole convent was dark except for the lamp in the front porch, which silhouetted him as he peered round before creeping along the building to the back stairs entrance. He paused at the door, then slid inside. From the Shoppe I could plainly see wavering torchlight move up the stairwell.

What to do? I needed to phone the police, but I also wanted to see what he was doing. I crept out of the Shoppe, thinking I might reach the phone in the front parlour – we still have no mobile – but the torch beam headed up the turret stairs in the opposite direction, so I followed. The figure moved along the passageway and stopped at the Retreat Cell door, then produced a key and unlocked it. He shone the torch at the lock in order to do this, and as he did so I could clearly see his face. It was Mr Wooler.

I said, "Oh Mr Wooler, it's you!"

He jumped and turned in the doorway.

"I didn't realize there was anyone here," he said, gathering himself. "I was just doing a security check. Perfectly routine."

"At midnight?"

"It won't take me long."

He and I looked at one another for a couple of seconds. We both knew this wasn't reasonable.

"If you could just allow me to get on..." said Wooler, turning back to the door.

"No, I don't think so." I said.

"You are preventing me from pursuing my proper business."

"I can't imagine what business would bring you here

in the middle of the night."

"There are documents I need. I intend to take them. It needn't concern you."

"We heard the Bishop had dismissed you, Mr Wooler. The police are involved."

"Nonsense," he said. "You were misinformed. Now step aside. I will not leave without my documents. They are important. I know you are alone here." He leaned towards me with a menacing expression, "I should warn you that I am prepared to use force."

Looking back, I have no idea why I didn't believe this. I just didn't. Wooler is not a large man, but he's wiry. He could certainly deal with me pretty well in a fight, but now, whether through divine intervention or a few weeks of Salsa fitness, I was surprised to find I didn't fear him at all. I can only think this must have shown in my eyes because, although I did nothing, he faltered and began to bluster.

"This is most inconvenient. I must insist..."

Then suddenly, with an awkward twist, he threw open the Retreat Cell door, jumped inside and slammed it closed behind him. All I had to do was use the second key to lock him in.

The Retreat Cell has no windows. He had nowhere to go.

I listened at the door and heard him unlocking the

safe. I heard its opening beep. There followed a brief pause and then a lot of swearing followed by a series of loud commands and some very dreadful threats, but the Retreat Cell door is particularly thick, so I just went downstairs and rang Detective Inspector Sylvia.

There was music in the background when she answered. Party noise.

"Hang on!" she yelled, and then a little later, "Right. What can I do for you?"

I explained about Mr Wooler and she said, "YES! Stay put. I'll get someone there fast. Just stay put, OK?"

It was lucky I didn't. I ran back upstairs to see what was happening in the Retreat Cell. It was very quiet, but putting my ear to the door I could hear something – shuffling noises – paper being moved.

At that moment I saw a flicker outside. The light over the side door of the chapel lit Hermione, well-wrapped against the cold, coming out. Her breath was clouding about her. I threw open the window and called down, "Help! Hermione! Up here, quickly." She dropped her bucket and ran, arriving, breathless, just as the first whisp of smoke appeared under the Retreat Cell door.

"It's Wooler," I told her, "I've locked him…"

"Fire!" she said, quite softly. She turned to me. "What's happening?"

"I've called the police. I locked him in."

"What's he doing?"

"He seems to have set fire to some papers."

"What papers? What's he doing here? He can't be allowed to set fire to St Win's," Hermione said. "He can't, Boniface, we mustn't let him. This place is too precious. He'll set fire to himself too! He must have lost it completely. Call the fire brigade, I'll get the extinguishers from the library."

I ran downstairs, called 999 and rushed back. By this time thick grey smoke was curling up from under the door. We could hear Wooler beginning to cough inside. Hermione handed me one of the extinguishers.

"Let me out!" Wooler shouted from inside. He began thumping on the door. The smoke was now thickening rapidly. "You've got to let me out. I'll die in here. Help!"

"Look," said Hermione, "we'll have to open it. He's going to suffocate. He can't get far. Let's just get the fire out. Pull the pin out and point the hose at the floor."

So I unlocked the door and threw it open. Brandishing a fire extinguisher each, Hermione and I reached in and started to spray. He had lit a pile of papers in a wastepaper bin, and he'd filled it well. The flames were already reaching the ceiling. A dense column of smoke rolled out towards us.

I don't know whether you've ever used a fire extinguisher, Emelda, but it's a powerful thing. Once you start one, it's difficult to stop. It just empties its whole contents wherever you direct the funnel. It made a tremendous noise, but the flames were out in seconds.

Wooler was nowhere to be seen as this happened. We couldn't have done anything about him anyway, but as the whoosh of the extinguishers died down, he darted out and ran towards us. The sensible thing would have been to let him go. We had called the police; they were on their way. But I can tell you that after finding an intruder and putting out a fire, the adrenaline is not very inclined to settle for such good sense. So, as he tried to slip between us and out of the door, both Hermione and I took action. She grabbed his arm and I hit him as hard as I could with my fire extinguisher. He went down like a shot buffalo face first in the foam.

Hermione gasped and fell to her knees on his back pinioning one of his arms beneath her. For a dreadful moment he lay there inert.

"Have I killed him?" I asked her. "Oh God forgive me!"

"He's OK," she said. "Yes, he's breathing..."

Wooler started to groan and struggle. We needed to restrain him somehow. So that's what we did. We found a roll of parcel tape in the Retreat Cell desk and wound about twenty yards of it around his wrists and ankles, lifted him onto the chair and taped him to that for good measure. He shouted and threatened the whole time, so Hermione rather matter-of-factly taped over his mouth too. He kept shouting, but at least it was muffled.

Constable Carl and another police officer arrived first, lights flashing up the drive. They saw the open door and ran up the stairs in their stab-proof jackets. They were gasping by the time they reached us on the landing. Carl was aghast at the sight of the trussed-up Wooler.

"It's not strictly speaking...I mean we don't recommend tying people up," he said. "It wouldn't be the safe option. What's happened to your face, Sister?"

Hermione looked at me too, and said, "Oh dear, does it hurt?"

I touched my eye, which, now I came to think of it, did feel odd.

"Has this gentleman assaulted you?" Carl asked in alarm.

"I think I overshot and hit myself with the fire extinguisher after I hit Mr Wooler," I told him.

"You know this man?"

"Yes, he's the Diocesan Accountant. He's wanted for fraud. He's stolen money from us and he came back in the middle of the night to..."

By now Wooler's wordless shouting had reached a bellow. Constable Carl leaned down and pulled the parcel tape off his mouth.

"She hit me!" he spluttered. "It's assault, I tell you. She hit me. It was totally unprovoked! I deny it all. I deny everything! I am a man of the Church!"

"You started a fire," Hermione pointed out. "We had to stop you somehow."

"You shouldn't have hit me. Not with an iron bar."

"Actually it was a fire extinguisher," I told him.

"You could've killed me," said Wooler. "Had my eye out. I could be in a coma."

"Yes. Keep calm now, Sir, I'm qualified in first aid and you're definitely not in a coma, are you?" said the Constable, reasonably.

"No thanks to them," said Wooler. "I am completely innocent. I want to press charges. You'll be hearing from my solicitor!"

"You're the one who broke in and set fire to the place," Hermione said. "We should be pressing charges, I think. Not you." Her glasses were steaming up with rage.

"You're only supposed to use reasonable force," said Wooler, "a fire extinguisher isn't reasonable force. I've got whiplash. It might be a broken neck."

We tried to explain what had happened, but Wooler kept up such a stream of loud complaint that it was impossible. By this time a fire engine was in the yard with its lights flashing and half a dozen fire officers were unreeling long hosepipes as their colleagues thundered up the stairs and along the passage towards us.

"I'm going to have to take you to the station, I'm afraid," said Constable Carl. "There's no choice."

"Quite right," Hermione and I agreed.

"All of you. I mean."

"What?"

"It was only that one hit me," said Wooler, pointing at me. "She's my, what's the word..."

"Attacker?" I said. "Assailant?"

"Yeah. She's my assailant. The other one tied me up, but she didn't go as far as to hit me with a fire extinguisher. Uncalled for, that was. Outrageous. Disgusting behaviour. Attempted murder, I'd call it..."

"Now that'll do, Sir," said Constable Carl. "Any more of that and I might forget myself and put the tape back on."

So Mr Wooler and I both had to go to the police station for statements to be taken.

It was my first experience in police custody. I wasn't put in a cell. I just had to wait in a side room without any windows, smelling very strongly of air freshener. Somebody had carved *Sean is a w* on the desk, a wobbly carved line trailing off after the w. It was easy to guess what was planned, but I passed a few pleasant minutes imagining alternatives: *Sean is a w---ell-brought up young man*; *Sean is a w---indow cleaner*; *Sean is a w---onderful tap dancer*, and so on. It seemed a long wait. Shouts and the occasional door being slammed suggested it was a busy night at the station. I wondered whether I would spend the night in a cell. Others nearby clearly would. My eye was beginning to ache. Eventually a tired-looking woman police officer came in.

"Do you wish to have a solicitor present?" she asked.

"Do you think I should?"

"Well, it's your right."

"I imagine it would cost money," I said.

"If you can't afford it, you might be entitled to legal aid. There'll be a duty solicitor."

"I'll manage without, unless you think it's really important," I said. "We usually rely on prayer."

"Prayer would certainly be a lot quicker than waiting for a duty solicitor," she said. "And will you be wanting treatment for that eye?"

I said, no, it was just a knock, but she picked up a phone and said, "Alan, you're a first aider. Pop in here to Interview Room 3. I've got a nun with a black eye, might need something for the swelling. No, a real nun. OK, Sister, let's make a start while we're waiting, just tell me what brought you here."

I told her the whole story, she wrote it down and I signed. At the end she said, "We won't make any charges at the moment, but the matter has been recorded. I should warn you that there may be action at a later date."

And that was that. They'd be in touch. They gave me an ice pack and I was free to go.

At the end she said, "Well, Sister, this was a first for me. I haven't interviewed a real nun before, especially not one with a very fine black eye. One for the memoirs! Now how are you going to get home at this time of night?"

"I don't know." I said, "I hadn't thought."

"Can I call you a taxi?"

"Oh no thank you," I said, "I haven't any money."

"Can somebody give you a lift? "

She was walking me towards the front door as she asked. I was hugely relieved to spot a friendly face in Reception. It was Alphonsus Dunn.

"There you are, Sister!" he said. "I thought you were facing a night in the slammer!"

"Alphonsus," I said, "how wonderful to see you. But why are you here?"

"Hermione said you might need a lift. That's quite a shiner you have there."

He led me out to his little sports car and I folded

myself in. He pulled away from the police station and I have rarely had such a feeling of liberation. "Free at last!" I said. "Thank you so much, Alphonsus! It would have been a terrible bus journey. I'm so grateful."

We drove through streets hung with Christmas lights reflected on damp pavements. It seemed very beautiful to someone just released.

"Are you alright, Sister?" Alphonsus asked. "Would you like to stop for something?"

I was absolutely desperate for a cup of tea, and I admitted it.

"There won't be much open at this time of night," Alphonsus said, peering around.

We pressed on until we were well outside the city, but as we approached a big roundabout he spotted a well-lit van in a lay-by.

"I think this might be all there is."

"Would they have a cup of tea, do you think?

"I expect so," said Alphonsus.

Mehmet and Androi, the boys who run the Star of Istanbul Kebab Van, welcomed us to their plastic chairs like old friends. They came out of the van to bring me a cup of tea and they generally treated us with such generous Turkish hospitality that we might easily have been in the finest café in their city instead of a rather muddy lay-by.

"You will eat, yes?" Mehmet said, waving towards the great rotating column of meat in the van. "Is very good food here."

I said, "I'll just have the tea, thank you."

"Wait," said Mehmet, "I bring you to taste. Is delicious! You try!"

"I couldn't," I said.

"You will pay for your mother, yes?" Mehmet said to Alphonsus.

"Of course, if she'll allow me."

"See? Your boy will pay! You will sit down and I will bring your food. Our kebab is good. Like Turkish, all people like it."

It was impossible to say no. Perhaps you've eaten a kebab, Emelda, I know you have tried many exotic foods. I found mine quite delicious. Mehmet carved it with a flourish from his rotating spit. Salad and flat bread came with it. Biblical food, really.

Alphonsus ate one too. The tea, the food, the peculiar setting; the jolly welcome at the kebab van; my release, the capture of Wooler; it was a special moment. We talked about the night's adventures and, greatly daring, I said, "Do you mind if I mention Hermione to you?"

"Of course not." He was adding chilli sauce to his kebab from a big plastic bottle.

"She seems very unhappy. I'm sorry to be so blunt,

but I thought you should know."

The boy looked serious and stopped eating. I didn't want his food to get cold. He was clearly hungry. "Eat up," I said. "The thing is, Alphonsus, we love Hermione and we all want her to be happy..."

"I love her too."

He said it quietly, looking down at the kebab he was holding with both hands.

It was my turn to stop eating.

"Have you told her?"

"No. Of course not. Sorry, that was completely inappropriate, I shouldn't have told you, either."

"She's leaving us. Did you know?"

"Is she? No, I didn't know." He set his kebab back on its paper plate. "Is she going to another convent?"

"No, she's going to work for a charity. She won't be in holy orders."

"Oh," he said, "she'll be...a civilian, an ordinary person?"

"Yes."

"Oh," he said. "Oh. I see." He frowned into the big white mug he was holding.

I took a sip of my tea, wondering what to say next. I'd just been arrested for hitting a man with a fire extinguisher – it seemed to be a night for taking chances, so I said, "You really should talk to her. She's very fond of you, Alphonsus."

A taxi drove by. The driver raised a small professional salute to the boys in the kebab van as he passed.

"I'm not much of a catch," he said, "no job and a criminal record."

"I thought you were working in a café."

"Yes, but..."

"Working in a café is a job. I should know that!"

"Of course it is," he said, laughing, then added, "it's just that I haven't got much money or anything."

"Well, I'm only guessing, Alphonsus, but I imagine someone who was willing to take a vow of poverty won't be bothered by that."

"And the criminal record..."

"Just explain it to her. Come and see her, talk to her. She's helping in the café for a few days."

"I can do that?"

"She's really just lodging with us now. Of course you can."

He picked up his kebab and took another bite.

"And don't wait too long, will you? She's been very unhappy."

"I won't," he said. He picked up his tea and held it up. "Cheers, Sister B."

I toasted him back, and in the kebab van the two boys joined in, "Cheers!"

So black eye apart, I arrived back in very good form. I am a free citizen – even if there may be charges to follow – Wooler is caught with all the evidence against him, and who knows, two young people we care about may possibly be on the right course.

It's been a long night, and it was a long day before that, but I'm writing this now because I can't sleep. It must be the excitement. Or possibly the kebab. I'm not used to either.

Prayers for your safety and happiness, wherever you are.

Best wishes,

Sister B.

32

St Win's
December 22nd

Dear Emelda,

This meditative moment comes at the end of a whirlwind of a day – St Win's has just hosted the Pensioners' Christmas Party. We agreed to do it some weeks ago, and over the last few days people have been queuing up to bring contributions into the Shoppe. Odge provided the turkeys and most of the vegetables, Intermediax delivered beer, sherry and wine, Mr Hedgby let us have a discount on Christmas puddings, and Mrs Dunbar from the college lent us all the extra china and tableware we needed from their training kitchens. All this was organized by Nesbitt, who is using it as one of her assessed projects.

Under her supervision we closed the café, decorated it with festoons of lights and tinsel, put all the tables together and laid them with crackers and candles and holly. The luncheon club regulars began arriving at 11.45 am. We had been warned to expect them early.

Father Humbert has lent Sister Bernard an electric piano, so she played carols in the background to set the scene. Nearly all the retired sisters came down to join in.

Some are quite disabled, others are just used to a very quiet life, but most took a little sherry and by the time everyone was at the table, all shyness had disappeared.

There were nearly as many helpers as guests. Nesbitt, Hermione and all the usual café team were in charge of serving food, and we were glad when Alphonsus volunteered in case any of the gentlemen needed help from another gentleman. Health and safety guidelines recommend it. He turns out to be a qualified first-aider.

I was so busy helping out that I missed the interrogation party surrounding Alphonsus until they were well into their questioning. I don't know whose idea it was to check his intentions were honourable, but to judge from the subtlety with which they approached the task, I suspect it was Sister Eustacia's.

"Have you had a lot of girlfriends?" she was asking him as I passed with a jug of gravy.

"Um... well, that depends..."

I would have intervened to rescue him, but Sister Prudence had finished welcoming everyone and come over to join in the questioning by then. Besides, elderly diners don't take kindly to gravy delays.

"What about your religious convictions, dear?" I heard her say.

By the time I was handing out cups of tea they were on to his GCSE grades. It seemed to be going surprisingly well.

"Now, about the criminal conviction..." Eustacia was asking, next time I passed, "we know the basics, but is there anything you need to add? Any other wrong-doing or dishonesty? We've only had one novice since 1998. We need to be sure we're not putting her in the way of a psychopath, or anything."

"No, I'm really not a psychopath." Alphonsus said, trying not to laugh.

"He'd hardly say if he were," Eustacia said in a loud aside, "but he seems a nice enough young man to me." She turned back to Alphonsus and said, "On you go. Go and talk to Hermione. Look, you can carry that pile of plates for her if you're quick."

With Sister Prudence leading, the convent choir gave a short concert, which was going beautifully until Mr Dawlish choked on a mince pie. He clutched his throat and started to go purple, and I was thinking, *Oh dear! Ambulance?* when Alphonsus moved smartly behind his chair and performed a very professional Heimlich manoeuvre, dislodging the pastry and saving both Mr Dawlish and the cheery atmosphere.

It didn't worry the other diners. "Ooh!" I heard one lady say to her friend, "nice young man like that, he can perform the whatsit manoeuvre on me any time!"

After the singing there was a little tea dance,

prompted by Dottie and George Chapman taking to the floor for a stately foxtrot. Lots of the others followed, until almost everyone was dancing.

Alphonsus, carrying teacups and watching, was given such an enormous nudge by Sister Eustacia that he almost dropped the lot, but he took the hint and sidestepped a dozen elderly couples to reach Hermione on the far side. I could hardly watch, in case she refused, but when I looked again they were both giggling and – not knowing how to waltz at all – managing some sort of dancing, and making it look fun.

Nesbitt had to ask each guest to give the party a star rating on the way out. Everyone gave it five stars, even Mr Dawlish. They hummed and waltzed their way through the rain to the waiting cars and even the guests who had fallen asleep in their wheelchairs had smiles on their faces.

The washing up was a marathon, but Sister Bernard kept playing, and there were a lot of us to help. I think we've started a new tradition.

Rain is thundering on the roof now. The chickens are brought to despair by days of it. They huddle, bedraggled in the doorway of the henhouse gloomily staring out, ruffling their feathers and shivering. The ducks, on the other hand, are delighted. They relish a downpour. Their pond fills to the brim and they love the fresh water, bathing and preening and cheerfully eating any slug careless enough to slide their way. We have extraordinary slugs here, Emelda, giant black, glossy things. They are almost large enough to feature in one of little Elvis's books. I haven't seen him with World's Mightiest Molluscs yet, but it's only a matter of time. (Is a slug a mollusc? I'll need to ask him, now that I think about it.)

We sisters fall somewhere between the chickens and the ducks in our mood at the moment. We are worried about you and concerned about the convent's future, but duck-like we are also buoyed up by our faith.

I probably needed to put that in a more poetic way, but you get the idea.

Best wishes,

Sister B.

33

St Win's
December 25th

Dear Brave Amazonian,

You'd love Christmas at St Win's. We considered braving the icy pond and the sub-zero temperatures in the big chapel and holding our Christmas Day service there despite the yellow and black tape and Keep Out signs. The elderly sisters themselves would certainly have been game, but the rest of us, their carers, dreaded the risk to their health, so we resigned ourselves to using the little retirement home chapel instead. Sister Bernard was in charge of decorating, and she worked a miracle, moving candlebra and lanterns from the big chapel as well as our treasured embroidered altar cloth. The plain little room was transformed by candlelight. She brought over the piano, so we had wonderful music – some of it newly-composed – as well.

Years ago things were far stricter. I don't know about yours, Emelda, but my first few convent Christmases were a series of exuberant extra-long chapel services, and a meal with – possibly, but not every year – a bit of chicken and perhaps a chipolata. I distinctly remember porridge with raisins for pudding one year. A Christmas tree and presents would have been out of the question. Things are a lot more relaxed now, but we still have a 'no extra money' Christmas policy, so we make everything we can, save up, and hope for a few donations when it comes to the food.

One present each – secret Santa – is the rule, and they must not cost money. Many of my sisters are such gifted craftswomen that they make a magnificent little glasses case or scarf out of found materials with no trouble at all. Those of us who are not so talented (I'm not the only one, thank goodness) give work tokens instead. These are an offer to take over another sister's kitchen or gardening duty, so she can have the time off. Free time – we hardly ever have it otherwise.

We still haven't had much very cold weather. Flooded water meadows nearby used to freeze. They were once used for skating. One of the elderly sisters, Sister Agnes, can remember going as a child. People from all round tying on their old-fashioned skating blades – hers were made by the local blacksmith – and sailing across the ice. There were races and games. Old photographs show cheery people in plus fours and tweed hats being presented with enormous cups. Have you skated? I only tried once, on a youth club visit. It was wobbly fun, but I mostly enjoyed watching, and it was noisy, like an indoor swimming pool, but out on a wide fen, under a vast sky – that sort of skating must have been very exciting. I imagined it on my Christmas walk by the river.

My gift was Christmas afternoon off. No washing up, no clearing of the tables after lunch, no moving firewood or wood pellets for the boiler – I didn't even have to feed the chickens. I just had to decide what to do for a couple of free hours. It was easy. The day was cold, but bright and even sunny. I went for a walk.

I strode along the towpath in the cold bright sunshine, watching grebe dive into the river's blue reflection of the sky and felt like the luckiest woman on the planet.

Happy Christmas, Emelda,

Sister B.

34

St Win's
December 27th

Dear Emelda,

We heard yesterday. It's weeks since we had a letter, so we guessed something was amiss. We were praying you were just on one of your adventures, but no, it does look like kidnap. Mother Maria Jesus at the convent in Valdepenas says only that rumours have reached them. We can only imagine how. Perhaps Raulito heard something at one of his stops on the river.

The convent emailed the sheet of instructions you left behind headed *In Case I Go Missing*. We were very touched that St Winifreda's came so high up on this list. "*2. Please inform Sister Boniface at St Winifreda's Convent. Tell her and the other sisters that they are not to worry, but ask them please to remember me in their prayers and to keep writing on the remote chance that either a letter will be allowed to me by my captors, or that, when I am released, I will have the comfort of several letters to look forward to. Please tell them I was following a call when I made my journey, and that I knew the risks, and believed them to be reasonable. Please forgive me if my situation causes any trouble or anxiety.*"

We discussed and prayed over the matter last night,

and have already divided up responsibilities: I will continue to write, whilst others set about researching the possible hostage-takers and contacting anyone who might be able to help. Another team, Sisters Prudence and Mary of Light, will rally the veritable army of prayer among your friends and supporters. Some people may think it unlikely that Sisters in a remote convent in the Fens of East Anglia can contribute very much to your situation, but, Emelda, we know better.

We've also sent word to Rev Mother Elizabeth, who is recovering with relations in Portsmouth. She is an ex-civil servant of some distinction. If you are lucky enough by some chance to read this, you should take heart. With or without crutches, Rev Mother Elizabeth Carpenter is the sort of woman who can do anything she sets her mind – and her prayers – to. The law-breaker, and more to the point perhaps, the government official, brazen enough to ignore her has yet to be born. We are perfectly confident it is only a matter of time before she pulls off whatever internationally-brokered deal is needed to set you free.

Meanwhile, my instruction from the Sister Emelda Release Team (SERT for short) is that I should write to you exactly as before. I have asked for guidance and the answer was to try to forget the danger you face and continue absolutely as normal with St Winifreda's news. I felt at first very daunted by this. How can I witter on about the café and the chapel puddle when you might be facing all sort of horrors? My mind keeps straying to an image of you bound and gagged... but when I admitted this, Rev Mother gave me a stern talking-to over the phone.

"You must summon the courage to overcome any such morbid thoughts, Boniface," she said. "Even if the chances of Emelda receiving a letter are remote in the highest extreme, it is vital that we keep the line of communication open. Stranger things have happened than kidnappers handing over a letter. It may be that something gets through and offers her the tiny glimpse of normality that stands between mere suffering and utter despair. We must all put our own anxieties behind us and keep going for Emelda's sake!"

So that was me told. From now on, although I shall be worrying every minute as I do it, I shall write to you absolutely as I have before. I probably won't be able to describe all the activities going into securing your release – some may be classified information – but I will let you know as much as I can and meanwhile it must be convent correspondence as usual. With the addition of extra parcels, more about which later. So, on to the art exhibition in the café.

It hasn't been too bad a winter so far. A lot of rain,

with floods elsewhere, but the fen here just seems to sop it all up. Any low-lying land does have standing water, but the clever women who founded St Win's chose the only ground for miles around that sits on a tiny incline. It's a Fenland incline, invisible to the naked eye and only discernible on a bicycle when the knees ache more in one direction than the other, but it pays off because, except for that one corner of the chapel, we have never been flooded in three hundred years. On the other hand the tiny elevation seems to act as a wind magnet. We have a force five here on a calm day, and when it blows, it really blows.

No umbrella has ever survived the distance from car to convent door on a windy day. I have a special place where I collect customers' mangled brollies. Last week I had five wrecks to dispose of. There's something sad about mangled umbrellas. Even Sister Immaculate Claire of Siena, who can recycle almost anything, is defeated by them. Until this week we just had to throw them away, but on Wednesday a young woman with very interesting rainbow-coloured hair came in and sat drawing at a table of the café, drinking a cup of tea.

Rain was lashing against the windows. It was that squally wind that drives rain at you from all directions at once. An umbrella is no use and it is madness to try to put one up, but we all try. We hope in vain for a little shelter, I suppose. So in swift succession three customers from the business units across the way struggled in, bedraggled and dripping, for their office kitchen supplies (instant coffee in the big tin, Chocolate Digestives, Gipsy Creams) and in each case they carried the jagged shape of twisted and randomly spiked fabric which was the remains of an umbrella.

"Ah well," said Bella from Intermediax, "I knew it was a mistake to go for the cheap one!"

"This is supposed to be storm proof!" the chap from Welney and Co, Estate Agents, remarked, annoyed.

And Jonathan from Intermediax laughed and looked at the remains of his large umbrella and said "Good heavens! It looks as if I put my umbrella into a giant washing machine. I fear there is no hope for it. But I used to be able to mend any umbrella at one time. It was a little business I ran with my brother. An umbrella was a rare and quite valuable item in Kenya in those days. It was worth the trouble to mend them. As a matter of fact, I am quite an expert! But I don't think many people repair umbrellas these days."

"Could you mend mine, as a special favour?" asked the drawing girl. "Only it was a present from someone and I've had it a long time. I'd love to keep it. I'd pay and everything."

Jonathan smiled at her. A smile from Jonathan,

I should add, is worth four or five from most people. Not only is he tall and gracious, but he has what Sister Prudence tells me is a Kenyan smile; a huge, generous beam. As a fellow Kenyan, Sister Prudence may be a little biased, but she definitely has a point. Jonathan has wonderful manners (all Kenyans do, according to Prudence) and his job is something high-powered.

"I am a little busy," he said, politely, "I am working on a special project..."

"Oh, sorry," said the girl.

"No, no, I only mean that I have not repaired an umbrella for a long time – since I was about nine years old – I may be out of practice."

"Don't worry," said the girl, "only my mum gave it to me and I was fond of it. Silly, really."

"Let me have a look at it," Jonathan said. He put his coffee on her table and took up the broken brolly as a vet might pick up a bird with a broken wing. "There is quite a lot to do, I'm afraid," he said. "Several of the struts are bent out of shape..."

The girl looked at him hopefully, "It would mean a lot to me."

"I will take it and see what can be done," said Jonathan. "Oh, I see you have made a drawing there. May I ask what it is that you are drawing? It is very interesting."

"I was sketching the broken umbrellas. They make really interesting shapes, don't you think?"

"I suppose they do! You have drawn them very skilfully too."

"It's what I do," she said, "I'm an artist. I think I'll make a painting from this one. Then, if my umbrella can't be mended, I'll still have a picture of it."

"I would like to have a picture like that," Jonathan said. "Could you paint my broken umbrella if I try to mend yours?"

"I'll give it a try!" She held out her hand to Jonathan. "My name is Angie Cooper."

"Jonathan Abasi." They shook hands and exchanged umbrellas.

And several things happened as a result. Firstly, Jonathan repaired Angie's umbrella and returned it to perfect working order, which pleased her enormously. Then, Angie brought her painting for Jonathan, and he loved it and hung it in his office. Everybody admired it. Several more people came to see her in the café and asked her to paint something for them, but one or two of them weren't sure what the subject of their painting should be. They didn't all have broken umbrellas. So I suggested – I happened to be passing while one of these discussions was taking place – I suggested that Angie could hang her paintings in the Shoppe. There's space on the walls, especially round the café area. And she said, "Oh! An exhibition!"

This was a bit grander than I had imagined, but why not?

"Can I sell them to customers?" Angie asked.

"Yes," I said, "and we can enjoy looking at them until you do."

"And what commission would you charge? Usually you would, as a gallery owner, charge a percentage on the sale of the paintings."

I hadn't even thought of that.

"Ten percent is quite normal."

"Let's say ten percent, then," I said.

So that is how we come to have Art at St Win's (as I see it's described on the website), seven very beautiful Angie Cooper original studies of broken umbrellas hanging in the café. And of course, as soon as they saw the exhibition my dear sisters produced their own paintings to go alongside them. Many of them are talented artists. Most make delicate watercolour landscapes, but Mother Martha's pieces are huge, startlingly vivid studies of oranges – always oranges. Hermione even brought over a few paintings that had been hidden away in the library. We're a proper gallery.

Angie sets the prices, and the paintings keep selling. Pavel's duck portraits are great favourites.

Last week one of the visitors to the tower bought one at £85 and the week before, a Finnish business visitor to Intermediax parted cheerfully with £125 for Angie's Polka Dot Umbrella 2. And all we have to do to earn our commission is enjoy having the paintings around us. Customers even buy more coffee and cakes as they sit and study the paintings. Art from broken umbrella; recycling of a particularly brilliant kind.

We will be sending parcels – but separately from the letters because hostage-takers prefer it that way. Sister Bernard read that somewhere. Anyway, good things will follow either for you, to cheer you, or for them, to put them in a better mood and make them reconsider their *very poor decision* to take you hostage. We are choosing books suitable for your situation – it won't be easy – we need physical lightness for easy transport, combined with psychological depth. They think you're strange in a bookshop, if you ask how much a book weighs, I got some funny looks in the Oxfam shop the other day, but one or two gems are on their way.

In case they read your letters, I urge your hosts to *hand you back to the convent in Los Santos unhurt so that you can continue with the vital good work you do with the people of that country.*

Emelda, take heart. Our prayers are with you, and the whole international prayer circle is churning out blessings on your behalf. It amounts to a mighty weight of prayer all together, so it's only a matter of time.

Best wishes and bon courage!

Sister B.

PS I am enclosing a KitKat with this letter. After much debate, SERT has decreed this to be the chocolate bar most likely to be delivered to hostages. Don't ask how they know this, *they just do!*

35

St Win's
December 29th

Dear Emelda,

The café now has a dedicated SERT table in the corner near the window and you can usually find two or three people at it, researching on Alphonsus's laptop, or making phone calls. Intermedix have donated a mobile phone. Sometimes there are meetings to discuss the next steps in the campaign. My brief is to keep them supplied with tea, coffee and cake of a particularly inspirational kind (easy – Nesbitt has moved on to chocolate skills recently). Alphonsus and Hermione are there a lot of the time as they are in charge of the social media part of the campaign.

Do you remember the artist who ordered 120 of your little boxes for an installation? His name is Georges Toussaint and he invited us to a private viewing of the work. The invitation itself was rather grand, a big embossed thing on thick creamy card. I pinned it on the noticeboard so that people could see that a famous artist was using the same little boxes as we were selling in the Shoppe. I never thought of going, but the eagle-eyed Sister Doris saw it and said, "Isn't that the same date as the Sisters Worldwide conference? How convenient, it means you can go to both on the same train ticket."

I had been trying not to think about the conference. The idea of speaking to a large number of people makes me want to hide somewhere dark. Finally I gave in and rang the organisers, hoping that detailed information might calm my nerves, or better still that they had decided to cancel the whole thing.

"Ah yes," said a jolly assistant, "we hadn't heard from you about a title for the talk, so we invented one. I hope it's acceptable, only the programme needed to be printed. We went with *'A Little Convent in the Fens: Sister Boniface, winner of the Copia Award, will talk about her letters chronicling daily convent life.'* I hope that suits you."

So definitely not cancelled then.

"How many people are you expecting?" I asked, dry-mouthed, when I had regained the power of speech.

"About 2500," she said, "all being well. Of course, yours is one of several workshops, so only a fraction of that number will sign up – it was 620 last time I looked.... *Hello?*"

"620?" It was about a hundred times as many as I had imagined.

"No, I'm looking at the bookings now, and it's up to 671! They're very keen, started signing up as soon as we put the title online. I expect you're thrilled! And of course we live stream to centres all over the world. At least another 1500 or so online."

"Is it a big hall?" I asked, stupidly.

"Oh yes, the main conference hall. We have every sort of audiovisual equipment. Just email your requirements. Any other queries we can help you with, just let us know. See you on the day!"

It was Sister Doris who heard me groaning aloud whilst cashing up in the Shoppe after this call. I thought I was alone.

"Boniface?" she called, "are you alright?"

"I can't do it," I told her. "I can't speak to 671 people. I can't!"

Sister Doris took matters into her own hands. She locked the Shoppe door and turned the sign round to 'closed'. She made us both a cup of tea. She sat me down at one of the tables.

"Would you like to tell me what all this is about?" she asked, "I might be able to help."

I told her the whole Sisters Worldwide prize and conference story.

"What is it that you fear, exactly?" she asked.

"Having nothing to say to hundreds of people."

"But of course you have things to tell them. Interesting things, too."

" I just scribble the letters down and send them. If I

tell them that they'll all be disappointed. They want to know the secrets of writing. I don't know any. My talk will last half a minute and they will all sit and stare at me. Of course, they will be kind. They're kind people, but they will all be disappointed."

Doris looked down at the table and smoothed a crease out of the tablecloth. "Maybe you should call it off. I'm sure they'd find a substitute speaker," she said.

"Could I?"

"Of course. With one phone call."

I thought for a moment. Sister Doris sipped her tea and continued to smooth the cloth.

"I don't want to let people down," I said.

"They seem pretty well-organised," Doris said, "they'll have a stand-by speaker who can take your place. No problem."

"Really?"

"Last-minute issues often force speakers to pull out; family crises, transport difficulties... cold feet. A lot of people get nervy at the last minute. It happens all the time. They'd just call on their usual stand-by speaker. Those talks are a bit generic, but they're fine if you haven't heard them before..."

"I don't want to call it off," I said. "I don't want to cancel. It's cowardly."

"Cowardly?" said Doris, "I see. So if you feel you

must go ahead, what would make it more enjoyable?"

"Speaking to 600 people is never going to be enjoyable."

"Bearable then. What would make it bearable?"

"Well, maybe if something good came out of it."

"What kind of thing?"

"I don't know!" I said. Doris said nothing. She seemed to study the paintings around the café. "Maybe it would encourage some other sisters to start writing letters," I blurted out, after a long silence.

"Mmm..." Doris said. She put her head on one side and looked at me mildly, "...what sort of letters?"

"They could write something that might help Emelda. They could even write to her."

"Yes, they could," said Doris... "or they could write to other people about her..."

"...like their MPs" I said, "or the Foreign Office, or the Bishop, or the Government of Peru, or Amnesty International!"

"That certainly is a thought."

"Six hundred, that's a lot of letters. People would take notice of that many letters. They could actually make a difference."

"Well, yes," Doris said, "I imagine so."

"I could just talk a little about my letters and St Winifreda's, and then spend the rest of the time telling them about Emelda and the campaign to free her."

"Yes. If you think you can manage it."

"I can manage that," I said. "Of course I can."

"Oh my," said Doris, tapping her watch, "time to start preparing supper. I left some bread rising. I should get back."

We had talked for less than five minutes. It was only some time later that I realized I had just been 'Dorised'. She's a clever woman, Emelda.

Emboldened by this, I booked a train ticket and rang the number on the artist's invitation. I think I expected another assistant to answer, but it was Georges Toutsaint himself. I told him I'd like to come, but could he tell me a little more about the installation.

"It's called *Please*," he said. "I've put nearly 5,000 little boxes – the ones I bought from you and lots of others – in a long spiral on the floor of the cathedral. Each one has a wish or request in it. They came from all sorts of people – charities, individuals, groups. I put out a call for them and people sent me their tiny pieces of folded paper. I don't know what they say, but I know each one is heartfelt, and I know the little boxes are all made by groups raising money for charity. I thought I'd stop at 3,000, but people keep adding to them."

"Could we add one?" I asked him.

"Of course," he said.

So one of the little boxes in the cathedral will soon contain a prayer for your safe release. It's has made us all very optimistic.

And now I'm off to try making a slide show on the computer. Powerpoint. Quite a macho name, isn't it? Hey ho.

KitKat enclosed.

Best wishes,

Sister B.

36

St Win's
January 2nd

Dear Emelda,

The ladies of Three Fens make a lot of New Year's resolutions.

"I'm going to go to the gym three times a week and eat no more than 1500 calories a day, starting tomorrow," I heard one say to her friend in the Shoppe yesterday.

"1500? Is that enough?" her friend replied. "We don't want you fading away. I might give up chocolate for the year, or maybe cured meats."

"Why cured meats?"

"They're bad for you – it's the additives."

"Are they? Does that include sausages?" her friend asked, leaning over the fridge. "Say no, please say no."

"It *does* include sausages and salami and ham and ..."

"Oh no, that's a step too far, I'm afraid. All the men in my family would go and live somewhere else if we couldn't have sausages."

"They'd probably buy them secretly. I worked with a man whose wife was vegetarian and he kept all sorts of meat in his car. The glovebox was full of pork pies. It smelt a bit funny, but you got used to it."

Rev Mother's resolution is to listen to more classical music. I went to her office yesterday for some stamps and found her doing paperwork to the sound of a particularly demanding Stockhausen opera. It sounded like two people impersonating an accelerating car engine. I must have winced because Rev Mother said, "I know, I know, I'm struggling myself, but it's important to keep an open mind."

There were deer across the fields this morning. I was on the way to feed the chickens and ducks when I spotted three of them on Odge's beans. They stood completely still, three elegant shapes, frozen, then turned and bobbed away across the field towards the woodland, their three white rumps visible after their brown coats had merged into the undergrowth. They're lovely things. We see their delicate hoof prints sometimes on our paths. Carmella lives in fear of them discovering her vegetables, but they don't seem to have done so yet. The rabbits are bad enough. Never mention rabbits to Carmella; or moles.

Sometimes I wonder what wildlife you see where you are. If I glance at the internet and ignore the insects, I see that there may be armadillos, sloths, tamarins, whiskery little monkeys, tapirs and huge gentle water mammals like manatees and dugongs. I hope you see dugongs, not many people do. They're very shy, and live in muddy places.

Our customers live in muddy places, but bargains make them a lot less shy. Nesbitt and I have been having a clear-out in the Shoppe. We've discontinued some lines and are selling the left-overs off at a discount, on the advice of Mr Hedgby the whiskery wholesaler. He lent us a round wire basket to put the bargains in, and it certainly does attract a lot of customers. There is nothing very interesting in it: one or two tins of beans, spaghetti hoops and sardines and a few packets of dried things like split peas, yet hardly a single customer can walk past it without rummaging.

"It's human nature," Hedgby said. "Everyone loves a bargain."

"Is it because people are desperate for those few extra pennies?" I said.

"I think it's more like hunting. That's my conclusion after 35 years in the retail business."

"How is it like hunting?" I asked.

"Well," he said, "in the old days it was woolly mammoths and dinosaurs or what-not."

"Sorry?"

"You know, you'd go out from your cave, and there'd be huge things, waiting to eat you before you could find some berries. And sometimes you'd spear them first, or sometimes they'd eat you first. You could never be sure, when you went out, what sort of dangers you'd walk into."

"How does this connect to tins of sardines?" I asked, but he was leaning on the counter by now, warming to the subject.

"It was exciting, you see. You might be eaten at any time, chewed up on your way to the water hole by any old passing tyrannosaurus, or whatever. And if you weren't, you'd be pleased. 'I survived another day. I lived to tell the tale, like. I showed that old tyrannosaurus a thing or two. I bested him, and now I'm home with this here piece of meat for us all to eat."

He'd lost me by now, but I was enjoying the scenario, which seemed to be more Flintstones than philosophy. "So this here bargain bucket, that's the same thing. They pick something out of there, and somewhere deep down they believe they've bested the shop, put one over on the shopkeeper and maybe on the whole world. Come out on top, sort of thing. Beaten the dinosaur."

He came back to reality and adjusted his tie. "That's how I see it anyway. Now, how about a few of these fancy teas? You've got Green Tea with Mint, but do you think Hog Fen is ready for Green Tea with Salted Caramel? They're selling quite well in Waterfen, but they're always a bit more advanced other there. Not like

THE POWER OF CAKE

Barham Bottom! It was 2008 before they'd even take crinkle cut crisps at Barham Bottom, talk about stuck in the mud!"

I was about to say no thanks to the Salted Caramel flavour tea, when Delphine Odge came up from behind Mr Hedgby and said, "Can I have a look?"

Hedgby handed her the box and she read the ingredients. Then she seemed to take a photo with her phone. Her phone bleeped and she said, "I thought so. It's free! On my diet, or rather, it's not a diet, it's a healthy eating programme. It's free. I can drink this and it's no points. I'll certainly have some."

So that's one box sold, anyway.

I asked Nesbitt whether we should put it on the menu in the cafe. "No, you're alright," she said, "I'm holding out for the Green Tea with Steak and Kidney."

I'm almost sure she was joking.

Best wishes,

Sister B.

PS Think of the Christmas song about what the True Love gave: Nothing twice, two dozen, calling birds, James Bond, gold rings, french hens, nil, when I'm (like the Beatles' song), nothing, more french hens.

(There's a short story in there somewhere!)

KitKat enclosed.

37

St Win's
January 6th

Dear Brave Amazonian Wanderer,

I think I mentioned the cockerel situation. All four of the youngsters have started both to crow and to fight now. It's serious. One in particular is very aggressive. He is slightly smaller than the rest and has inherited a flat comb – Odge calls it a scrambled egg comb – on the top of his head. This bird picks a fight at every opportunity. He stalks around the run eyeing his brothers menacingly and flies at them suddenly with his claws aiming for their eyes. Chicken world is a cruel place. We've segregated him now, so he is in prison, which makes him very angry.

I put a sign up in the shop advertising free cockerels, and a customer, Mrs Farringdon from Withy Fen, took one after hers was stolen by a fox. Mrs F is a lifelong chicken keeper and, despite being in her late seventies at the very least, strode into the run and caught the cockerel she wanted without it even being given the chance to run. She just grabbed it instantly, tucked its head under its wing, and sent it to sleep. We were very impressed. Our attempts at cockerel-catching usually result in a twenty-minute chase with at least one headlong dive into the mud.

"You got a lot of old cockerels here, ant you?" she remarked. "Those'll eat you out of house and home, if you in't careful."

"They've already been doing that for some time." I said. "You wouldn't know anyone who could dispatch a couple of them for us?"

I half thought Mrs F. would offer to do it herself, but she said, "I shall send Nick over. He's a nice lad. He'll kill anything you want killed."

Quite a reputation.

So a couple of days later a very large lad in his twenties presented himself in the Shoppe. "I hear you need a couple of birds dispatching," he said. "I don't mind doing it, like. You're on my way home. That was Hazel Farringdon sent me over. Up Withy Fen. I kill most things, deer, foxes, rabbits. They always send for Nick. I do a bit of hunting too, like, but not because I like killing animals, it isn't that. It's just they got to be killed sometimes. When there's too many of 'em or when they cause trouble. Or when they get injured or something. They always call for me, the farmers. It's not that I like killing things. I got a soft spot for most animals. I like rabbits, mostly. If it was up to me I'd leave them alone most of the time, but they overrun a place, and they have to be stopped. I never kill a hare, mind you. Not a hare. I like hares. Some people will go for a hare, but not me. Leave them alone, they don't do no harm."

As he uttered his manifesto, the boy's eyes were ranging over the cakes.

"Would you like a cake, Nick?" I said. "On the house, as a thank you for doing us this favour? We're very grateful. What would you like?"

"Oh no," he said, "I don't want nothing for helping you out."

"Just as a gift?" I said.

"No, no, I don't need nothing in return. I'm happy to do it. I won't take nothing off you. Nice little shop you've got here."

Nesbitt heard this, and came out of the back kitchen.

"Is that you, Blue Nesbitt?" Nick asked her.

"Hello Nick."

"I en't seen you since school! You working here, then?"

"Yeah. Apprentice chef," Nesbitt said.

"Oh that's great. You never made these, did you? They look like beauties."

I leave you to imagine the way he pronounced 'beauties' in his accent. It was lovely. Nesbitt took a cake box off the shelf and began to fill it.

"Really nice, they look. Can't believe you made

them yourself. Proper professional-looking! Did you do cooking at school? I can't remember."

"Hated it at school," said Nesbitt. "Mrs Barton."

"Oh, yeah. Mrs Barton," Nick said. "I remember her. Dragon or what? You still living up here with your mum, then?"

"Yeah. And my little girl."

"Oh yeah. She'd be, what, three now. D'you see her dad?"

Nesbitt folded down the lid on the cake box. "No," she said.

"You here a lot then? Full time is it?"

"Here or the kitchens, when I'm not at college, yeah."

"I might drop over, then," Nick said.

And Emelda, that little conversation had the feel of something important. Even if it did peter out at that point.

"Shall I show you the birds?" I asked.

I led Nick into the chicken run. Walking beside him reminded me of how large he was. He must be six foot four and well-set-up with it. Carmella was there, feeding them.

"Which ones am I killing?" he said, "good-looking boys, en't they? Nice birds."

Carmella was pleased with this. She is proud of her flock.

"We kill this boy here – she pointed to Flat Comb the Fighter and – "what do you think, Boniface – this white one, Pol Pot?"

I agreed. We spared Prince William. Carmella and I left Nick to his work. He was back in the shop in less than ten minutes.

I said, "Is it already done? That was fast!"

"Cockerels don't take long. I left them by the tree."

We thanked him again, and he left, offering to come back any time and leaving his number.

"What a nice boy," I said to Nesbitt. "He obviously wanted a cake, but wouldn't take one."

"I put half a dozen in his car," she said. "I've known Big Nick since school. He's alright."

"Do you still see Roselily's father?" I was nervous about asking this. We were folding tablecloths.

"No. He never knew I was expecting. He went away."

"You were very young," I said. "It must have been difficult."

"Yeah. It wasn't what Mum wanted for me." She paused for a moment, "But it changed, soon as the baby came. We loved her so much, we never thought about anything else after that. It's been hard, with the money, but we always manage. And now I've got the apprenticeship."

This was an unusually long speech for Nesbitt. A

pair of office workers from the business units came into the Shoppe and she recovered quickly and went back to serving food.

I was so relieved at the extreme cockerel problem being solved that I had not thought much beyond the actual dispatching. Now, of course, there were two dead cockerels to be dealt with. We had already had a high-minded discussion at convocation about how to dispose of them. The general feeling was that it was more or less our duty, as proper chicken keepers, to eat them ourselves. In doing so we completed the cycle of chicken-keeping properly. I can't really remember the logic of it, but it seemed to make sense at the time. Nobody got as far as to wonder *who* would draw and pluck the birds, but somehow it seemed to fall to me.

I waited until the bodies were cold, then put on some rubber gloves and collected them from under the tree. I won't go into the details, Emelda, you may have done this many times, but it's fair to say that if people had to kill, draw and pluck a bird every time they ate one, we'd all eat chicken a lot less. When it was done, though, I must say there was a certain sense of achievement. I was covered in gore and feathers and it took me an hour to clear the bench I'd been working on. Nesbitt was not allowing it to happen anywhere near the café and Gertrude excluded me from the convent kitchen, so I was working on a far-removed garden bench. When I handed them over to Sister Gertrude for cooking, I felt I had earned supper in some vaguely primeval way.

Gertrude looked the birds up and down with a raised eyebrow and held them at arm's length. I had hoped for a tiny bit of enthusiasm, but without their feathers they looked surprisingly small, and they were a bit tufty, still. Frankly the pale little bodies were a bit pathetic.

Sister Joy joined us for supper; she's staying overnight in case the presentation on her report runs late. "I thought I'd present it personally," she said. "It's good practice, and it means I can assure the correct focus of attention. In case you need any pointers, so to speak."

"You are very kind," Sister Prudence said with a gracious smile, "but I'm afraid we are distracted at the moment because of our friend in Peru."

"You have a Sister from this order in Peru?" Sister Joy asked.

"No, not from here, from a nearby convent in Suffolk."

"Oh, is that your pen pal, Boniface, what's her name again? Araminta?"

"Emelda," I said.

"Is it that one you won a little prize for writing so many letters to?"

"Yes, that's the one."

"How did you meet her, then?"

"I've never met her, I just..."

"Well, I wish I had time for all that leisure writing. Goodness, it must take you *hours*," Sister Joy remarked. "Are you not having any of the chicken?"

"Cauliflower cheese for me, please."

Yours, vegetarian (at least for a while),

Sister B.

PS And in case you're wondering: yes, we did miss them the next morning.

38

St Win's
January 9th

Dear Emelda,

The most beautiful sunny day here; still and cold, but bright with that stark winter clarity that comes from a low sun. In all the fuss and bother of preparing my talk, I had forgotten the pleasure of the train journey to London. Holiday visitors and cheery families off to pantomimes or bargain-hunting filled the carriage, chatting amiably as the bare branches of the trees slid by, three-dimensional silhouettes against a dazzling alpine sky. Little flocks of deer in the fields near Cambridge raised their heads warily, and a pair of tall white birds, egrets perhaps, landed in a wheat field somewhere near Royston. I never even opened my book.

You left the country before they modernised King's Cross. They added a vast glass dome between the old station building and St Pancras. Its lofty white supports fan out like an elegant umbrella. It was hung with stars for Christmas; a Salvation Army band played carols. I sat in a balcony café to listen and watch station life below. It was better than a box at the theatre.

After that it was on to the cathedral where lovely

George Toussaint helped me, and many others in a long queue, add our prayers in little boxes to his growing sculptural design.

"Are you religious yourself, George?" I asked him.

"Not really," he said, "but I have been changed by doing this. We all have. There are six of us working on this installation and we've spent nearly a month in the cathedral surrounded by people praying because they're sad, or lost or lonely or desperate or because they're happy and grateful for their baby, their new house, their aunty's cure. All of life is here." He laughed. "It's pretty full-on!"

I could have stayed forever, but instead of quiet meditation in a holy place I was due at the conference venue for – if you can believe this – a sound check and microphone fitting. It was a huge converted cinema complex, a thickly carpeted warren of windowless rooms with names like "Calm" and "Harmony". No, seriously.

"You're speaking in 'Peace One'," the reception volunteer told me, pointing it out on the leaflet and handing over a badge and a little canvas bag. "You can relax in 'Serenity' until someone comes for you."

Relax in serenity. If only!

But Sister Doris's hard work paid off. I did the deep breathing, I did the positive self-talk – "Come on

Boniface, you can do this! Best foot forward!" – that sort of thing. As long as I remembered to hand round the sign-up sheet drawn up by the Release Team, I could just get the rest over as quickly as possible and head for the 5.15 train. Or even the 4.15, if I was lucky. The more people signed, the greater the chances of letters being written and pressure being applied in the right places. The rest didn't really matter. A very sweet girl came and took my photo for the report afterwards and promised to include the details.

"We can Tweet that too," she said. "Can we use your photo?"

"Why not?" I said, "if it helps." I'd forgotten about the black eye.

Have you done much public speaking, Emelda? I imagine a crowded lecture hall would not daunt someone who treks solo across rain forests, braving tropical diseases and giant insects in order to comfort the despised and outcast, to say nothing of the dangerous and unpredictable. It would probably be nothing to you, but as I heard myself introduced and stepped forward onto the stage, my knees were wobbling and my carefully written notes seemed suddenly to have translated themselves into Ancient Greek. I could make out the odd letter, but nothing like a whole word. My glasses had disappeared. For a vast expanse of immeasurable time (15 seconds probably) I gazed at the assembly dry-mouthed and panic-stricken, then realised the glasses were in my hand all the time. The relief made me smile. I looked up at the audience and they were smiling back, expectant. I remembered my first line, "I am Boniface, the correspondent for hand-written letters at St Winifreda-in-the-Fen, and this (cue first slide, photo of you, a distant dot on the end of a rope hanging over a 500 foot waterfall) is Sister Emelda Griggs, adventurer, nurse, teacher. Emelda is missing, believed kidnapped. Please, I need your help to find her."

The rest is a blur. I can't remember a word. I showed the slides. There was laughter. There were questions from the floor. The sheets were passed around and came back covered in signatures and offers of help. At the end people crowded round in the hall, then later in the corridor and a side room. More photos, more email addresses given, more ideas, more offers. I missed the 5.15 by five hours and wasn't back much before midnight. There were lights on all over the convent. In the common room I found a dozen sisters in deep discussion.

"Is something wrong?" I asked them.

"It's Joy Vernon's report," Sister Bernard said, "she's recommending immediate closure."

"What? What about the retired sisters?"

"She recommends dispersal to a variety of local authority care homes where they will receive, I quote," she flicked through the document to the right page and read *"a far higher standard of professional personal care and more meaningful opportunities for socialisation."*

"She never even went and talked to any of them. It's all bollocks, if you ask me," Eustacia muttered. "I'm going to bed. How was your talk, by the way?"

So just as we seem to have retrieved enough money from Mr Wooler to keep St Win's going for a bit longer, Sister Joy, management consultant and diocesan PR advisor finds 41 reasons we should close. I know the exact number because I couldn't sleep again, so I read the whole report. It is as indigestible as a bad kebab and, in my opinion, Eustacia's summary is spot on.

Let's comfort ourselves, Emelda, with the thought of George Toussant's swirl of tiny prayer boxes sweeping in a wave around the cathedral. They're quiet in the dark now, and the little prayer for your safety is among them, doing its powerful work.

Best wishes,

Sister B.

PS *Limited edition* KitKat enclosed. I found a fancy one in London.

39

St Win's
January 13th

Dear Emelda,

I'm just back from the easiest trip to Outpatients ever. We drove there, we parked and after the appointments, we drove home. We were warm, we were dry, we even listened to the radio: we have a new minibus! New to us, anyway. It isn't an actual miracle, but it's something close.

It all started to happen after the Copia Award. Sisters Worldwide have a publicity department. Pictures of all the prizewinners were sent to the papers with a little report, me included.

I never guessed – how could I? – the effect a photograph of a nun with a black eye would have on news editors. The next morning I was hauling a sack of carrots into the Shoppe when Sister Bernard ran across the yard and said, "Boniface, I've had three phone calls about you in a row, you'll have to deal with them, I'm supposed to be rehearsing. The numbers are by the phone in the office."

No sooner was I there than the phone rang again. The *Daily Telegraph* wanted to speak to Sister Boniface.

"Speaking." I said.

"Just checking a few details from the press release," the reporter said. "You won the, er, the Copia Award. Is that right?"

"Yes, that's right," I said.

"And we have a photograph of you here... you seem to have, er, well, it looks a bit like a black eye..."

"Yes," I said. "I had an accident."

"Oh dear," said the reporter, "nothing serious, I hope?"

"I hit myself in the face with a fire extinguisher. Accidentally, obviously," I said.

"Oh!" said the reporter. There was a pause as if she was writing something down. "How did you come to...?"

"Well I was trying to stop someone, a burglar, on Christmas Eve, he broke in and..."

"Sorry?" said the reporter, "Can I just ask you to repeat that? Did you say you were trying to stop a *burglar*? With a *fire extinguisher*?"

And that was all it took, really. I think they call it going viral.

They put the story on their website and ran it in the national papers the next day, and people tweeted it. Social media is a mystery to me, Emelda, but perhaps you understand it, and then the local papers started to ring and send reporters too. Round here it's the local papers that really count. For several days I did little else but tell and re-tell the story of the burglary and pose for more photographs. I mentioned your long-term visit to the loggers every time. If you've ever done it, Emelda, you'll know how embarrassing and absolutely exhausting this sort of thing is. You hear your own voice telling the same story over and over and with each repetition it sounds sillier. How anyone stands it for any length of time I can't imagine – my respect for people in the public eye has grown enormously – but all the sisters agreed that it was very good for the campaign, so there I was, posing away in paper after paper, hoping someone might read it who could somehow help get you released.

It was only right at the end, in the interview with the Three Fens edition of the *Littleport Post*, that they printed the whole story accurately. They gave it a double-page spread with photos of the convent, the falling-down tower, the chapel with yellow tape and Keep Out over the door, and a charming shot of Carmella, Cambridge United scarf knotted under her chin, pushing a wheelbarrow full of compost up the long walk. (She'd be furious, I haven't shown her.)

People have been rushing into the Shoppe ever since to ask more about your kidnap, the campaign to free you and the intruder. Their generosity has been amazing.

"I see you in the paper," Wol remarked. "You done a brave thing there, a very brave thing. And that Sister in – where was it now?"

"Peru," I said, extracting a pair of Americanos from the Rocket.

"That's the place," Wol said, "that one wants a medal if you ask me. Held hostage."

"It's not right," Wil agreed, "and her a Suffolk gel. Not right at all. And that wrong'un breaking in here at night. That's a poor show alright. You make a good cup of coffee too."

"We decided to do something," Wil added, "din't we, Wol?"

"We did," Wol agreed. "We'll go for a couple of Armadillo biscuits too. He likes an Armadillo, don't you Wil?"

"I do," Will agreed, "'herem Sister, there's a cheque for you here too."

I handed them their coffee and biscuits and they gave me a cheque.

 "£2000 for the repairs and £1000 for finding that lost nun."

"What? But that's a huge amount of money!" I said, "it's far too much! Are you sure?"

"Oh yes," said Wol, elbowing Wil affectionately, "he looks rough, but he's got a few quid. He can afford it."

I was staggered. "That's very generous. Thank you very much indeed."

"Least we can do," Wol said. "The boy give us the idea, din't he, Wil?"

"Yeah. Elvis. He's coming later, got some homework. Maths, that'll be, on a Tuesday."

And so it went on for several days. Farmer Odge quietly handed me an envelope with a cheque for £500. Bob Fairbrother gave us a new little computer and offered to pay for a special system that will make the internet work and stop doing those whirly circles all the time. It was overwhelming. I was quite glad on Thursday when the interviews all seemed to be over and the only extra appointment I had was Antonio's lesson. I was happily at work composing more super-challenging tongue twisters for him, (*Hurry, hurry, Aunt Harriet, there's hardly an hour before the huge, angry hippo arrives again*) when he dashed into the Shoppe waving a copy of a newspaper.

"You are famous, Sister! Is terrible what happened! How are you? Look at your eye in this picture! *Dio mio!*"

"I'm fine, absolutely fine," I said.

"Is 'orrible! Antonio cried, "a Sister is kidnap! This convent here is a robbery! Terrible, terrible!"

"Well, we've had lots of offers of help, and I'm fine now, shall we get on with the lesson?"

"Sorry Sister, I have no time. I came to give you this. You need something to get around. You must be able to travel if you want to get back your sister from Peru, eh?"

He handed me a bunch of keys. I was puzzled.

"Is a car, a little bus thing, for you. Then you can travel, eh?"

And outside, a smiling Carla was waiting in Antonio's big car and beside it was parked a big steely grey vehicle.

"Is yours," Antonio said, with a casual shrug in its direction. "Enjoy! Now I must go to Tottenham. Drive careful, eh?" He climbed in beside Carla and they drove away with a wave.

I was left, keys in hand, standing in amazement.

Roger Collis appeared.

"He wanted to get you something completely new," he said, "but I told him you wouldn't want that. Hope I was right."

"It looks new to me," I said.

"It's five years old," he said, "but it's quite low mileage. I chose it and chipped in too."

"Thank you, Mr Collis," I said. "I can hardly take this all in."

"Can't have you sisters stuck in Hog Fen, can we? I certainly wouldn't like to be here for long without transport. It'd drive me mad."

"Are you still hoping for a big new corporate headquarters in Cambridge one day?" I asked him.

"Yes, and it won't be much longer now. Intermediax is doing pretty well," he said. "Now, shall we take your new motor for a spin?"

So that's how we come to breeze through our hospital appointments today, and how I was able to give Hermione her lift to the station this evening. She's on her way to London on behalf of the Sister Emelda Release Campaign. She'll be meeting the South American people from the Foreign Office and two representatives of charities who have managed to secure the release of hostages in different part of the Andes. We're doing everything that can be done, Emelda. Chin up!

The black eye is almost healed now. Elvis was very sympathetic. "I had one of them once," he told me. "I fell off my bike. Can I give you some money in pennies?"

"It's very kind of you to give us money, Elvis" I said. "Are you sure you can afford it, dear?"

"Yeah! I did piggybacks for all my friends at school, 20p each," he said, and he handed me £3.20 in warm coin, which represents a lot of piggybacks, when you work it out.

"I'll tell her all about you, Elvis," I said, "and I know she'll want me to say a big thank you to your friends, but especially to you. And she'll also want me to give you a big slice of any cake you choose."

He chose chocolate. It somehow seems very important that you know that.

Best wishes,

Sister B.

(Hog Fen's very own Have-a-Go Sister, according to the *Littleport Post*)

And kidnappers, if you can read this, please be aware that the number of supporters who signed up to the campaign to free Sister Emelda has now reached close to 90,000 and continues to rise. It's time you let her go. We know you have your problems, and we are sympathetic, but kidnapping is no way to achieve greater understanding of your cause.

Think of the extra energy that will go into seeking you out, now that the kidnap is a matter of international discussion. If you end this now, you may still be able to return home and lead the rest of your life in peace and at liberty.

I've put two KitKats in this time, so you can have one. Don't forget to give one to Emelda, though.

Blessings to you and your wives and families,
Boniface

40

St Win's
January 18th

Dear Visitor to the Oppressed Loggers,

We spoke on Wednesday to Sister Helena of the Order of St Lucius in Rio di Janeiro. We did it on the computer. There is a shouty arrangement you can use nowadays where the person you talk to is on the screen. They're always blurry and sometimes it freezes – our broadband signal still isn't perfect – but it enabled us to ask her about loggers and their lives, and also about how they might treat a long-term visitor, which is the phrase we have decided to use instead of "hostage" or, even worse, "kidnap victim".

Sister Helena was a long-term visitor herself a couple of years ago. She was there a while – I won't say exactly how long. The good news is that they treated her with kindness more or less all the time. The bad news is that it cost a lot of money to get her released. She doesn't even know how much, it was handled through intermediaries. We won't be taking that option. St Win's kidnap policy is against it, and so, I know, are you, so we depend on going through channels. You'd be amazed at how effective East Anglian channels are. Hermione has made a social media campaign and I put a sign up in the Shoppe and a remarkable number of customers know someone or have a friend who knows someone in Peru. We've been deluged with offers of help. Some of them very surprising. Some of them from security experts. I can't say more at the moment.

The day before yesterday I was cashing up when a young man in black leather with his hair tied back came into the Shoppe and stood looking around. He did this by standing in the middle and rotating his head on his shoulders, like someone stretching the tendons in their neck, it was odd. Finally he said, "Yeah. I need to talk to someone."

"Anything I can help with?" I asked.

"Only I was going to offer to make a film. For your campaign."

"How kind," I said. "What sort of thing were you thinking of?"

"The missing Sister in Peru. Thought I might be able to help. I've done a few campaigns before, charity things, quite big stuff."

I didn't know what to say. It's not that I didn't believe him, exactly, it's just that he was out of the blue. Whatever did "quite big stuff" mean?

"Yeah. I'm pretty busy, but I could do something short. They work well on the internet. I've got a team. I live locally. I've got a few days' spare. Maybe think about it and give me a ring, yeah?"

He gave me a card with a picture of a film camera on one side and a telephone number.

He turned to go, but then stopped. "This is a cool place, right? It feels calm. It's nice. Anyway, give me a call. Anytime."

I put the card by the till and didn't think much about it until the next day when Tilly Matthews dropped in for scotch eggs and Peruvian Egg cake (Nesbitt's latest experiment). She read it and jumped.

"Oh! Gabriel Muncie! He's famous. He's won prizes. Look!" She pulled out her little flat computer and tapped until a picture of the same young man appeared. Only in this picture he was wearing an evening suit and a bow tie and clutching an award. "He's won a BAFTA! Look."

A BAFTA is a very important prize, apparently.

"It must be Divine Intervention," Sister Bernard said. "Film directors don't wander into the Shoppe for nothing. I'm not sure how we can use him, though. Any ideas?"

I left them thinking and went to salsa class. All the salsa ladies had read the papers and were full of commiseration. They had a plan. Paquita said, "We dance to raise money. Yes? Maybe a sponsored thing? Here in the hall?"

"I think we can do better than that," said Iris, one of the ladies. "Let's go big. Go national. Go *international*. Try for a world record or something. Salsa for Sister Emelda, we'll call it. My Diane's an event organiser. Leave it with me."

They took Gabriel Muncie's card and set about organising. So next Wednesday, there will be a world-wide simultaneous Salsa workout over the internet. Gabriel is going to film it. Everybody who joins in pays some money – it all happens online, I don't know how – Alphonsus is dealing with the computer side of things. All I have to do is dance in the class as usual. In the back row, if I have any say in the matter. I practise, but I still can't remember the steps. Sometimes you're expected to turn twice on the same foot *and do things with your hands at the same time.*

Item 35 on Sister Joy's list of reasons for closing St Win's was that "certain members of the Order have taken up public dancing in lewd costumes". I read it quickly the first time, and thought she'd written "dancing in *loud* costumes", which was a fair enough description, I thought, even though Sister Joy had never seen my salsa clothes. But on re-reading it was "lewd". I looked it up, wanting to know exactly how indignant to feel. "Belonging to the lower orders, common, low, vulgar" were all given; no problem there, but so was "lascivious, unchaste".

Blimey! As Nesbitt would say.

Sister Joy recommends sacking Nesbitt immediately and wants Pavel out of Pigpen 1. She thinks the chapel should be demolished to avoid further costs. The Shoppe and the café should cease trading and the gardens should be offered to the local authority for a shopping mall. This would "maximise its financial potential". The other convent buildings should be mothballed pending redevelopment, possibly as a regional logistics hub. Sisters over 70 should go into local authority care, and those under 70 should be "redeployed appropriately" or apply to a housing association for accommodation and go on benefit. All this, she says, would "upgrade the religious presence in Three Fens and boost diocesan coherence going forward".

Re-booting in safe mode sounded even more attractive when the computer started playing up again last night. Hey ho, I'm off to practice my salsa. Guess how many people have signed up to join in so far?

127,368!

Best wishes,

Sister B.

KitKat enclosed.

41

St Win's
January 21st

Dear Emelda,

I often wonder what your mornings are like. We're early risers here at St Win's, what with prayers at 5 am, so we're used to being up on dark winter mornings. My favourite kind are the misty ones like today where drifting veils dangle above the fields as the sun rises and then roll cleanly away as if they are being wound back into the ditches at dawn. As I walked to the Shoppe there were a lot of bird calls, as if they were foghorning for safety in the gloom. The noisiest are the partridges who live in big busybody families just over our fence. A brood of ten or twelve isn't unusual. Their ritchety ratchety call is like someone scraping a saucepan with a stick; it makes cockerels sound positively musical. Partridges are very beautiful close up, as I'm sure you know, a lovely plump shape with very delicate markings. I'm watching a little group now, pecking their way in a line over the grass towards the Shoppe. They look as if they're posing for a wildlife calendar.

I hardly know where to start describing last night's salsa event. One minute the ladies at the village hall were planning a modest little sponsored dance at our next evening class; the next, dozens and dozens of people were Latin dancing under arc lights on the convent lawn. There was a live orchestra! Where did that come from? There was a sound stage. There were several TV camera crews – one from Japan! I'm serious!

I did none of this. It was out of my hands from the moment I handed Gabriel Muncie's card over. I did a fairly ordinary few days' work, but I was aware of the atmosphere around me gradually becoming charged with excitement. Customers started to be high-spirited – giggly, even. Mrs Odge said she could hardly wait, and did a little cha cha move as she bagged up her onions. Nearly all the elderly sisters announced they were joining in, three of them in wheelchairs.

Joining in *what*?

Lorries came and went, delivering large, mysterious pieces of equipment and crews of men in matching shirts to assemble them.

Every time I looked something in the garden had changed. At some point an enormous dance floor arrived, was assembled and tested by twenty people who appeared to be professional dancers.

"I think we should offer refreshments, don't you?" Sister Bernard suggested, watching an enormous loud speaker being rolled into place by four men with "Stage

Crew" on the back of their shirts. "Let's dig out the urns. And maybe cake. Yes, tea and cake. But I don't want you to do it, Boniface – we'll delegate it to Gertrude and Clementine. You'll be dancing, obviously."

Would I?

The day before, there were sound checks, "One two, one two. Testing." It went on for hours. Banks of lights were turned on and off. I could see Gabriel setting up cameras all around the dance floor. An orchestra came in their ordinary clothes and asked if they could hang their suits in the outhouse until they needed to change. I said, "of course," as if orchestras arrived at the convent every day.

The café was busy feeding staff involved with the performance or local people eager to see what was going on.

Bob Fairbrother and four of his clients came and saw the poster that someone had put up in the Shoppe. *"Salsa for Sister Emelda"* it said. *"Charity Salsa Flashmob at St Winifreda's Convent! Support the release of a Suffolk sister held captive in Peru. Event filmed by local director Gabriel Muncie for unique documentary. Come and strut your stuff to save Sister Emelda Griggs. Sign up now. £5 buys a salsa workout routine, £100 puts you in the front three rows, £300 and you dance with Robbie or Trixie Silverside, Gold Medallists in the National Salsa Championships."*

"Well, I'm up for it, if you guys are," Bob said.

"Ach, salsa! Jah!" they all agreed (they were German).

And into this melée there came the Bishop and Sister Joy. It took me a moment to spot them, the place was so busy.

"I came to see you in particular, Boniface," he said. "I'm here to congratulate you on... Whatever are all the preparations?"

"It's a salsa flashmob," I told him, trying to sound well-informed, "to raise funds."

The Bishop walked over to the poster, put his half-moon reading glasses onto his nose and leaned in to read it. I wondered what to expect, but to my surprise he wheeled round with a grin and said, "What fun! I used to cut a rug myself in my youth. Took a blue for ballroom at Oxford, as a matter of fact."

I said, "Well, my Lord, for only £5 you can join in."

I thought I was joking.

"Oh, I think I can do better than that!" he declared. "I fancy stepping out with Trixie Silverside! I won a cup for my Rhumba. There might be slightly more of me, but I bet I could still show her a thing or two." He tripped his feet nimbly around under his robe as he said this.

Sister Joy had been preoccupied on her phone until she overheard this last remark.

"Oh Bishop, I don't think...!" she said in alarm.

"Now don't tell me I can't join in, Joy, it's for the most excellent cause!"

"Yes, but, we have to consider..." she leaned in to speak to him confidentially. I caught the words "dignity", "Twitter" and "disrepute".

"Nonsense," said the Bishop, "it's far worse to appear stuffy and stand-offish. Count me in!"

People began to file through the gates. They paid collectors standing along the drive, they took their places on the dance floor and the warm-up dancing began. I stood in my coat handing out cups of tea and I swear I saw everyone I've ever met in the whole Three Fens area. The Odges bustled by, as did Hedgby the wholesaler with his wife, and Hari Menon, my old Retail for Beginners tutor with his. Customers from the Shoppe and the café came with their whole families. Nearly all the Sisters joined in. The staff of Intermediax were there, and so was Constable Carl, looking quite different out of uniform. Nesbitt was handing out drinks, but I was pleased to see her mother and Roselily had come too.

At the appointed time, under the arc lights, the orchestra struck up, the workout leaders, with their head microphones in place, took up their positions, and off we all went. On giant screens around us we could see similar groups of people from around the country and around the world, all doing the same thing at the same time. It was loud; it was bright; it was extraordinary.

The beauty of dancing in a vast worldwide crowd is that nobody can tell if you go wrong. It was wonderful, and it all seemed to go by in a second. After the flashmob, the professionals took the floor and danced with the people who had paid extra. I was heading back to the café, when I spotted Rev Mother Elizabeth arrive in a cab. She was using a stick, but walking steadily.

"Welcome back, Elizabeth. I hear you had a little injury," the Bishop greeted her, as he left the floor slightly out of breath.

"And I hear your accountant made off with our funds," Rev Mother replied.

"Now, now, Elizabeth, that's all been sorted out. The man's been arrested."

Sister Joy spotted the conversation and began to ease herself closer.

"He has," said Rev Mother, "thanks to the police and the outstanding courage of one or two sisters. But the fact that he was able to commit embezzlement suggests poor oversight at the very least, you must admit. Now about this report. I've seen a copy. What's its status, exactly?"

Sister Joy leaned in and was about to speak, but Rev Mother continued, "Shall we go to my office? I can't stand for long yet."

"Shall I join you?" Sister Joy asked, bobbing along beside them.

"That won't be necessary, thank you, Sister Joy," the Bishop said, and they left her standing on the drive.

You'll see the Salsa for Sister Emelda one day on the internet. Perhaps you already have. I'm the one in the back row who usually goes left when the others all go right. I'm very hard to see. You can't miss the Bishop, though, he's the one in purple dancing with the lady in the mostly invisible dress.

It's raised a huge amount of money.

Best wishes,

(still salsa-ing a little, as I write)

Sister B

To the kidnappers, in case you are able to read this:

We know your lives are difficult, but holding Sister Emelda is a bad choice. Please free her. Thank you very much.

God bless you.

Boniface

42

St Win's
January 27th

Dear Emelda,

The SERT have been busy this week. They have been on the phone to the Foreign Office almost every day and Annunziata rings the convent in Los Santos every morning for updates. No news so far. This week we're sending *Far from the Madding Crowd* and *Dombey and Son*. Hardy and Dickens; hard to beat in terms of literary heft per kilo. Let me know if you need something less 19th century.

A mysterious little box of some kind has appeared in the television room, attached to the retired sisters' set. According to Sister Gertrude it allows many more programmes to come into the television. It was a Christmas present.

"Is that wise?" I asked. "We have enough trouble monitoring the programmes that come from the ordinary channels. If dozens of others become available, how are we to select the best programmes for the retired sisters? Remember the *Embarrassing Bodies* debacle last year?"

"There are loads of wildlife programmes. They always like them," Gertrude said.

And there are, but many of them of the lovely-pictures-but-not-much-else variety, which our seasoned viewers in the old people's centre despise.

"The three-toed sloth – there's practically nothing I don't know about them," I heard one of the elderly sisters say yesterday, "and as for the fruit bats of Madagascar, I could pass an exam on their habits. I'd prefer robots, sci fi – that sort of thing. Just because I'm old doesn't mean I want to watch hippos swimming under water every day of the week and keep pretending to be surprised."

At convocation we discussed the vast possibilities for television watching now available. What to do? In the end we decided two hours a week would be devoted to box tv, on a Wednesday and Thursday evening and the retired sisters would take it in turns to review and choose the programmes to watch themselves. There seem to be robot and sci fi programmes available, but whether they are the kind of things sisters want in their heads is another matter. I glanced at the listings, and I have to say I doubt it. Most of them were about serial killers or drug dealers. One called *Game of Thrones* might be a safer bet. They always like history and the royal family.

Best wishes,
Sister B.

KitKat of the week (mint – we'll try *anything*) enclosed.

43

Dear Emelda,

It's much colder here now, and the soil is sodden. It's proper Three Fens damp. You can tell it's normal for these parts, all the village names are so watery; our neighbours are Wetbeach, Mudde Fen, and my favourite: Little Puddoo.

In all the excitement over Christmas we forgot about the big box that had been delivered. I found it a couple of days ago and asked Pavel to help me move it. I still didn't know what it was or who it was for.

Pavel read the writing on the side and laughed. "No, Sister, this means 'Happy Christmas'. This is in Polish language."

"But what is it?" I said, "Is there another label?"

"Is a present," said Pavel.

"But, how do you know?"

He shrugged a little shyly. "Is from me, this present," he said.

"Pavel, is it you who leaves useful presents around for us?"

He shrugged, "Maybe; maybe not. But this one, I did

buy this."

"You shouldn't spend money on us, Pavel," I said.

"You came when I was in the police station, Sister. I don't forget this," he said.

So I called the other sisters and we opened the box and, Emelda, it was a beautiful, shiny, brand new bicycle. It needed a little assembling, but that took no time at all, and soon we were testing it up and down the lane. It was cold, but the pleasure of sailing along on that lovely new machine, I can hardly tell you.

We hadn't exactly forgotten about Wendy Wooler – we'd just assumed that she'd been arrested. We hadn't seen her here since she was taken off to talk to the police. Pigpen 2 was empty of her possessions. Then, the morning after the Salsa event, I happened to glance out of the Shoppe window and saw her blue car drive up. It turns out she was on bail.

She stepped out carrying something in her hand and wearing a clear plastic raincoat with a matching rain bonnet tightly tied under the chin. This was odd, since it wasn't raining.

As I watched, she walked briskly towards our lovely new vehicle, held a bright canister at arm's length and began to spray red paint over it. She worked in a determined and unhurried way, starting with the windscreen and moving clockwise. I was too shocked to move at first.

She seemed absorbed in her work, spraying a wavy line all along the passenger side and then walking around to the back. From that angle she could have seen me if she had looked up, but she didn't. She obliterated her own view with red paint over the back window. I could hear the canister rattle as she shook it between sprayings. This sound attracted Baz's attention, he and Animal were cutting hedges along the drive. They were some way away, but I saw their heads turn.

I was running her way by now, shouting, to stop her, but Wendy Wooler was working with an odd, hypnotic concentration. She continued the wavy red line over the bonnet, paying particular attention to the radiator. By the time I reached her, she had coloured it in completely.

"Oi!" yelled Animal and Baz. Seeing what she was doing, they both dropped their hedge cutters and began to run down the drive, shouting.

"Stop!" I shouted, "stop or I'll..."

Wendy Wooler paused for a moment and then turned and looking annoyed at the interruption, lifted the canister and pointed it straight at me.

"You won't stop me," she said.

"Please stop, Wendy, or I'll have to call the police."

"Call them. I'm going to prison anyway."

She turned back, shook the canister briskly and began again. Scarlet paint shot out of the can, hit the shining panels, congealed for moment and then started to run down in vertical stripes and drip onto the ground.

"Half the money was mine," she said, over the noise of the spray can. "Half of it, that was the deal. And I'd have it, if it wasn't for a bunch of bloody interfering nuns!"

With this she swung round and aimed the canister my way.

At that moment, Sister Joy's car pulled into the car park. She stepped out, completely oblivious to the scene around her, picked her briefcase out of the boot, and started to walk past, heading for the garden door. This meant passing Wendy Wooler. As she did so she suddenly spotted the blood-red paint all over the car. Her face registered confusion, followed by outrage, then fear. Her step faltered. Wendy Wooler swung the canister around and pointed it straight at her.

"I hope you're not..." was all Sister Joy managed to say, before a jet of red paint hit her in the chest. It splashed her face, making her shriek, jump and drop her laptop.

Treading carefully around puddles of paint, Wendy Wooler walked over and sprayed the prone Sister Joy thoroughly up and down from veil to shoes.

"I lived with that man for years, *years* while we planned this. I hate him. I hope he goes to jail and never comes out. I hope I never have to see him again as long as I..."

There were footsteps, a crazy confusion of impacts and falls, and then the sound of a metal canister hitting the ground and rolling, followed by a shriek of anger and frustration. Animal and Baz had rugby tackled her.

"I dread to think how much paperwork it'll take to explain this, but I suppose it's in a good cause," Ted said, later, after Constable Carl had taken Wendy Wooler away. Animal and Baz, stuffed with cakes and many times thanked, were waiting in his van. "Still, it does them good to be on the right side of the law, for once. They're good lads, really. Don't tell them I said so."

When she was arrested, Wendy Wooler was wearing a tidy grey tracksuit and training shoes under her plastic mac, as if she had considered an outfit suitable for vandalising the convent's new vehicle carefully before setting out. There wasn't a spot of paint on her.

"It's the neat ones I always worry about most," Sylvia said, when she dropped in later. "They can't believe it when their plans don't work, they often go a bit loopy, don't they, Ron? You probably got off lightly."

Ron was looking at the poor, red-smeared vehicle. "Ooh, dear, oh dear, she really did a thorough job there.

You were insured, I hope."

We were, but we're still without transport while the garage removes its thick covering of warpaint.

I must stop now and cycle this to the post. The lovely new bike came with splendid lights, but fen ditches are deep and black in the dark and I need to be back for convocation and a SERT meeting later. There's progress. I'll report next time.

I keep finding traces of red paint. There are one or two smudges on the KitKat wrapper, but only on the outside.

Courage! We're hard at work on your behalf.

Best wishes,

Sister B.

44

St Win's
February 6th

Dear Emelda,

Sister Prudence formally handed St Win's back to Rev Mother last night at convocation. We had expected Sister Joy to be there, presenting her report, but she had left looking crestfallen in the borrowed baggy jeans and bobbly sweater that had replaced her paint-stained habit. She'd had only a short private meeting with Rev Mother, but that seemed enough.

"I must admit, Rev Mother," Prudence said, "that I stand down with some relief. It has certainly been... eventful. I will be glad to get back to my studies."

"Thank you, Prudence. By all accounts we should be very grateful to you. Well, Sisters, you have packed an awful lot of incidents into the time I've been away. I find you have opened a community café and an art gallery, begun hosting pensioners' lunches, started a small kindergarten and besides all this you have hosted a fund-raising event featuring the Bishop giving the whole world the benefit of his Latin American dance skills. I could hardly keep up with it all, while I was away. I'm sorry there have been some difficulties, but a couple of problems are now resolved: the Woolers have both been charged and the police are confident of tracing the money."

"Will we be able to start work on the chapel?" Sister Bernard asked. "I'm worried about the state of the organ. It's bad for it to be so damp, and it should be played, but it's too dangerous even to go in there now."

"We'll prioritise the chapel, certainly," Rev Mother agreed.

"How can we do that? How can we do anything at all, if Sister Joy's report recommends we close down? I'm worried about Nesbitt, in particular," I told her, "Sister Joy wanted her sacked and the Shoppe and café closed. 'Nesbitt's the breadwinner for her whole family. It would be disastrous for them if she lost her job."

"Several of the elderly sisters are scared out of their wits," Eustacia added. "They think they're going to end up on the streets. I've tried talking sense into them, but not having working teeth has made them gloomy."

"And what about poor Pavel?" someone else started to say.

Rev Mother held up her hand.

"Sisters, we certainly have a few things to worry about, but Sister Joy's thoughts about our future need not concern us."

"But what about her report?" we all cried.

"It carries no weight at all," said Rev Mother.

"She was always saying how closely she worked with the Bishop," Sister Bernard said. "She was writing it on his behalf, surely?"

"She wanted us to think so, but she wasn't. She was acting on her own misguided initiative. The report was a project she dreamt up, probably because she wanted to impress the Bishop and his team. She was looking for promotion, perhaps. I don't know what her motives were, but I checked, and it turns out she has no remit and nobody in the Diocesan office is the least interested in her report. I doubt if anyone else will read it. We can forget it ever happened. I recommend recycling the copies we still have. They'll burn nicely."

"Did you ask Sister Joy about this?" I asked. "What did she say?"

Rev Mother adjusted her reading glasses. "We had a frank exchange of views and Sister Joy decided to take up a posting she'd been offered...elsewhere.

We must all have looked puzzled.

"All that matters is that she won't be back. So, at least for the time being, Pavel can stay where he is, Nesbitt's job is safe, and nobody will be sending the retired sisters to a home. Longer term, we can't be so sure, but it's best to deal with the threats one day at a time, Sisters. That's what our predecessors always did."

"Let's put the Sister Joy Report in the Bad Things box," Hermione suggested. "It'll keep up the tradition."

So that's what we did.

I'll stop now, so I can cycle to the post.

Best wishes,

Sister B.

PS Rev Mother also updated us on SERT activities. I can't tell you about that yet. Courage, Emelda, things are happening.

45

St Win's
February 11th

Dear Emelda,

A bright, clear sky this morning, sunlight glittering on the frosty grass. Carmella's row of bird feeders in the vegetable garden is attracting goldfinches. They swoop down in playful flocks, fluttery, chattering dots of red and gold shining like treasure among the bare branches. In fact, birds are thriving all round the convent. We have put up all sorts of boxes and nesting places, and buildings in poor repair suit owls and sparrows, and bats as well. There are barn owls in the dormitory roof, which we're pleased about, although they hiss in the most extraordinarily fearsome and devilish way.

Oh dear, here I am rambling about birds in the Fens when you might be locked in somewhere. Horrible thought! It's my job to keep writing, and I will; prayer apart, there is little else I can do at the moment.

Rev Mother and Hermione, on the other hand, have plenty of things they can do. They went to London yesterday for a meeting at the Foreign Office. They took a taxi to the station. This fact alone will give you some idea of the priority we are putting on the matter, but

I won't say more, except that via Sister Doris almost every religious sister in the US is now on board with prayers. Your captors must be feeling the effects by now. Thousands upon thousands of people praying for you to stop what you are doing; it must have an impact. I picture even the most hardened and brutal kidnapper beginning to feel at least a little unsettled: a slight queasiness, an unexplained shudder, the dawning of the thought that what he is doing is grossly and utterly wrong...he remembers his mother; the words of the prayers he used to say in the little church in his village on Sundays keep coming into his head; sleeplessness, doubts, odd arthritic pains in the joints, palpitations...

The Foreign Office gave us a telephone number anyone can call. It is on the little paper enclosed. A small separate piece of paper is apparently a good idea. Either you or your captors can ring that number. Someone will answer immediately and will be able to speak a long list of languages and to begin negotiations. In case the separate piece of paper goes missing, I am also instructed to give you the number in other ways in every letter, but not be too obvious about it.

Working on the principle that the men who are holding you speak poor or no English – apologies all round if this is mistaken – I will do so this time by using a song you will remember about green rushes. The song has no nought in it, so I am using the word green for that. Green, green, lily-white boys, gospel makers twice, green, green, stars in the sky, symbols at your door, rivals, green, proud walkers, gospel makers, green, rivals. Remember, phone it any time.

Stay brave, Emelda. Sometimes we comfort ourselves here by imagining you have already been freed and are making your way slowly back to the convent, or that you have chosen to stay and work with your kidnappers, who no doubt have their reasons and probably haven't had many chances in life. We never doubt your courage or your resourcefulness.

Best wishes from your friends in the Fens and those working hard in the Foreign Office too,

Sister B.

46

Dear Emelda,

Hermione rushed into the Shoppe this morning and said, "I've been doing some internet research. Do you think Emelda had insurance?"

"Travel insurance?" I asked, "in case she lost her suitcase or her ticket or something?"

"No, kidnap insurance."

"Can you insure against kidnap?"

"You can. With Lloyds of London, actually. And if she did, they can help with finding her."

"Wouldn't the Foreign Office have checked this already?" I said.

"They may have, but they wouldn't tell us. They seem efficient, but they don't tell us what they're doing. The problem is that we don't really have any direct connection with Emelda – she doesn't even come from this convent, Boniface. We don't even really know what she looks like, do we? We couldn't give a description. How old is she, for example?"

I didn't even know that. I've written to you for more than a year and I suddenly realised I didn't know even these most basic facts. A horrid discovery. I went through the photographs you've sent us in the time we've been writing, but there is no recognisable image of you among them, Emelda. Mostly they are breathtaking views of the scenery you live in or the schoolchildren you work with. You are the photographer, not the subject. The nearest thing I could find to an image of you was the one of your mountaineering expedition some time ago, when you are a dot on the end of a rope about 50 yards from the camera. By squinting we can just about make out that you are probably of medium height.

At convocation Hermione mentioned the insurance possibility.

"The sisters at La Santa don't know anything about it; I've asked their Rev Mother already," she said, "but that doesn't mean she didn't have any insurance. It just means she didn't want to involve them, and there seems to be quite good evidence that she was keen to keep the convent there out of things as far as she could. Perhaps she was worried about implicating them, if there was a kidnap demand. They are a very poor convent and she was always very aware of how dependent she was on their hospitality when she was there."

"What difference does it make, anyway?" Rev Mother asked.

"If you have insurance," said Hermione, "the

insurance company will send a kidnap expert to advise and even take part in negotiations. Cases of kidnap are often not very clear cut. There aren't always ransom demands; sometimes the kidnappers want only to take the possessions the person has at that moment. They might take them to a bank and make them draw money and then let them go."

"But that would be in a city, surely," said Sister Mary of Light. "It happened to me once in Argentina on my gap year. My own fault. Of course I had no money, but it took a while to convince them."

We all admired her calm.

"Even if she had no insurance, we could surely employ someone to help us, couldn't we? The fund now has quite a lot of money," said Sister Bernard.

"How would we find the right person, though?" I said.

"We could ask the man whose website I read. He's a security expert who works internationally. His website is full of tips for staying safe and avoiding kidnap all over the world. What to do on a hijacked plane, that sort of thing. It's amazing reading!" Hermione told us.

"What is he then, some sort of private detective?" I asked.

"No, he just calls himself a security professional; his job is to stop people being kidnapped."

"Well, I can't see why we shouldn't ask him for help," said Rev Mother. "How much would he charge? Did it say on the website?"

"He's used to protecting celebrities, I imagine. Oil company executives or film stars, that sort of person," Hermione said.

They'd definitely have lots of money, we all agreed.

"Well, we'll just have to ask, I suppose, but if it's more that £20 per hour..."

I said, "Rev Mother, £20 is not very much these days..."

"£25?" she said, "£30?"

"I think even more..."

"Good Lord!" Rev Mother said, "that means more than £200 in one day! It seems a fortune."

It's possible that we are a little out of touch. It was the same with bathrooms, I remember. It was a shock to us that guests expected a bathroom apiece. Even quite smart hotels had bathrooms down the hall in my youth.

This is how we met Hugh Snipe of Snipe Security (*NB kidnappers, this is a false name and other details in this letter may be deliberately misleading. Sorry.). It is actually as easy as that. You can email a website and a security man with contacts all over the world will come to see you almost immediately.

"What will he be like, I wonder?" Hermione asked,

as we were waiting for him in the café. "Square and tough, with sharp eyes?"

"No," I said. "Scottish, surely. Dark and good-looking; elegant suit; dazzling car."

We were just thinking of the James Bond of our youth, weren't we?

Hugh Snipe could hardly be more different. Mr Snipe is consciously average and invisible – which, when you think about it, is much more what's needed. He is about 40, tallish and dressed in a slightly rumpled grey suit with a jumper under the jacket. If you were forced to guess, you might say he was a school teacher or perhaps an academic – a historian maybe, or an archaeologist. He has sandy hair and large spectacles. His whole demeanour radiates mildness, yet according to his website he is a black belt in four different martial arts, one involving sticks.

What Mr Snipe does best, we soon discovered, is listen and absorb information. We told him your situation in some detail. He listened, sipped Earl Grey tea – he prefers it to coffee – and listened some more. He wrote nothing down, but sat with the tips of his fingers pressed together, looking at the floor, frowning. Occasionally he held up a hand, stopped the speaker – usually Rev Mother – and asked for a detail to be repeated. When it was clarified, he nodded, and the briefing continued.

At the end he looked up and asked very mildly, "And what is it, Sisters, that you would like me to do, exactly?"

We all blinked for a moment, wondering how to put it into words.

"We want to know that Sister Emelda is well," Rev Mother finally said. "Ideally we would like her to return, in good health. But she may not want that. She may prefer to continue her work in the Amazon. We simply want to know that she is well, wherever she is, and that she is not being held against her will, or, or suffering in any way."

"So, just to be clear, if someone were to locate her, you would want them to confirm that she is safe and well and not being held against her will. And what if she *is* being held against her will?"

"The authorities..." Rev Mother started to say.

"Yes," said Mr Snipe, "let's assume for a moment that the authorities have drawn a blank, or found themselves, for diplomatic reasons, say, unable to act very swiftly, or very directly."

"Does that happen?" I asked.

"International relations are complicated, delicate and often very slow-moving," Mr Snipe said, as if he were apologising. "Very often we find, in the field, that direct action is the most efficient policy."

"When you say direct action...?"

"Well, basically, that would mean obtaining some sort of access to the place and getting the principal out."

"The principal?"

"Forgive me," said Mr Snipe, "technical term; it's what we call the person we are being paid to protect."

"Wouldn't that be dangerous?" I asked.

"There are risks involved, clearly, but we have done this before. Our success rate is reassuring."

"We may need some time to discuss all this," Rev Mother said.

"Understood," said Mr Snipe, "but I need to warn you that time is critical in such cases, and there has already been a very considerable delay."

"Would you allow us an hour?" Rev Mother asked. "You are very welcome to eat lunch in the cafe while we call an urgent convocation."

"I'm sure that would be delicious, but I'm afraid I have calls to make," Mr Snipe said. "Shall we rendezvous back here at 2.00?"

He left with a slight bow. He reminds me, for some reason, of a Wimbledon tennis umpire. I suppose it's the combination of authority and self-effacement.

"Whatever are we getting ourselves into?" Sister Bernard asked, once we were all summoned to the urgent convocation. "How do we know we can trust him? He might be anyone. He might be going to go straight to the kidnappers and..."

"Shall we begin with silent prayer for a moment?" Rev Mother asked.

We all fell silent and even if our brains did continue to whirr, our ears and our hearts had a few moments' peace. It never fails.

"Now," Rev Mother began, "what we need is someone we can trust. Are we agreed on that?"

"Yes," we all said, "agreed."

"Fundamentally, we have to decide whether we can trust Mr Snipe and his associates. We will be trusting them with money given to us in good faith by our supporters and people who have been moved by Emelda's situation. They didn't mean us to keep it in the bank. We need to take action. So, we must decide, and really, we must decide now, whether Snipe and his people – his operatives, as he calls them – are reliable people who will act as we would want them to act. We can only put this in God's hands. I suggest five minutes' silent prayer, then a vote."

"I vote yes," said Hermione, when the time was up. "I don't see we have any other option."

"Yes from me too," Eustacia added.

One by one every sister there voted yes. We can be pretty snappy over big decisions when it's necessary;

I've always liked that about St Win's. (Small decisions are another matter.)

At 2.00 on the dot, Mr Snipe returned to the same table at the café and became our man in South America.

"How will you... go about things?" Rev Mother asked.

Mr Snipe poured himself a little more tea, and stirred it. "In a case like this, we usually find it best for the commissioning party – that is to say, our clients – to know as little as possible about the detailed activity on the ground. Ideally, we liaise with someone local. We will probably base our communications in Los Angeles, simply for ease of access. I have colleagues there. Do you have anyone there who could communicate for you?"

"We need to talk about money," Hermione said. "How do you charge us? How do we pay? How much?"

"We will provide you with a fully itemised list of expenses on our return," Mr Snipe said. "These will include travel costs and accommodation. There may be local staff to hire, guides and drivers, for example. This is insurance-funded, I take it?"

"We don't know," Hermione said. "We have raised some money and meanwhile we are looking into her insurance position."

Mr Snipe's face was momentarily crossed by a shadow. "So you're not sure, then, about the funding?"

"You're not charging more that £30 an hour, are

you?" Rev Mother asked.

Mr Snipe coughed slightly on his tea. "I'll go ahead on the principle that the insurance is going to step in," he said. "Now, if we're to carry out this... commission on your behalf, I think the sooner we can begin, the better. I'll leave tonight. You won't hear from me directly, but give me your LA contact when you can."

He said other things, but I won't risk writing them down.

This letter may not be sent. I can always keep it for after he finds you.

He will. Somehow.

Best wishes,

Sister B.

47

Dear Emelda,

This week the SERC reported that talks with important official bodies – I won't be more specific in case this falls into the wrong hands – had been very useful, but that the bodies in question were a bit unforthcoming with the details. They claim to be making progress, but there is no way for us to know what, where or how much. It's frustrating, but the email and social media campaigns have certainly had an effect. Hermione tells me they put her straight through when she phones now – that's what happens when a campaign has nearly one million Twitter followers, apparently; people in high places pay attention.

Here in the café – a low place (but only geographically) – Elvis is paying attention to his homework. He comes most days after school, buys a piece of cake and sits over his books at one of the tables. Wol and Wil have taken him under their wing and I sometimes see them pondering a homework question together.

I was passing on Monday, and heard Wil say, "He's

got to put them whotsits in these sentences, Wol. You know the things."

"I en't brought me glasses," Wol said, "I can't make it out."

"What're they called? I forget the name of them."

"I can do arithmetic better. English, that was never my thing. Never could spell."

"Speech marks! That's it! What d'you need to do with them?" Their three heads were together, two white and one sandy, bowed over an exercise book.

"I just need to put them in these sentences," Elvis said, "I've had a try, but I'm not sure they're right."

I once asked Nesbitt if she knew Elvis's family, since he's obviously a local lad.

"Yeah," she said, "his mum's not around, but everybody knows his Dad."

"Are they a nice family?"

"Not really," she said.

A brief but eloquent summary that left me rather glad Wol and Wil were taking an interest in the boy, even if their punctuation advice might not be the best.

Sister Doris, Rev Mother and Hermione breezed into the café yesterday afternoon looking determined – they make a powerful trio. Rev Mother was carrying a letter.

"Can you join us for a minute, Boniface?" she asked.

"We'd like to ask you something."

I sat with them and she showed me the letter. It was from Sisters Worldwide. "They want you to attend the prize giving."

"I already have," I told them.

"Those were the heats," Hermione said. "If you remember the Copia Award was just an interim thing; you have been put in for the international prize now."

"Oh dear," I said, "really? I've had enough prizes."

"I told you she'd say that," Rev Mother said. The other two nodded.

"They've offered to pay your fare," Rev Mother continued. "There would be no expense to us at all."

"And you can stay at my old convent when you get there," Sister Doris added.

"Get where?"

"California."

The Rocket suddenly hissed very loudly in the background, making us all jump.

"*California?*"

Rev Mother shrugged, "That's where the award ceremony is held."

"But that's ridiculous!"

"Please, Boniface, just listen before you decide," Rev Mother said.

"*Please,*" Hermione added, "for the Release

Campaign. We need someone out there, in California."

"What's wrong with emailing, or phoning?" I asked.

Hermione leaned forward and lowered her voice. "They don't like using open channels like email, or even the phone. They worry a lot about being listened in on."

"We just thought," Rev Mother joined in, "we just thought you could combine the two things. You could go to the prize ceremony and while you were there, you could have one or two quick little meetings. It's very difficult to stay in touch from here. It's much better to have someone on the spot. Oh, and it can be a little holiday too. You need a break."

All three were smiling and nodding at me in a wide-eyed, encouraging-the-difficult-teenager sort of way.

"I know LA," Sister Doris added. "You'll be fine, absolutely. And as for the prize-giving, you nailed that speech last time, Boniface. Oh, and if you have any spare time, the convent runs a homeless shelter and they always need help. You might even enjoy it."

"I don't think I'm the right one to go," I said. "Wouldn't you be better, Hermione?"

"We need someone more experienced," Rev Mother said. "Besides, Hermione is on a course next month."

"I thought Hermione was leaving us."

Rev Mother brushed that aside. "Well, technically yes, she's not joining the order, but we need her skills, so she's agreed to stay on for a while."

"What about Sister Bernard?" I suggested.

"She's in the organ competition. Besides, only you have the perfect reason for going on the trip – the Sisters Worldwide prize. We can find someone to stand in for you in the Shoppe and the café easily enough."

How expendable I am. I was still dithering that evening, but as I sat thinking about it in the retirement home chapel, the answer came to me as clear as day: *of course you must go.*

So I agreed.

Emelda, you travel the globe constantly, as do many of my sisters here, but I am a stay-at-home. I have taken pleasure in the details of life here in Hog Fen. I haven't travelled much. Flying to California; I can hardly imagine it. I am secretly worried about the journey; not its dangers, but its practicalities. How do people sit so long on a plane? Obviously they do have bathrooms, but how do they work? Can you take sandwiches? Should I take a cake for my hosts? What kind? I am too embarrassed to ask these things. They never seem to occur to anyone else. It's been very foggy lately. How do pilots see in fog? Do they just plunge their huge machines upwards into it and hope for the best? We're saying a special rosary for my journey tomorrow. I'm hoping that will help with the nerves. It's all God's will, anyway.

Mufti clothes, mercifully, are not needed, I can wear the habit every day, but my sisters have unanimously decided that swimming in the Pacific Ocean is on the agenda, and a swimming costume has been located. It was handed to me by a delighted Mother Martha this evening. "Look!" she said, "I knew we had one somewhere!"

I know they mean only to be encouraging, Emelda, but I took one look at this costume and decided the balmy waters of the Pacific Ocean were never going to be coming near either it or me. It must date from the 1960s. It is made of dense, crunchy fabric and has a pleated skirt. If hippos wore swimming costumes, this would be their style.

Sisters keep coming into the Shoppe with useful items for the journey. I have had lavender bags from one and a shower cap from another. Sister Clementine presented me with a tiny wrapped bar of fragrant Savon de Marseilles, and Sister Bernard has contributed Kendal Mint Cake, which looks remarkably similar (I must be careful not to confuse the two). Then there are elastic stockings donated by the retired sisters. These compress your legs so that you avoid...something with letters – TVP? – on the aeroplane. They've read about it on the internet. Unless TVP is very bad indeed – I have avoided reading about it myself – I will not be wearing them. I tried putting one on as an experiment and it took so long, and involved so much effort, that I would need to start 24 hours earlier in my preparations. Not only that, but the sensation of having a leg pressured by this powerful tube of the strongest elastic was extremely unpleasant. My foot went blue and the thing cut into the back of my knee and then it took a quarter of an hour to get out of it. If all my fellow passengers on the flight are wearing these stockings, good luck to them, but I predict a rather bad-tempered journey.

Mother Hilda is the most recent contributor to my collection. She dropped in to the Shoppe on her way to the old people's home, in her leathers. From the crash helmet under her arm she produced a white paper bag of the traditional sweet shop variety. "Barley sugars, dear. You suck one on take off and landing, and it stops your ears from popping. I've had these since my last BOAC flight to the mission in Mombasa. Perfectly good, though. Nothing wrong with them at all. I knew they'd come in useful."

So now I add popping ears and TVP to the many hazards of air travel that lie ahead, to say nothing of the dangers of boiled sweets several decades past their sell-by date and a shared convent suitcase with locks that don't work and rusty hinges. Hostage negotiations are beginning to sound like the *easy* part of this trip.

All prayers welcome. Ours are with you all the time.

Best wishes from a very infrequent flyer who can't tell her soap from her mint cake,

Sister B.

48

Heathrow Airport
February 23rd

Dear Emelda,

People are nervous in airports, aren't they? I have rarely had so many requests for prayers as here at Heathrow. I can't sit down without people passing me notes or telling me about the time the undercarriage failed on the 747 and asking for a blessing. I'm happy to help, obviously. And then there are the other travellers who want to be your religious friends. I've already sidestepped a couple of Franciscan fathers and I'm only just inside the door.

The airport bus options weren't good, as you can imagine. It was either 5 am and be hugely early, or 9 am and risk being late, so I'm here with many hours to spare. The check-in desk isn't even open. I have found a quiet spot in the Bienvenue Continental Café and lovely Aneeza says I can sit here for as long as I like with my tea. I'm glad of this because the shared suitcase has developed an ear-splitting squeak on one of its wheels. People wince and look round. I was wondering whether butter might work on it. Someone's left some on the next table.

Hugh Snipe has been gone a week now. We have only had one message, an email saying "Arrived safely. All going well." As bland as a decaf vanilla latté. I was secretly hoping for something a bit more action-packed: *"Arrived Narco hideout. Armwrestled El Gato into submission. Heading to hidden loggers' hideout immediately,"* but that isn't how Hugh Snipe (or real life) works.

I'm working with the Little Sisters in their homeless hostel, near Venice Beach. If there is news, someone will come and find me there.

Sister Grace, who runs the hostel, emailed yesterday.

"Hi Boniface, how are you with substance abuse and prostitutes?"

"Ignorant but willing," I replied.

"Welcome aboard!" she replied. "See you tomorrow. We're glad of the help."

She's been there for 34 years, so I'm hoping she can train me up enough to be useful, even if it's only for a few days.

I wonder how they're getting on in the Shoppe.

Best foot forward, Boniface.

Aneeza has just brought me complimentary toast and marmalade. No reason. Just delivered it with a little wink. No zero hours contract could harden that kind heart.

A jolly group of elderly Americans are playing cards across the way. I met one of the ladies looking for a teaspoon. "So, Sister, what brings you to Heathrow so early in the morning?" she asked.

"I'm flying to Los Angeles," I said. It's still hardly believable, even to me.

"Well, so are we! I'm Lucy-Ann, by the way, Lucy-Ann Radzinski."

"Sister Boniface."

"Come and sit with us, Bonny. Bob and the Diepental's would just love to meet you. Come on, there's room, and if you sisterhood folks are allowed to play gin rummy, we'll deal you right in."

So instead of letter writing and quiet meditation, it was gin rummy and friendly conversation until the check-in desk opened.

I explained a little about SERC and you being held and so on. It's easy to tell people things in the odd, transitory surroundings of an airport coffee shop when you've never met them before.

"Jeez, that's some story," Bob said. "You take care now, Bonny."

Somewhere in the complicated route to the next stage of departure, the Americans were directed off to one side. They waved goodbye, wishing me luck, as I did them. More passengers had arrived by now. I reached the front and the uniformed lady told me it was small enough, so I could keep the shared suitcase with me.

This was good because I needed access to all seven books if I was to be ten hours on a plane. Besides, the suitcase wasn't strong enough for manhandling. I did think about buying a webbing strap to hold it together, but it would have cost all the money I had for the fortnight.

Then it was through the security scans, through the buzzing archway and the pat-down for hidden weapons and into the next vast waiting area: Departures. It's like a small town in its own right; a crazy town where people shop only for luxuries and need ten thousand kinds of perfume. Restaurants, bars and whole parades of glossy shops and everywhere you look enormous animated advertisements, which repeat and repeat the same brightly-coloured sequence.

Towing the squealing suitcase, I ambled around, exploring, and saw a sign saying "chapel". It was a little complicated to find, but a staircase and long corridor later, there it was, a peaceful haven in a sea of frantic activity. I ♥ chapels (in text speak).

Rev James and I chatted. I told him about your story and we said a prayer. He knows Peru.

"The people are very kind," he told me. "We mustn't judge them on the basis of the few outlaws."

"Of course not," I said. "Emelda loves the people she works with. She'll probably stay, when she's released."

"I'll add a prayer for her every day," he said. "Tell her

to drop in and see me whenever she's passing."

Thus fortified, I stepped back into the sensory overload of Departures and almost immediately the wheel came loose on the suitcase. The squeak was replaced by a thump and a clunk as the little axle lurched. I could still wheel it, but only by leaning it on one side. All I could do was to limp it over to a bench and settle down to watch the slow changing of the flight departures board until my plane began boarding.

I ate my packed lunch. The boiled egg was particularly good. I knew which hen had laid it.

After a while I heard a tapping sound, and looking round I saw the Americans behind a glass wall up in the first floor. They were knocking on the glass, jumping up and down, gesturing to attract my attention. At first I just waved back, thinking, how extraordinarily friendly Americans were, but they were all pointing to the big soundless TV screen suspended in one corner, gesturing to me to go over and look.

When I got there the screen was showing a row of people sitting behind microphones at a table almost overwhelmed by press photographers. It was such a throng that it was hard to tell what was happening. I walked closer to the TV so that I could read the words scrolling along the bottom of the screen. They said, "... *missing nuns in North Peru.*"

The picture changed to confusing images of a crowd of photographers surrounding people being rushed out of an official-looking building into a car. *"Officials deny ransom claim,"* said the scrolling words. A woman reporter clutching a big microphone began talking, but she was somewhere else, in a studio. Still images looking like grainy passport photographs of two women appeared behind her. The scrolling words began to repeat themselves, *"Release of missing nuns in North Peru. Officials deny ransom claim."*

The missionaries were waving and shouting, but I couldn't be sure what I was seeing. All I could do was shrug at them and point to my ears. *I can't hear. I don't know what they're saying.* They were disappointed. I looked around, but, even though I was surrounded by people, I didn't know who to ask. The picture on the TV screen was of the overcrowded press conference again. There were two women, the ones from the photographs, both looking thinner and tired. They leaned forward and said something briefly into the microphones and flashbulbs went off like fireworks exploding around them.

The handle slipped out of my grasp and the suitcase lurched and hit the hard floor. Its hinges broke immediately and it fell open, just as I had dreaded. My spare habit, the Kendal Mint cake, the Savon de Marseilles, underwear, shoes and all seven carefully chosen books tumbled out around my feet. I fell to my knees, scrabbling in my rucksack for the bin liner, but I couldn't take my eyes away from the screen, so I was fumbling and blindly jamming things together when one of the two women on screen leant towards the cameras and held something up. The camera was not steady, whoever was filming was struggling with the crowd. When it finally settled we could see that in her left hand the woman held what looked like a very muddy envelope. She was talking, explaining. She smiled, looked down and picked another object up in the other hand. The camera shot zoomed in – it was red. It was the torn and badly crumpled remains of a KitKat wrapper.

The rest is not very clear in my memory. I certainly shouted. I definitely waved and cheered. There may have been some jumping up and down. The Americans escaped their glass-walled lounge and came noisily down the escalator to hug me and dance about. Rev James sprinted down the stairs from the chapel and shook my hand.

"Are they sure?" I asked him. "Really sure?"

"Is her name Griggs?"

"Yes."

"Then it's her."

People in all directions turned and stared. I tried explaining, but the words were a jumble. A kind young woman picked up my things and soon a large pair of airport security men appeared.

They had the elaborate good manners of people in uniform who carry handguns. "Would you mind stepping this way please, Madam? My colleague here will carry your bag."

"Am I being arrested?" I asked. "I'm sorry I shouted, it's just that..."

"If you would just accompany us, Madam, there is a private area over here."

A kind and rather senior uniformed lady was waiting. She did two wonderful things: she confirmed that you had been released and were safe and well, and she provided a new suitcase. They keep a few spares, she said, for emergencies.

We watched the TV with the sound playing. They showed your press conference several times more. Right in the background, hardly visible at all, I thought I caught a glimpse of Hugh Snipe, but I couldn't be sure.

You're safe! I've no idea where to send this letter.

Toasting your safe return in English Breakfast in the VIP lounge at Heathrow International (I never imagined writing *those* words).

Best wishes, Emelda,

Sister B.

49

St Win's
March 20th

Dear Emelda,

It's just light these mornings at 5.30. Pale along the horizon, anyway.

The chapel puddle is definitely still growing. I saw an odd movement in it yesterday – a quiver, which sent gentle ripples out from a strange bobbly prominence. Frogspawn. Now, I am as keen on the new life of spring as the next sister, but frogspawn in the chapel! We will have a thousand froglets flipping around the place in no time. It can't stay. The problem is that although I can (just about) gut a chicken, picking up frogspawn turns out to be beyond me. I tried. I put on rubber gloves and went back with a bucket. I was willing, but my hands refused to reach out and pick it up. It has a sort of gelatinous shudder when you touch it – even thinking of it makes me want to run away.

I had to confess this to Sister Bernard, who came in to check on the organ.

"Oh dear," she said, "I'm pretty sure I'm not the one to help with that."

We both stood wincing at the wobbly egg mass. For about 20 minutes we tried to encourage each other, and said things like "Oh, come on, Boniface, it's only a bit of frogspawn..." and, "...perhaps if I close my eyes..." and, "...if I sort of ease it towards you and you hold the bucket..."

Rev Mother, came in and found us, "There you are!"

She laughed when she saw us cringing, took the bucket and without even putting the gloves on, scooped the spawn up one swift movement. It was a perfect illustration of the decisive energy and lack of squeamishness that makes her such an admirable leader.

The café, while I was away, was bustling and well-ordered under Nesbitt's supervision. Alphonsus has started part-time as a faster barista than I ever was, whilst also keeping the website up to date, and helping out in the Shoppe. I pushed aside thoughts of what Sister Joy would say about his National Insurance situation.

Roselily made a very beautiful painting of me on a plane, a black blob with stick arms and a radiant smile on a dart heading for the sun. It's hanging in the café, but is most definitely not for sale.

Hermione is on a course with the homeless charity. There's talk of opening a hostel somewhere nearby. I can have a job there, if I want one. Two weeks' work at the hostel in Los Angeles makes me a qualified candidate and Rev Mother thinks I need a change.

Hermione and Alphonsus are engaged.

"Old-fashioned pair, aren't they?" Eustacia remarked. "I told Alphonsus she's only on loan and we can reclaim her, if he misbehaves. A lifelong bodyguard of nuns. I think it made an impression."

Sister Bernard's composition, "Fenland Sky", was called "uplifting, profound and highly original" by the judges. It's going to be performed in London this summer. You can hear it online – Alphonsus put a link on the website.

It's quiet around the convent this afternoon, partly because the sisters are preparing for a special benediction and thanksgiving, partly because Norwich are playing West Ham. I don't watch the matches, but I enjoy the post-match interviews. Antonio's verb tenses are a little better, but I can't claim much progress on the accent.

We went for LIBERAM TANDEM for the new inscription on the re-cast bell – "free at last".

We're still waiting to hear about the stolen money. If and when it comes, there are a lot of decisions to be made about the future of St Win's. Is it right to spend so much on keeping these big old buildings going? Longer term it may not be. Meanwhile we have applied for a loan, like everyone else. They start work on the drains this week and the chapel floor soon after. We'll meet, perhaps, if you come back.

Best wishes, as ever,

Sister B.

PS Sister Layla won the Sister Worldwide letter-writing prize. Her letters saved the lives of 23 sisters and led to a campaign that freed 16 others in Sudan.

Respect (as Nesbitt would say)!

B.

Acknowledgements

Chris Bristow read drafts and laughed; Claire McMillan and Margaret Smith were careful early readers; Kit Johnstone is a nicely opinionated source of comedy ideas, and Cathy Byfield checked the manuscript.

Nicola Doherty and Helen Bryant at Cornerstones provided advice when I needed it.

Lovely readers kept asking when it would be ready, which was very encouraging. Jennie Rawlings' cover is fantastic, and Yasmin Standen at Three Hares is the one who makes it all happen.

Thank you all.
Fran Smith
March 2017